Too Far Under

Also by Lynn Osterkamp:

Too Near the Edge

Stress? Find Your Balance (nonfiction)

How To Deal With Your Parents When They
Still Treat You Like a Child (nonfiction)

Too Far Under

a novel

by

Lynn Osterkamp

PMI Books

Boulder, Colorado

Published by
PMI Books
an imprint of
Preventive Measures, Inc.
254 Spruce St.
Boulder, CO 80302

Printed in the United States of America

For information regarding special discounts
for bulk purchases, visit our website at:

pmibooks.com 

The water can be deceptive.
Please be aware of strong undertow and crashing waves.

Beach Sign

Prologue

Mirabel's last day on earth was a late August scorcher, but the heat melted away when the sun slipped behind the mountains. The evening air had a delicious mountain crispness and piney smell. Mirabel was overdue for a soak. She dropped her clothes in a pile on the bathroom floor and slipped into a terry robe. On her way through the empty kitchen, she grabbed a chilled bottle of Chenin Blanc, a wine glass, and her ipod. Then she headed out to the secluded hot tub in the backyard of her house in the outskirts of Boulder.

"My favorite part of the day," she said to herself as she turned on the jets, tossed her robe on a chair and slid into the bubbling hot water. "Yes," she sighed in relief as the throbbing in her muscles and joints eased. Mirabel refused to accept limitations to her active life, despite increasing arthritis pain. Some days it was all she could do to get moving in the morning, but she pushed through the fog and kept her commitments. Mirabel was proud that people who knew her said that once she set her mind on something she moved forward like a rocket and got things accomplished.

Today she'd spent hours with the Prairie Dog Action group she chaired, working on strategies to take action against Hugh Symes, a vicious developer who plowed a colony of prairie dogs under—killing them instead of relocating them. Then she delivered meals-on-wheels, worked on promotional materials with the Colorado Sierra Club, and had a short Scientology session with India and Brian.

As usual, her husband Derrick wasn't around for dinner, so she and her daughter Angelica picked up some fruit smoothies and black bean tempeh burgers at the Boulder Co-op café. They ate downtown on the courthouse lawn while listening to a local jazz group at the weekly Bands on the Bricks concert. It was after 9:00 when they got home and by the time she'd checked her phone messages and had her usual bedtime heart-to-heart talk with Angelica, it was about 10:30, which was slightly past her usual soaking time.

Angelica, an unusually perceptive ten-year-old, had offered to forgo the bedtime ritual so Mirabel could get right to the hot water. But Mirabel treasured Angelica's nighttime confidences too much to miss one no matter how much her body ached. She wished she had spent this quality time with her three older children, but somehow life had gotten in the way and that opportunity was long gone.

A familiar sadness overwhelmed her as she thought about her older children, now all but lost to her. Her ongoing arguments with her two oldest—Shane, twenty-four, and Lacey, twenty-three, left her frustrated and disappointed. Somehow neither of them had found a steady path in life. She had tried to teach them the importance of contributing to the community, but they insisted she had already contributed enough for all of them. Had she neglected their emotional needs to serve her social causes? She never meant to, but looking back she did have regrets.

Worst was Kari, dead at thirteen. It had been two years now, but Mirabel still missed Kari every day and blamed herself for not doing more to save her. Tears trickled down her cheeks. Her precious babies. She may not have been the best mother, but she loved them all so much. At least she was close to Angelica. She vowed to do whatever she needed to do to keep that, and to redouble her efforts to reach Lacey and Shane.

As Mirabel's physical tension yielded to the swirling water, she turned her thoughts away from her family. Other worries nagged at her. Life was confusing lately and she didn't know who to trust or believe. She wasn't naïve. She was quite aware that money—or the desire for more of it—could motivate people to evil. But until recently, she'd thought she was a good enough judge of character that no one could take advantage of her or of people she loved. Now she wasn't so sure. Things were happening that she knew she needed to stop. It was going to be an unpleasant month.

As she soaked and sipped her wine, Mirabel tried to quiet her reactive mind and move toward clear as she'd learned to do as a student of Scientology. But it wasn't working—maybe because of a combination of alcohol and painkillers in her system. She'd resisted taking any medications for at least a year after her arthritis began to interfere with her daily life, and even now hadn't found the courage to tell her fellow Scientologists that she was taking pills they believe to be poison. Actually, she had other issues with them these days that had eroded much of their mutual trust, so the pain killer thing was probably minor.

She sat up to reach her wine bottle, poured herself another glass, leaned back against the side of the tub, and drank deeply. As the wine level dropped in her glass, Mirabel slid down further into the water, focusing on relaxing her body and again trying to clear her mind. Gradually her thoughts dimmed, her body loosened, and she felt the floating calmness she sought.

She had almost lapsed into a stupor when she felt a hand touch her head. She couldn't see who it was, but in her groggy state she didn't really care. The hand squeezed her head lightly, which felt soothing and she drowsily wiggled her head to snuggle into it. But soon the touch felt too firm and aggressive. She roused herself enough to push back and finally tried to turn her head to see who was there. But the person behind her held her head tightly in both hands, thrusting her face under the warm water.

Mirabel kicked at the bottom and sides of the tub, struggling to get a foothold to push herself up and raise her head out of the water. But it was too late. The pills, the wine and the hot water had left her body and her mind too slack to act forcefully in her own defense. The hands pushed her head deeper into the tub.

Fear and panic came over her in waves as water gushed down her throat. Her chest burned and she gasped, trying not to breathe in the water that surrounded her. But finally the irresistible urge to breathe won out. Mirabel's last thought before the water filled her lungs and she lost consciousness was that if she drowned she'd be letting down all the people who were counting on her to show up tomorrow and the next day and all the days after that.

Chapter 1

Two months later

When I got the urgent early-morning call from Shady Terrace Nursing Home, I thought it was my boyfriend Pablo calling to say he missed me already. He had spent the night and was on his way to work while I dozed lazily under my puffy down quilt enjoying the afterglow and procrastinating getting up for a few more minutes.

I flipped open my cell and saw the Shady Terrace number instead of Pablo's. My heart sank. "Cleo Sims," I answered, dreading what could only be bad news from the nursing home calling so early. It was Tanya, one of the nurses on my eighty-seven-year-old grandmother's unit.

"Get ready for a shock, Cleo. Shady Terrace is closing and all the residents have to move out! They just told us, and the residents don't even know yet. There's a big family meeting this morning at 9:00. Can you make it?"

Too stunned to ask for details, I said I'd be there. I wanted to scream and throw my phone against the wall, but instead I grabbed a robe and stepped out onto my front porch, hoping my mountain view would have its usual calming effect.

It was a mild sun-drenched October morning, but I shivered as if winter had arrived overnight with a blast of arctic air. Tanya's words bounced around in my head as I paced around the porch, struggling to absorb the unwelcome news. Fury prodded me to fight back, but at the same time I wanted to curl up in a corner and cry. How could this be happening just when Shady Terrace had finally gotten its act together and was providing such good care? Where could Gramma go?

Her Alzheimer's disease has progressed to the point that she doesn't always recognize me, but she's been at Shady Terrace for eight years and the staff knows her ups and downs and how to make her comfortable.

I was a wreck, and the mountain view wasn't soothing me at all. As a grief therapist I know there are times when you need to stop and absorb bad news and there are times when you need to take action. This moment called for action. So I went back inside to grab a quick shower and get dressed. As I showered, anger and sorrow continued to fight for control of my emotions, while my saner professional side tried to start making a plan.

It was going to be a busy morning. It was Friday and I had a class to teach at the university at 10:30. I couldn't be late for that. The department head had made it clear that my paranormal psychology class was an experiment and that some faculty did not approve of hiring an unorthodox therapist like me to teach even as a lowly instructor. I was on trial and I wanted to measure up.

For the moment, though, Gramma's well-being was my top priority, so I had to make this meeting. I jumped into my Toyota and headed to the nursing home. Of course the main parking lot was full and I wasted time looking for a space before I went over to the auxiliary lot. The meeting was just getting started in the central lobby when I dashed in, so I didn't have time to go to Gramma's room and check on her. Instead, I found an empty chair at the back of the room and sat down. This lobby was designed to look like an old-fashioned town square with fake storefronts, an ice cream parlor and a popcorn wagon. The theory is that the residents will feel comforted by a setting that takes them back to a happier time of their lives.

Maybe it is calming for them. But I felt like I was sitting in Disneyland listening to Cruella De Vil. I'd never seen the woman who was speaking, so I figured she was from corporate headquarters. She was a tall, large-boned woman, dressed in a snazzy black business suit that was overkill for a fake main street in a Boulder nursing home but would have fit right in to Donald Trump's boardroom. Unfortunately, her message matched the boardroom image.

"We know that Shady Terrace is a vibrant community of seniors," she began in an incongruously upbeat voice. "But, our building is in need of significant and costly repairs that we can't afford to make with our current operating budget. So, after careful deliberation, we have entered into a sales agreement with Hugh Symes Development Company, which will require the closure of the Shady Terrace skilled nursing center. You will be receiving a letter this week that will be your official sixty-day notice of closure as required by Colorado law. We know this decision will be difficult for our residents and their families, but we assure you that we will do everything possible to assist you in making a smooth transition to another living situation."

I squirmed in my chair. What did she mean they would do everything possible to assist us? Do these corporate executives go to a special class where they learn to sugarcoat horrible news and lie easily to suit their purposes? I wanted to scream at her, "Doesn't this corporation have a slogan that says, 'Caring for you is what we do'?"

Listening to her, it sounded to me like what they do is go for the big bucks. Tears welled up in my eyes. How could they care more about their bottom line than they did about people like my Gramma who couldn't speak out for themselves and were dependent on all of us for their care?

Boulderites tend to be assertive, especially when it comes to issues of human rights vs. big business. Hands shot up all around me and a man in front plowed right in without waiting to be called on. "It took my mother a year to adjust to this place and now you're saying she has to move? It sounds like our family members are just dollars to you and if they don't bring in enough, they have to go." His anger and disgust were front and center.

"I assure you that this is not personal. It's just business." Cruella spoke evenly, not matching his furious tone. "We understand that this is an unsettling and difficult time for you and your loved ones and we will do all we can to make it go as smoothly as—"

"I assure you that it is very personal to me and to my mother," the man interrupted. "And it's not going to go smoothly for you because I'm going to do all I can to stop you, starting right now with a call to the newspaper."

A woman on the other side of the room, tired of waiting for her raised hand to be noticed, jumped up and joined in. "Isn't there something we can do to save Shady Terrace? It took me forever to find this place and now that Mom is doing well, I don't want to move her."

"We understand that this is difficult, but after exploring all the possibilities, we determined that closing is the best option," Cruella continued in her condescending I'm-being-patient-with-you tone. "Now I need to catch a plane, but the Shady Terrace staff and your local long-term-care ombudsman are here to help you get started on making new arrangements." With that, she picked up her briefcase and ducked out the front door.

I needed to get out of there myself if I was going to get to my class on time, but Mary Ellen, the Director of Nursing, and Betsy from Social Services were walking up to the front and I wanted to hear what they had to say. The both looked like they'd been crying. "We're checking on openings in other nursing homes and we're going to help you all look for places," Mary Ellen said. "And Tim, a volunteer ombudsman from the county, has offered to help you with information about other facilities." She beckoned to a tall thin bald man in the second row, who stood up to join them in front.

My eyes nearly popped out of my head! Tim Grosso, Ph.D., the Chair of the university Psychology Department—the very Tim Grosso who had reluctantly hired me to teach a class—was a volunteer ombudsman? I hated to miss his comments, but I knew the students wouldn't wait for me if I was late for class, so I slipped out.

As I drove up to the university, I agonized over Gramma's plight. This was one more in a long line of indignities she'd faced over the last twelve years. Before Alzheimer's eroded her mind, she was a top-ranked Boulder artist, whose colorful oil paintings commanded high prices and won national awards. And she was the sweetest, most patient teacher, whose students—including me—learned to paint better than we ever thought we could.

She and my Grampa, who taught philosophy at the university, had a storybook marriage for more than fifty years before she began showing signs of Alzheimer's at age seventy-five. At first, it was forgetfulness and confusion. But she kept getting worse, being argumentative and accusing us of hiding her things. She began wandering out at night in her nightgown—probably to go to her studio in the backyard. She had always been a night person. If Grampa locked the door, she would wake him up to let her out. If he refused, she sobbed and screamed. If he left her alone in the studio, she often fell and hurt herself.

It was horrible for all of us. Gramma because she couldn't make sense out of the world any more, and Grampa and me because we were losing her at the same time that she was still here needing us to take care of her. Grampa tried hiring people to be with her, but she hated having them around and didn't want them in her studio. He wasn't getting any sleep at night and he couldn't deal with her constant arguments or keep her safe at home anymore, so after four years of that he finally decided to move her into Shady Terrace. He picked it because he thought it was the best place. The whole thing was terribly hard on him. He visited her every day, even though it was painful when she kept begging him to take her home.

I visited a lot too and I still do. It was easier for me when Grampa was still alive because we could share the sadness. But he died of a heart attack a year after Gramma moved to Shady Terrace and I've been in charge ever since. My grandparents practically raised me and I want to do as much for them as they did for me. They were never close to my mother—their only child—so Grampa set things up for me to be Gramma's guardian after he died. I miss him more than I can even begin to describe and I do everything I can to live up to his trust. But today I felt scared and overwhelmed. Even though it wasn't my fault that Gramma would have to move, I had a sinking feeling that I was letting Grampa down.

Chapter 2

I raced along the sidewalk to my class, feeling unprepared because I hadn't had time to review my notes, and my focus was on Gramma instead of on my upcoming lecture. The campus is a treat in the fall when the turning leaves match the buildings' red roofs, but I was too rushed and distracted to enjoy the scenery. Because I'm a temporary university employee, the parking permit I'm allowed to buy isn't valid in the best lots, and I had a ways to walk in a hurry to get to class on time.

I was thrilled when the Psychology Department hired me to teach this class in paranormal psychology as part of their new initiative reaching out to nontraditional students. Every stamp of respectability I can get for my work is important to me. I have a doctorate in psychology and I'm a certified grief therapist, but my practice has recently taken a somewhat unusual turn. I've found a way to help people see and actually talk with dead family members or friends to resolve incomplete issues.

I know it sounds like one more flaky new-age Boulder fad, but it's actually based in scientific exploration. I use a process developed by a medical doctor who spent years studying the experiences of people who had seen and interacted with apparitions of the dead. His method is based on ancient reports of deceased persons spontaneously appearing in a mirror or other reflective surface usually in dim light. Based on these accounts, he created an apparition chamber in which some people were able to contact spirits.

My homemade apparition chamber emulates his. It's a four-foot square mirror on the wall, surrounded by a black velvet curtain that creates a small booth with an easy chair inclined backward so the sitter can gaze into the mirror and see only darkness. I prepare people and set them up in the apparition chamber. Then I leave them in there alone to relax and focus on the person they are trying to contact. If the process is working for them an apparition appears as they gaze into the mirror's shiny surface. At that point they can talk directly to the departed and also make their own assessments of the reality of the experience. Those who are able to contact a deceased loved one often go through a breakthrough healing experience that resolves much of their grief.

After some of my grief-therapy clients found that this process helped them, they encouraged me to offer it to more grieving people. So I created the Contact Project, funded by an endowment from a local dot-com multimillionaire who was able to contact a family member and wanted to help other people do the same. I'm very selective about who I accept into the Contact Project and I insist that participants also be involved in traditional grief therapy.

As it turned out, my ruminating about the Contact Project right before I ran into Lacey Townes was an omen. But I had no clue what was coming as I screeched to a stop in front of the petite young woman with long dark hair standing in the doorway to my classroom. I recognized Lacey, the girl blocking my way into the room, as one of my students who usually sat near the front of the class and actively participated in class discussions. Lacey didn't move to let me in—just stood firm in a graceful dancer-like stance and stared at me with probing deep blue eyes. "Dr. Sims," she said in a breathless voice, "I desperately need to talk to you right away."

I tried not to sound impatient. "Lacey, I'm already late for class. I can't talk now. Maybe after class." What was going through her mind thinking I'd keep the whole class waiting while I talked about whatever was bothering her?

I squeezed past her through the door, tossed my stuff on the table, apologized for my lateness and started right in on my lecture. It was the sixth week of class. We'd been gradually working our way through research that supports the existence of paranormal phenomena as well as evidence that discounts the validity of many psychics and mediums. That day's class focused on the work of the internationally famous psychiatrist Ian Stevenson who, until his retirement, was the head of the Division of Perceptual Studies at the University of Virginia. He spent decades traveling all over the world recording and attempting to verify cases of children who claimed to recall past lives. While he never was able to prove reincarnation, the more than 2,500 cases he published raise interesting questions that suggest that it is possible.

The students involved themselves in the topic right away, raising provocative questions on both sides of the issue. But I noticed that Lacey, sitting unexpectedly in the back of the room, looked as distracted as I felt myself. I already had to work to keep Gramma out of my mind and focus on the class, and now I found myself preoccupied by Lacey as well. I shook off those thoughts and pulled myself back to the discussion.

"If reincarnation is real, how come most people don't remember past lives?" asked Logan, one of my most talkative students who loved to challenge.

"Maybe it's hard to remember. Most of us don't remember what happened when we were babies, so why would we remember past lives?" said Josie, a short fortyish woman, one of my several older students.

"Maybe most people do remember but keep it to themselves because they're afraid people will laugh at them," said an intense woman named Aimee, who always sits in the front row.

This led to a discussion in which a woman named Daphne told a fascinating story about being haunted by dreams in which she lived in Taos, New Mexico in the early 1900s. "I eventually did genealogical research and discovered that the woman I was in my dreams had lived in Taos and died in childbirth in 1931," she said. "Then last year I visited Taos for the first time and it was amazing how familiar it all was and how much I felt at home. I'm sure I lived there in another life."

I made notes as she related her story and students pummeled her with questions. The discussion was so exhilarating at that point that I momentarily forgot about Gramma. By the end of our two-hour class, I was rejuvenated, but Gramma's problems quickly rushed back to the front of my mind. I was ready to get out of there, grab some lunch, and find out more about her predicament.

But Lacey, looking more troubled than ever, lingered behind as the students left class. She stood directly in front of me blocking my way to the door once again. Very determined young woman. "Dr. Sims, you absolutely have to help me. My mother drowned in her hot tub last August. You probably heard about it—Mirabel Townes? It was in all the papers." Her voice rose as she went on. "My life has been a huge mess ever since and it's getting worse every day."

She did sound desperate, but right at that moment I couldn't summon the energy to listen to her concerns. I was starving and I had a lot on my mind and I had issues about taking on a student as a client. I looked her in the eyes with what I hoped was a sympathetic look. "Lacey, I did hear about your mother, and I'm so sorry. You must be going through a difficult time. But I can't do grief therapy with one of my students. I can refer you to someone, though."

"No, no that's not it." Lacey held her hands out in front of my face to stop me. "I'm not looking for grief therapy, although I could probably use some because when Mom died, I hadn't even gotten over my sister Kari dying of anorexia two years ago. But I can't worry about myself with what's going on now. Have you heard of Indigo children?"

Whew! She was all over the place. How to respond? I dredged up what I knew about Indigoes, while trying to edge toward the door. "They're supposed to be psychologically and spiritually gifted—sort of a more highly evolved new generation—right?" I said as I maneuvered gingerly around to her other side. This girl was persistent.

"Exactly," Lacey nodded vigorously, while at the same time moving to again block my way to the door. "And my ten-year-old sister Angelica is one. She sees below the surface. She's been telling me that our mother didn't die by accident. Angelica knows that someone pushed Mom under and drowned her! But she doesn't know who did it. And we can't get anyone to believe us and investigate. We need your help to contact Mom and find out what really happened."

She was drawing me in, but I resisted for so many reasons.

"Lacey, I really need to go," I said. A cold sweat came over me. I was overwhelmed, not like myself at all. I could see that she wanted me to get involved with Mirabel's death, to become her partner and ally. But I just couldn't. I had to be careful.

Unfortunately, I got some very bad publicity last summer when the father of a client I was helping to contact her dead husband filed a complaint against me with the mental-health licensing board and it got in the local paper. He accused me of engaging in fraudulent and unsafe practice that placed his daughters' safety and welfare in danger. He also charged that I was mentally ill, and delusional. None of it was true and the complaint was eventually dismissed, but I've had to work hard to maintain my professional image. So I've been trying to lay low and not take on any cases that might get me back in the news.

"No, you haven't heard the whole story yet!" Lacey held up her hands in front of me to stop me from leaving. Her eyes filled with tears. "You have to help us. We have money. We can pay whatever your rate is. We really need you to help us."

"I wish I could help you, but I don't have any more time right now," I said. I pulled out one of my cards and handed it to her as I jumped around her into the doorway. "Here's my number. Call me and I'll give you some referrals to people who might be able to help."

Then I'm ashamed to say I turned my back on her and ran out of the room.

Chapter 3

Talking on a cell phone while driving is not a practice I support. It's too easy to get distracted and do something stupid. But I have to admit that when it comes to my own need to make a call, I figure I'm the exception who can eat and chew gum at the same time. So while I drove back to my office, I called Pablo to share the bad news about Gramma. I was looking for some commiseration, but instead I had to leave a voicemail message. He's a police detective, so he's hard to reach. Next I called my best friend Elisa. This time I got a sympathetic ear.

"The corporate goons are selling Shady Terrace to a developer, who's going to plow it under," I wailed, "and Gramma and all the residents have to move out. Can you believe it?"

"Ohmigod, that's unexpected!" Elisa's gravelly voice had an overtone of shock. "How soon does she have to move out?"

"I think it's sixty days, but even if it was a year, I don't know how I'd find a good place and get her moved and adjusted to it. I feel sick just thinking about it."

"Hold on, Cleo. You need a plan, and you need it soon. But I have to run out now to teach my class. Anyway, we can talk about this better over some strong drinks. Can you meet me at the St. Julien after work? How about 5:30?"

"Thanks, I'll see you there." A wave of relief flooded over me. Not that I thought Elisa could change the situation, but just having someone to share it with was major.

When the St. Julien Hotel opened in 2004 it was the first new hotel in downtown Boulder in nearly fifty years. I love its big-city air of classy sophistication combined with a smidge of Colorado casualness. The red and buff-colored sandstone building almost melts into the surrounding mountain landscape, and it's situated to take the best advantage of the stunning views of the Flatirons rock formations. But my favorite part is the intimate T-Zero martini bar's daily happy hour with reduced-price wine, beer and drinks, and half-price bar food menu. It's quickly become a favorite after-work spot to see and be seen, catch up with old friends, and meet new ones, so it's always crowded. The crowd spills out into the spacious lobby furnished with stylishly comfortable chairs and couches that mirror the reds and browns of the outside of the building.

Elisa had already snagged a good spot with two comfy oversized chairs and a round glass-topped cocktail table facing the glass wall on the south side of the room with the best view of the mountains. I noticed a guy by himself at the table next to her checking her out. No surprise there. She looked sensational as always. Elisa is a woman you notice because of her natural good looks—tall and thin with thick blonde hair—and because she dresses in a casually elegant way. Today she wore a soft cotton patchwork jacket of muted greens, blues and browns over a simple black tee and flared skirt. What totally made the outfit was a low-slung metal belt with glass stones that echoed the colors in her jacket.

As usual, I felt a little plain in comparison. I'm only 5'4," with medium-length brown hair and green eyes—my only distinctive feature. I had on my favorite jean skirt and a long-sleeved lavender ribbed cotton sweater. Adequate, but nothing special.

Elisa jumped up as soon as she saw me and enveloped me in a huge hug. "Life sure sucks some days, and today is one of those days," she said. "It's so unfair. Just when everything was going smoothly for you, this has to happen."

"Well, my Grampa always told me that no one ever said life was supposed to be fair," I said, as I positioned my backpack under my chair and sat down. "But pushing all those old people out of their home seems beyond unfair to me."

"I talked to Jack to see what he knows about it," she said, referring to her husband who is a Boulder real-estate developer. "He said Hugh Symes has wanted that land for years and saw his opportunity recently when the corporation that owns Shady Terrace was having some financial problems. Symes made a good offer and the corporation went for the money. It doesn't sound like there's much chance of stopping the sale. Especially if you know Symes. When he makes up his mind to move on something, there's no stopping him."

"Evil money-grubber. How does he sleep at night?"

"He's a strange bird," Elisa said. "Doesn't fit the Boulder liberal image at all. A political conservative who thinks Boulderites tend to be whiny do-gooders who don't understand the real world." She stopped short, shrugged her shoulders, then moved on to more immediate business. "But enough about Symes. Let's get a drink."

We looked around for a server to take our drink orders. The room was filling up quickly, and there were way more people looking to order drinks than the three young waitresses could keep up with. Elisa caught the eye of a perky dark-haired girl with a wide smile and huge silver hoop earrings. We each ordered one of the T-Zero signature Kettle One martinis that come with three giant olives. And a mozzarella melt to share. My mouth watered in anticipation.

Elisa and I have been friends for about fifteen years and we know each other inside and out. She turned forty this year, which makes her three years older than me. We're both psychologists, but she has a full-time faculty appointment at the university, where she teaches in the doctoral program in clinical psychology and serves as both a research advisor and clinical supervisor. Aside from the one class I'm teaching, my work is not at the university. I do mostly clinical work with my grief therapy practice. Elisa is also my therapist and clinical supervisor when I need one, so I can tell her anything, even about my clients. She keeps my confidences and she's never shy about giving me her straight-up honest opinion.

"I know I'm going to have to find Gramma another place," I

sighed. "But she's been getting along well there lately and finally stopped wandering around in the middle of the night. I'm afraid she'll go downhill in a new place. I promised Grampa I'd take care of her and now I don't know if I can." Tears welled up and trickled down my face as I thought of letting down my grandparents who had always been so good to me.

"Cleo, you know they wouldn't see it that way. None of this is your fault. It's just been dumped on you. Is Shady Terrace going to help people look for new places?"

"They say they are. Oh…and here's something amazing. Did you know that Tim Grosso, the head of the Psych Department, is a volunteer long-term-care ombudsman? He was there at the Shady Terrace meeting this morning to help families with information about other nursing homes in town. I didn't get to hear what he had to say because I had to leave for class, but I plan to talk to him later."

Before she could respond, the waitress arrived with our drinks, and we took a moment to sit back and enjoy the scene. Couples sharing intimate moments, groups of friends catching up, all looking relaxed and happy, releasing the day's tension like the air from a balloon. Conversation mingled with the soft sounds of a live Brazilian band to form soothing waves of sound that ebbed and flowed around us.

We talked on about Gramma's situation for twenty minutes or so, Elisa helping me explore various possibilities until I had a semblance of a plan in mind. I would collect what information I could from Tim and from the Shady Terrace social workers, choose two or three places to visit, and see how well Gramma might fit in there.

I felt much better by then, maybe because the martini was working its magic, but I did need some food to balance out the liquor. Just as I realized how hungry I was, our mozzarella melt finally arrived. The waitress apologized for the delayed service, which we knew was typical for Friday evening.

"Yum," I said, breaking off a messy piece of the gooey cheese, tomato and basil on crusty bread. While I chewed, I decided to move the conversation on to a different subject.

"Did you know Mirabel Townes?" I asked. "You know, she was

that local activist who drowned in her hot tub last August."

Elisa was about to eat her own cheesy bite, but stopped to give me a quick answer. "Sure. Knew her for years. You probably met her at some of our parties," she said as she popped the morsel into her mouth.

"Where did you know her from?" I asked, taking another sip of my martini.

"Her husband Derrick is a real-estate developer who's done some projects with Jack. And their daughter Kari was the same age as my daughter Maria," Elisa said, tearing off another piece of mozzarella melt. "Kari and Maria were great friends. I felt terrible for Mirabel when Kari died of anorexia two years ago. Don't you remember me talking about it?"

I searched my memories. "Now that you remind me, it's coming back," I said. "You asked me to spend some time with Maria helping her cope with the loss. And I did. But I'd forgotten that Maria's friend was Mirabel Townes' daughter." I ate another bite and wiped my messy hands on my napkin while I thought about Mirabel's loss. As a grief therapist I know the agonizing pain that follows the loss of a child.

"Poor Mirabel," I said. "Losing a child is always tragic, and even worse when you feel like you could have prevented it. There's so much guilt along with the grief. It must have been horrible for her."

"It was. Mirabel was never the same after that."

"What do you mean, 'never the same'?"

"Well she crashed, like you'd expect after losing a child. I don't need to tell you, you're the grief therapist. I don't know what I'd do in her situation. What Mirabel did was join the Church of Scientology. Apparently thought they could help her cope with her grief. She got very involved with them, dropped a lot of her old friends who I guess weren't big fans of Scientology. Why are you asking about her?"

I scraped the last crumbs from our appetizer plate, then launched into my explanation. "Mirabel's oldest daughter Lacey is in my class and apparently knows about my Contact Project. She stopped me after class today to say that her little sister Angelica—who she says is an Indigo child who sees beneath the surface—says that Mirabel didn't drown by accident. Lacey says that Angelica insists someone pushed Mirabel under and drowned her, and they want me to help them contact Mirabel to find out what happened."

Elisa gave me a quizzical look. "Why don't they get the police to look into it? If someone drowned Mirabel, I think the police would want to know. I mean Mirabel was a big-time Boulder activist—on boards, supported all the liberal causes like open space, prairie dog preservation, affordable housing, homeless shelters, anything progressive." Elisa was getting so wound up her voice was rising.

I didn't want anyone listening in to our conversation, so I put my hand lightly on her arm to calm her. She got the message instantly and stopped for a sip of her drink. Then she went on in a softer voice. "Look, Mirabel Townes was rich. Inherited tons of money from her mother's family's cattle ranching fortune. I know the Boulder police don't have the best reputation for murder investigation, with the whole JonBenet thing and all, but it's hard to believe someone could drown Mirabel and the police would just overlook it."

I frowned at her. "Come on, Elisa, that's a low crack about the Boulder police. The thing is—the police can't do anything if there's no evidence of a crime. I'm guessing the coroner ruled Mirabel's death an accident and that was that," I said, a little defensively.

Even though my boyfriend Pablo works for the Longmont police, not Boulder, and he does drug enforcement, not homicide, I get a little touchy when people rag on the Boulder police. Most of the cops I've met are like Pablo—hard workers who are passionately committed to their work. Pablo, for instance, became a cop after his younger brother Miguel got involved in a street gang selling drugs and ended up in prison. Pablo works in drug enforcement trying to keep young kids like Miguel from ending up like him.

Elisa put her hand on my arm. "Down, girl! I'm not insulting your boyfriend and his buddies," she said. "Just trying to figure out why Lacey Townes needs you instead of the police."

"Lacey said she and Angelica can't get anyone to believe them and open an investigation," I said, squirming a little in my seat.

"Yeah the police probably wouldn't put much stock in what a kid thinks, even if she is an Indigo child," Elisa said. "How old did you say the little sister is?"

"Lacey said Angelica is ten. Do you know much about Indigo children?"

Elisa leaned back and looked up at the ceiling as if she expected to find the answer written up there. Then she looked back at me. "Some people say they're a new kind of children—a unique generation of highly sensitive and psychic kids, independent, bright, creative, but easily bored and resistant to traditional authority," she said, using her teacher voice. "Other people say there's no such thing, that these are kids with attention deficit disorder whose parents won't accept that and insist on seeing them as spiritually gifted."

Elisa's eyes began to wander away from me and she stopped to wave at someone across the room. I knew I was losing her, but I wanted a better response.

"What do you think about Indigos?" I prodded.

She turned back to me. "I have no idea. I haven't seen any research on it one way or another. But you might want to look into it more before you take her word on what happened to Mirabel." She grimaced. "Anyway, do you want to get involved in another possible murder case?"

She was referring to the mess we'd gotten into last summer helping her friend Sharon find out how her husband died. Elisa had gotten me into that, and she'd paid as big a price as I did in the end. But I didn't want to rehash it, so I plowed ahead. "You know I'm not looking for another murder case. But Lacey seemed so desperate. And Mirabel did so much for the community. If someone did kill her, doesn't she deserve justice?"

Elisa polished off her drink while giving me a fixed stare. "Why is that your responsibility, Cleo? What about her husband Derrick? But come to think of it, maybe he doesn't care that much. He's been having an affair with Judith Demar for years. I don't know whether Mirabel knew about it or not."

I ignored her question by asking one of my own. "Who's Judith Demar?"

"She's a faculty member in the sociology department. Not one of my favorite people. A legend in her own mind."

"So maybe she drowned Mirabel?"

"Hold on, Cleo," Elisa grabbed my shoulders and stuck her face in mine. "You say the police need evidence before they investigate a crime. Shouldn't you hold yourself to some standard like that before you start speculating?"

"Well, I'm not the police, so—"

"Whoa—thinking of police," Elisa interrupted, grabbing my arm. "Isn't that Pablo over in the corner? And who's the gorgeous chick with him? Maybe his sister or a cousin? She looks a lot like him."

I whipped my head around to the direction she was looking, and my stomach churned. There, over by the giant open fireplace on the west side of the room was my boyfriend, Pablo. His back was towards me and across from him was a stunning young woman whose dark curly hair matched his own. I've known Pablo since college and I know his family and I'd never seen this woman before. And the way she was looking at him had more of a romantic than a cousinly feel to me. I stared at them, speechless. Pablo and I have been in an on-again, off-again relationship for years. Right now it's on, but not in an exclusive, committed way. Still, I don't expect to run into him with another woman gazing dotingly into his sexy brown eyes. If you had asked me how I'd feel seeing him with another woman, I would have said, "I'm fine with it. We've both agreed to have an open relationship." Surprisingly though, I didn't feel fine. I felt like another woman was moving in on my boyfriend. I decided to take action.

"Wow. I wonder who she is," I said. "I've never seen her before. I think I'll go find out." I stood up and took the last swig of my martini to fortify myself. "I wonder if I should introduce myself to her as his girlfriend or wait and see what Pablo says first?"

"I'd see what he has to say. You've got surprise on your side, girl. Use it."

I strolled over in what I thought was a sexy, yet confident and casual sort of way. But I couldn't take Elisa's advice. Instead I came up behind him, threw my arm across his broad shoulders and marked my territory with a quick kiss on the back of his neck. "Hey, Pablo,"

I said, trying to sound cheerful, like I'd just run into him by himself.

He turned toward me with a start. "Oh…hi Cleo. I thought we were meeting at the gallery for my show opening at 7:00." He gave me a big smile as if nothing out of the ordinary was going on.

"We are …were… meeting there. But Elisa and I came for a drink first. Did you get my message about Gramma?"

"Oh, right!" Pablo smacked himself in the forehead. "I did get it and I was going to call you back, but something came up and it slipped my mind. Sorry."

"Hi, I'm Mia." The dark-eyed woman stuck out her hand in my direction. She must be what had come up to erase my phone call from Pablo's memory.

"Oh, sorry." Pablo turned back toward Mia. "Mia's just here for a visit. We met years ago when I was studying art in San Miguel de Allende. She's an artist, too, so I invited her to come to the opening tonight to see my work. Mia, meet Cleo. Cleo and I were art students together at the university. She's a very fine painter."

"Nice to meet you." I shook Mia's hand and tried to smile, but suspected my real emotions showed through. The San Miguel de Allende chapter of Pablo's life is one I'd rather forget about. And he'd introduced me like I was some casual art colleague rather than a girlfriend. I definitely had some burning questions to ask him, like who is Mia staying with and for how long.

I didn't want to ask in front of Mia, though, so I backed off. "I should get back to Elisa," I said. "It's almost 7:00 and we need to get our check before we go to the gallery. We'll see you over there."

Chapter 4

"Her name is Mia." I stomped harder than I needed to on the brick pathway imagining it for one brief moment as Mia's head. Elisa and I were walking the few blocks over to the West End Gallery. "She's an artist and he met her years ago in San Miguel de Allende. It's that artsy town in Mexico where Pablo went to nourish his creative spirit a few months after we graduated from college."

"Sure, I remember you telling me about that time," Elisa said. "Didn't he just take off with no notice when you thought he was your soulmate destined to be with you forever? I met you a couple of years later and you still weren't over him."

"Not true," I said as I folded my arms and made a fake pouty face at her. "I was involved with Brian by then."

"Whatever. I never liked Brian. Good riddance on that score. But when you and Pablo got back together—or whatever you call it—a few years ago, I thought you were asking for trouble. Someone who's left you once is likely to do it again. I know, I know—you don't want commitment, you just want a dishy guy for fun and good sex, and keep your independence. But why are you so steamed about Mia if you and Pablo have such an open relationship?"

"Who says I'm steamed? Anyway, here we are, so let's leave this conversation for another day."

West End Gallery, named for its address on west Pearl Street, is a small modern art gallery that specializes in interesting shows by local artists. Its location in the now-fashionable west end commercial area, surrounded by high-end shops and trendy restaurants is ideal for drop-in traffic. Pablo's show there tonight was part of First Friday Boulder, a monthly event where downtown galleries introduce new shows, often with the artist in attendance. Most galleries include refreshments—usually wine, fruit and cheese trays, nuts, chocolates and such—which attracts art lovers but also some college students who make the rounds of galleries like a free bar tour.

Pablo's contemporary abstract metal sculptures stood together like an infantry unit just to our right as we walked into the gallery. Elisa hustled off to the wine table, but I headed over to my favorite of Pablo's pieces, a tall thin stick-figure man, built from rusty steel tools, blades and gears. Pablo had named him Cliff, but I thought of him as Rusty G. He looked much spiffier here in the gallery than he usually did in Pablo's garage. I could almost imagine Rusty G. was feeling as proud as I did at Pablo's artistry on display.

"Hey, Cleo. Where's Pablo?" I turned away from the sculptures to face a petite woman with short, spiky auburn hair and a wide smile that crinkled her whole face. Her outfit—ivory silk pants and tank topped by a short Asian-styled gold jacquard-woven jacket with a standup collar and square wooden buttons—more than lived up to her reputation for decking herself out in expensive designer ensembles.

"Hi, Faye. Great outfit! He's on his way. Just got sidetracked briefly by the St. Julien happy hour." I'd known Faye Whitton, the gallery owner for years. She's a great admirer of Gramma's painting, which she continues to exhibit and sell as part of her commitment to showing high-quality local art. "Wow, the display looks great," I gushed. "Isn't it amazing how much better artwork looks when it's well lit and given some breathing room?" As I heard myself rattling on, I realized I was trying to charm Faye, so as to deflect her attention from Pablo's lateness. And I also realized that it was not my responsibility to make excuses for Pablo, especially when he was hanging out with Mia.

Fortunately we were interrupted before I could embarrass myself further. A husky dark-haired athletic-looking man wearing a cotton sweater and designer jeans grabbed Faye in a bear hug, lifted her up and twirled her around. "Great show, Faye. Judith and I love the way you hung Angelica's work," he boomed.

A slim woman standing next to them watched with a disapproving look. Her long blond hair was swept away from her face in a way that emphasized her scowl. "Derrick, don't forget that one painting that is hung too high." The woman's frown deepened as she reminded him. "It doesn't serve the work. We really need to have it lowered."

Faye flinched ever so slightly, but quickly regained her composure. "Derrick have you and Judith met Cleo Sims? Her grandmother is the painter, Martha Donnelly." She grabbed my arm to draw me closer to them. "Cleo, this is Derrick Townes and Judith Demar. Derrick's ten-year-old daughter Angelica is a gifted painter. We're showing some of her work here tonight for the first time."

Suddenly lights were flashing inside my head. Derrick and Angelica Townes. This must be THE Townes family here. As in the drowned Mirabel Townes whose daughter Lacey thinks she was murdered. And the blond woman with the long neck is Derrick's girlfriend Judith Demar, the sociology faculty member Elisa doesn't like. And Angelica the Indigo child is also an artist? At this point I can't wait to meet this kid.

"Nice to meet you both," I said. "Derrick, you must be very proud of your daughter. Is she here?"

"Great meeting you, Cleo." His smile was charming and slightly sexy, the kind that makes you feel instantly welcome. "My older daughter Lacey is bringing Angelica, but they haven't showed up yet. I was just about to call them and find out what's up."

Judith chimed in with another negative comment. "You can never depend on Lacey. She acts more like an irresponsible teenager than the twenty-two-year-old she is. She always gets involved in some crisis that makes her late. I told you we should have brought Angelica with us."

I thought about mentioning that I knew Lacey, but didn't want to be drawn into their argument. Instead I excused myself and went off to find Elisa, who to my surprise was deep in conversation with Tim Grosso, the Psych Department chairman. Tim is a tall, bald ascetic-looking man, who looks like he spends hours meditating every day—and maybe he does. I don't actually know much about him, except that he's a mild-mannered, agreeable guy who gets top teaching ratings and is generally liked by most people who know him. While he had made it clear to me that my teaching at the university was on a trial basis only, I didn't take it personally because I figured he had to act on the concerns raised by faculty in the department who think my Contact Project is new-age quackery.

"Cleo, where did you get off to?" Elisa asked, handing me a glass of red wine. "I got you this wine ages ago and then I ran into Tim and we started talking about your Gramma's problem. I thought I'd get some more details for you from Tim's volunteer work at Shady Terrace. From what he says, it sounds like you need to get Martha on a list for another place soon because there may not be enough openings in Boulder for all the residents who need to relocate."

"Thanks for the wine," I said, although I didn't feel much like drinking it. My gut had begun to churn again at the thought that Gramma's choices might be even more limited than I'd thought. "Good to see you, Tim. Sorry I had to leave for class before your talk started at Shady Terrace this morning. I really wanted to hear what you had to say. I hate the idea of moving Gramma—and it's even worse if there's a shortage of places for her to go. Do you think there's any chance the sale won't go through?"

"Unfortunately it looks like a done deal," Tim said gently. His eyes were warm, but his expression was grim. "They wouldn't have a big family meeting announcing they're closing unless they're sure it's going to happen."

"Do you know of other good places she could go?" I asked. "I don't even know where to start."

Tim asked me about Gramma, her care needs, her history, her likes and dislikes and such. And he made a few suggestions as to places I might want to check out. But he said he couldn't make specific recommendations. "I can tell you which places have had the best health department surveys and the fewest complaints against them, but you'll need to visit them to see how you think your grandmother would fit in. And like I was telling Elisa, there's the question of what places have openings. With sixty plus residents needing to move, everything will fill up fast."

None of this was sounding good to me at all. "Gramma has money. She's paying privately there. Maybe I could bring her home and hire a caregiver to stay with her." This was scary because I remembered the problems Grampa had with Gramma before she moved to Shady Terrace. But I love her so much and I owe her and Grampa so much, how could I not consider it? Tim gave me a sympathetic smile. "You could look into doing that, but the agencies charge a fortune for round-the-clock care—and you'd probably need that even if she's living with you, since you say she wanders at night and you'd need to be able to sleep."

"Maybe I could find someone I could hire privately to live in so we wouldn't have to pay the agency fees," I said.

"Maybe, but you have to be really careful who you hire. I've heard some horror stories. In fact my own father was ripped off by his housekeeper and I didn't even know it until after he died."

"Were you able to—" Before I could finish my question, we were interrupted by shouts from the other side of the room.

"This is *unbelievable*! What are *you* doing here? You ruin *everything* for our family! Couldn't you let us have *anything* special just for us?" Across the room, my student Lacey Townes stood eyeball to eyeball with Judith Demar, screaming at her. Judith did not reply but jutted her sharp chin closer to Lacey's face.

"Enough, Lacey." Derrick Townes stepped in back of Lacey, gripped her shoulders and pulled her back away from Judith, who looked disgusted.

"And *you*! I suppose you *invited* her here," Lacey screeched. "Don't you even *care* that this is Angelica's special night? You can screw whoever you want, but please don't bring your whores around for family events."

The gallery was completely silent by then, except for Lacey's tirade. All eyes were on her. What a drama queen! I was already congratulating myself that I hadn't agreed to take her on for the Contact Project.

Then a young girl in a white dress with long dark hair down to her waist walked confidently toward Lacey and put her hand on Lacey's arm. The young girl paused, gazed into Lacey's face and spoke in a calm, clear voice. "Lacey, our joy is within us. She can't touch it. Don't give her power over you."

Lacey closed her eyes and took a deep breath. I could almost see waves of tension leaving her body. She opened her eyes and turned to Angelica with a smile. "You're right, Angelica," she said, "Let's go look at your paintings." She clasped Angelica's hand and they walked off toward the back of the gallery.

As I watched them move off together, I marveled at the ability Angelica had to calm Lacey so easily. She was clearly a powerful ten-year-old. I felt strangely drawn to her, almost as if she radiated energy that connected with me in some spiritual way.

Chapter 5

As other guests gradually returned to their conversations, I pulled my attention back to the people around me, thanked Tim for his help and excused myself. I considered going to the back of the gallery to meet Angelica, even though I had reservations about getting into a conversation with Lacey. But as I looked around I saw Pablo, who had finally shown up and was standing over by his work. Mia wasn't with him. He beckoned me over with such a big smile that I couldn't resist.

He gave me a huge hug and I relaxed and hugged him back, loving as always the solid feel of his well-muscled body. I hung out there for a while with him, listening as he answered questions about his sculptures. I love to hear Pablo talk about his art because while he's serious about it, he doesn't take himself too seriously. I heard a man ask, "How do you manage to breathe so much life into sculptures you create out of rusty gears and tools?"

"Basically they're reincarnated from discarded stuff into new creatures and they come alive in the process," Pablo said. "As I sculpt them, each cat or frog or chicken or person reveals its distinct personality to me. Most of them come out humorous—kind of like they're laughing at being made out of stuff people threw away. But some seem to have something serious to say—mostly about recycling." I laughed along with the crowd and felt proud that Pablo is a guy who is able to combine being a hard-nosed cop with being a soft creative artist as well as a witty outgoing conversationalist.

Of course it's his outgoing personality that leads to situations like him taking Mia for a drink before tonight's show. And whoops—there she was, walking slowly through his sculptures, carefully checking out each piece. "Great work, Pablo," she said, giving him a hug. Then she stood beside him like she belonged there.

I was tired of doing the jealous girlfriend thing by then. He knew we were both there and it was his problem to solve. I wasn't going to hang around looking needy. So when I noticed Lacey and Angelica leave, I went off to the back of the gallery to look at Angelica's work.

Her paintings were impressionistic new-age-type portraits of faces, each surrounded by a unique swirling multi-colored pattern. Vibrant colors and well-rendered, especially for a ten-year-old. It's not easy to tell how a child artist will develop or whether she is a prodigy, but Angelica did seem to have talent. I wondered how Faye had discovered her work.

It was almost time for the gallery to close by then and my day had been long and stressful. I was so ready to go home and crash. But there was Pablo to think about. We were going to a wedding in Estes Park the next day but we hadn't made any specific plans about tonight, whether he was coming home with me again or going back to Longmont. We tend to sort of go with the flow on that stuff. I knew that if he came home with me, we'd get into a big fight about Mia and I didn't have the energy for that.

I noticed that Mia had moved on to look at some work at the other side of the gallery. She was absorbed, examining the art with an artist's eye, which gave me the opportunity to talk to Pablo without her. So I walked over to him and said, "Hey, great show. But I'm on my last legs, so I'm going home and get some sleep. What time do you want to pick me up tomorrow?"

Pablo looked surprised. "I thought we could all grab some dinner after I get done here—maybe hang out and talk a while," he said.

All? He wanted me to go to dinner with him and Mia? No way I had the energy for that. "Thanks, but I'm too tired and I'm not really hungry," I said. "It's been a long day."

He put his arm around my shoulders and gave me a sideways hug. "Oh, right. I'm sorry I haven't had time to talk with you about the Shady Terrace closing. Are you sure you don't want to go for dinner so you can tell me about it?"

The hug felt good and I was briefly tempted to go with him but I was too exhausted to cope with Mia. "Pablo, I appreciate your concern, but I don't think I can talk about it any more today," I said. "We can catch up tomorrow. What time is good for you?"

"How about 1:30? That will give us time for a hike before the wedding."

"Perfect. See you at 1:30," I said moving toward the front door.

Elisa came out the door right behind me and offered me a ride home, so we walked back to the St. Julien parking lot to get her car. I live in west Boulder, only about ten blocks from there and my office is in the 200 block of Pearl so I had walked over to the St. Julien after work and I could have easily walked home. But the evening had cooled and a breeze had picked up, so I was glad for the ride. We hustled along the sidewalk trying to stay warm. "So you decided to let Mia win out?" she asked.

I knew Elisa had a point, but I didn't want to think about it or talk about it right then. "I don't want to confront him until I've had some sleep. I'm too tired to even think about it right now. So it can keep until tomorrow." As we dodged a couple of cars on Walnut, I decided to change the subject to get Elisa off my case. "By the way, how come Tim Grosso was at the opening?" I asked.

"He and Faye have been in a relationship for a while now. You didn't know?"

I stopped dead in my tracks. "No way! Really? I had no idea. But I don't see Faye that often. And we don't talk about personal stuff, just painting."

Elisa put her arm over my shoulders and pulled me along. "Come on, girl. Let's get out of that cold wind."

I picked up my pace. "Do you know why Faye is showing Angelica's work?" I asked. "An unknown child artist is unusual for her."

"One reason might be that Mirabel Townes was her silent partner in the gallery."

"Wow, I guess I really don't know Faye all that well. But you know everything as usual."

"Honey, you know me. I like to be in the middle of everything and know all about whatever is going on," Elisa said. We'd reached the parking lot by then, got in her car and drove out.

"That Lacey Townes sure is a piece of work," Elisa said. "After what we saw tonight, I'd say she's not a prime candidate for your Contact Project."

While I'd had the exact same thought myself while watching Lacey's over-dramatization, somehow hearing Elisa say it aroused my oppositional side. I have real problems with anyone telling me what to do, even when the advice-giver is a good friend. So I said, "Maybe Lacey truly is desperate to find out what happened to her mom and that's why she's behaving this way. So tonight could be a sign that she really needs help."

"Suit yourself, but I'd say you're the one who's going to be needing help if you get involved with her. Remember you heard it here first."

"I'm still thinking about it," I said, "Interesting family. So I guess Derrick Townes is Faye's business partner now that Mirabel's dead?"

"Or maybe the kids," Elisa said, turning into my driveway. "I heard they inherited a lot."

"Right. Lacey did say she had money to pay whatever my going rate is. I could use a little influx of cash about now. I lost a few clients during that mess we were involved in last summer."

"Give it up, Cleo. Not worth the money."

"Maybe not, but I'm not sure," I said as I gave Elisa a quick hug and jumped out of the car. "Thanks for everything. Talk to you later." She waited until I unlocked my front door, got inside and turned on the lights before she drove off.

I wasted no time getting ready for bed, but once I lay down I was suddenly wide-awake worrying about Gramma again. I kept running the problem through my mind, hoping a new solution would somehow pop up.

Instead what popped up was Tyler, a spirit who visits me now and then—usually when I'm wrestling with a problem. I guess you'd have to call Tyler a ghost. I never knew him as a live person. He originally showed up one day when I was trying to contact my dead grandfather.

Instead of Grampa, I got this blond, blue-eyed spirit-guy in a faded gray "Never Stop Surfing" tee shirt, black nylon shorts and gray rubber sandals. I know enough about spirit contacts to believe Tyler is real. But I don't tell people about him. I did tell Pablo and that was probably a mistake—but I've learned Tyler comes for a reason, and it's important for me to follow his directions.

Tyler always visits without warning. It's as if he drops from the clouds. I'm not always glad to see him. He's not only dead, he's bossy. He speaks in this stupid surfer slang and tells me what to do like I'm his flunky, and he won't leave me alone until I do what he says. But even though it can be problematic to figure out what he's telling me, I know I need to take him seriously when he says someone needs my help.

Today I needed his help, so he was a welcome sight sitting cross-legged on the end of my bed. I sat up but stayed at my end. "Tyler! Great! I have a huge problem."

"Yo, Cleo. You're into some mean waves, dude."

"What about Gramma and how she has to move? What should I do?"

"She's in the impact zone. Got snaked. Might take a nose-dive and wipe out."

His cryptic answer was more and at the same time less than I wanted to hear. Frustration surged through me like one of his waves. "What do you mean, *wipe out*? What can I do to stop it?" I shrieked.

Tyler answered calmly like he always does. "That's not my dog, Cleo. Angelica and Lacey are in the waves you need to grab."

"But Tyler," I begged, edging closer to him on the bed. "Won't you help me with Gramma's problems first? At least ask Grampa what he wants me to do. He's dead too, so you should be able to ask him."

Tyler bounced—or whatever he does when he moves—over to the corner of the room, where he floated in midair. "Back down, Cleo. I'm not in that channel. You need to help Angelica. She's out there alone body surfing in those mean waves."

"How about you help me and then I'll do what you want?" I said boldly.

"I don't do deals. Angelica needs you. You can't just splash around.

Get out there and get on before the wave starts to break."

"Tyler, I don't—"

"I gave you the word. Now I'm gone," he said. And he disappeared.

I flopped back down in my bed, disappointed and confused. So Tyler wanted me to help Lacey and Angelica, but he had nothing useful to say about Gramma's problem. His visit had just added to my distress.

I had plenty to think about but I was beyond fed up with this day. So I put it all out of my mind and went to sleep hoping that somehow life would look better tomorrow.

Chapter 6

When Pablo picked me up the next day, he was in a great mood—all smiley and affectionate. He gave me a big kiss, then said, "Faye called this morning." A guy who was at the show last night came back this morning and bought two of my pieces."

"That's terrific news," I said, hugging him and kissing him back. "A great way to start this beautiful weekend."

"Exactly," he said with another big smile. "We're headed for some fun. The wedding's going to be a great party and today is a perfect day to drive into the mountains."

We decided to take the slightly longer route to Estes Park along the Peak-to-Peak Highway where we'd get the most stunning display of fall color. In Colorado we don't have the full palette of autumn color that many other states do. Our dominant color is the brilliant golden yellow of aspens. The sight of luminous yellow leaves sparkling in the sunlight, set off by the dark green evergreens, is truly spectacular. It was a gorgeous day and I relaxed into it for a while as we drove up Boulder Canyon.

But my thoughts kept drifting back to Mia. I needed to know more about her and why she was visiting. I waited to see if Pablo would bring her up. Big surprise—he didn't. So as we got close to Nederland at the top of the canyon, I turned toward him and said in what I hoped was an interested-but-not-accusatory tone of voice, "I don't recall you ever telling me about Mia before."

Pablo kept his eyes on the road. "Nothing to tell. I knew her a long time ago."

I waited a minute to see if he'd go on, but he didn't so I forged ahead. "So what's she doing here now?"

He continued to look straight ahead. Well okay he was driving, but a few seconds of eye contact wouldn't be all that dangerous. His answer was brief. "She's visiting her cousins in Denver and checking out a couple of job possibilities. Hey, look at that bunch of aspen on the right up ahead." He pointed at a gorgeous stand.

I took a minute to enjoy the sight. I'm used to Pablo changing the subject when I ask a sensitive question. He doesn't like confrontation, even when it's gentle. I respect that to a certain extent, but this time I felt he owed me at least some explanation. So I got back to business. "Mia's looking at jobs—does that mean she might be moving here?"

"Maybe."

"Are you hoping she does?"

"What's with all the questions, Cleo? Mia's just a friend. Here we are lucky enough to have hit the peak weekend for fall color. Let's enjoy it."

I took a few minutes to think and admire the scenery before I answered. I was frustrated with his responses, but he had a point about the peak weekend. It can be tricky to get into the mountains at just the right time to see the aspens turning and today as we drove along the winding highway, curve after curve revealed yet another stand of glowing trees. I didn't want to ruin a good time by continuing to push him.

It occurred to me that Pablo's and my relationship had as many twists and turns as this road. Sixteen years ago when we were twenty-one-year-old art students in love, I thought Pablo was my soul mate. Back then our future together stretched out in my mind's eye like a long sandy beach where the sun reflects off the crashing waves day after day as we stroll hand-in-hand through the surf. But Pablo's mind's eye held a different vision—one that left me here in Boulder while he went off traveling the world to find his artistic voice. It took me nearly a year to accept that he was really gone and not coming back any time soon. Once the shock finally wore off, I got over being left, and began to see my future without Pablo. I moved on with my life and into other relationships—some intense and even serious.

When Pablo moved back to Boulder ten years ago, I was so over him. No way did I want to open myself up to that kind of hurt again. But in the last few years we've gradually drifted back together. One reason is that we know each other inside and out and we have fun together. Another is great sex. But I don't have those old illusions about where we're headed. Now that he's a cop I'm not thinking he'll leave town on a whim and be gone for years. But he likes to keep his options open. And I'm liking that freedom too. We don't have any claim on each other.

Like Elisa said, I don't want commitment right now, so why does it bother me when he pays attention to someone else? Am I like some petulant two-year-old who wants only the toys someone else is playing with? I knew I needed to sort out my feelings about the Pablo and Mia thing and he clearly didn't want to talk about Mia, at least not right now. So I decided to drop the questions until I had more time to think about what I wanted to say.

"You're right," I said. "It is a gorgeous day and I'm ready for some relaxation. This thing with Gramma is driving me crazy."

"She has to move? That's a shame. What's the deal?"

I filled him in on the meeting at Shady Terrace and what Tim Grosso had told me. "And from what Tim said last night I'll have to act quickly to get her a place," I continued, "so this morning I dropped in on one of the possible nursing homes she could maybe go to. Tim said visiting unannounced is the best way to see what a place is really like, especially if you go on a weekend when staffing is lighter."

"Where did you go?"

"Easy Living Care Center. I picked that one because one of Grampa's old friends, Dr. Loberg, moved there after his stroke and I've been meaning to visit him. I figured I could check the place out and look in on Dr. Loberg at the same time."

"How was it?"

"Not great. When I got there it was nearly 11:00 and Dr. Loberg was in his room, still in his pajamas. Then an aide came in and told him he needed to stop fooling around and let them dress him in time for lunch. I left and went down to the dining room. There were a bunch of residents slumped in wheelchairs outside the door waiting for lunch. When lunch got started at about 11:15, I noticed three nurse aides standing by the wall chatting instead of helping residents who couldn't feed themselves. That's definitely a deal-breaker for Gramma, since she eats pureed food and usually needs help at the table."

"Sounds grim. I'm so sorry, Cleo. Your grandmother is a terrific lady and I know how much you care about her." He reached over and gave my hand a squeeze. "Do you think there's any possibility Shady Terrace won't go through with the closing if enough families complain? Or what about calling the paper and getting the corporation some bad publicity?"

I teared up a little at the love and sympathy I felt from Pablo. He knew me so well and he'd known Gramma before the Alzheimer's hit, so he could really understand what I was going through and how much I was worried about her.

"No," I said, wiping my eyes. "I don't think any of that will help. Elisa says the developer who's buying the place—his name is Hugh Symes—has been trying to get his hands on that land for years. Apparently he's not the sympathetic type who'd care that he's displacing a bunch of old people."

"You've got that right. Symes is one of those guys who does what he wants and then later says, 'Oh did I run over your foot? Well you shouldn't have been standing so close to my car.'" Pablo suddenly swerved off into a turnout where we could look at the trees back down the valley. We got out of the car, Pablo gave me a big hug, and I kind of collapsed on his shoulder for a minute. Then we turned arm-in-arm to the stunning display of leaves below, oohing and ahhing like tourists.

When we were back in the car driving along the highway again, I asked, "So you know Hugh Symes?"

Pablo clenched his teeth and tightened his face in that way he does when he takes a dim view of someone or something. "More like I know about him," he said grimly. "There are lots of nasty Symes stories out there. Like last year he was getting ready to build on some land he owns when the animal-rights activists started protesting that he was going to be destroying prairie dog burrows and that those prairie dogs had to be relocated before he could build. You know Boulder has those laws against killing prairie dogs or damaging their burrows unless you have a permit. Well, those permits aren't easy to get. First, you have to make what they call reasonable efforts to relocate the prairie dogs to an approved site."

"Who approves it? The prairie dogs or the city? Do the prairie dogs insist on mountain views like everyone else in Boulder?" I'm not unsympathetic to wildlife preservation, but sometimes the way we talk about issues in Boulder can be so holier-than-thou I can't resist poking fun. Plus I wanted to see if I could get Pablo to lighten up.

I succeeded. His face relaxed and he laughed. "Very funny, Cleo. Maybe you're more like Symes than you think. Anyway if developers can't get the prairie dog colony moved, they can apply for a permit to use lethal control, but the permits can take more than a year to get after all the reviews and cost thousands of dollars, and Symes didn't want to mess with all that. He just wanted to get on with his development." Pablo shook his head and took on that disapproving look again. "Somehow some of his workers plowed the burrows under, which Symes later said was all a big mistake, that he wasn't there when it happened, the workers didn't speak English, yada yada yada."

I shook my head right along with him at that point. "Wow! Power triumphs again! Didn't the city do anything about it?"

Pablo gave an exasperated sigh. "One of Boulder's local activists was pushing the city attorney into filing criminal charges against him, but then she drowned in her hot tub and I guess the other people in the prairie dog group didn't feel like pursuing it, so Symes got away with it."

Wait a minute! I gasped and almost grabbed Pablo with both hands as I tried to digest this stunning news. But even in my agitated state I realized that pouncing on him physically wasn't a good move while he was negotiating mountain curve. Instead I pulled back and screeched at him. "Drowned in her hot tub! Was that Mirabel Townes?" How did this woman's name keep popping up? Could Tyler be sending me hints?

"Right," Pablo said. "Did you know her?"

I could have just said, "No, I don't know her," and left it at that, which probably would have been better, but I decided to go ahead and tell him about Lacey's issues. I took a deep breath and said, "No, I never met Mirabel Townes, but her daughter Lacey is in my class and yesterday she told me she and her younger sister think someone pushed Mirabel under and drowned her. They want me to help them contact her to find out what happened."

"What?" Pablo turned to face me and nearly slammed into the back of a car that had slowed down to take in the view. His good mood had taken a definite nosedive this time. "Dammit, Cleo. I thought you had enough of that last summer when you almost got yourself killed."

I knew he didn't want me getting involved with another possible murder. But I'm an adult and bottom line I get to make my own choices. So I didn't give an inch. "Back off, Pablo," I said. "You're going to kill both of us if you don't pay more attention to your driving."

But he didn't back off. He scowled and said, "How about you don't smack me with ugly news while I'm driving then?"

What happened to enjoying the day? I took a calmer tone "I wasn't trying to upset you. I was just telling you what Lacey said to me, what she asked me to do. Why do you have to react so fast and get all bossy and overprotective?"

"Cleo, I don't want to tell you what to do, but I don't want you in danger either."

"I hear you," I said. "And I know your concern comes from caring about me, but I have a lot to consider in this situation. I haven't decided what I'm going to do yet, so can we let it go for now?"

"Okay, Cleo," he said with a sigh. "I hope you use good sense making your decision, and I don't want to talk about it now either. We're almost to Estes, so how about we head straight for the park so we can get in a hike before the wedding. We could both use some exercise to work off our stress."

I agreed, so we went right through the town of Estes to Rocky Mountain National Park, home of some of the most fantastic mountain scenery in the world. It's only an hour from Boulder, but I don't go there nearly as often as I wish I did. It's one of those places people come from all over the world to see, but because I know it's right next-door—well, you know how that goes.

October is elk mating season at the park so there were lots of elk and tourists everywhere. We stopped briefly at Moraine Park to watch some male elk butting heads, each trying to win the right to mate with a nearby female elk. As I watched, I couldn't help but think that while facing conflict head on may be violent, it has the advantage of being clean and quick.

We sat silently as we drove on along the curvy Bear Lake Road to the Glacier Gorge parking lot where a popular trail leads along Glacier Creek to Alberta Falls, less than a mile each way. I wanted to focus on the scenery, but I couldn't get the Townes family out of my head. I truly didn't know what to do about Lacey and Angelica Townes' suspicions about Mirabel's drowning. Tyler had been—for him—very clear about what I should do. And Tyler is a determined spirit who finds ways to get me to follow his directions. But if Lacey is a drama queen and Angelica some sort of precocious psychic kid, Elisa might be right about them being trouble for me. And—despite what Pablo might think—I'm not looking for trouble.

Plus, it had only been twenty-four hours since I'd found out that I had to find a new place for Gramma to live, and apparently I'd have to act quickly. So should I start with that and put other unpleasant stuff out of my mind?

As we hiked along the creek, I played a game I sometimes use, where I mentally toss my problems into the creek and let them pitch and bob along beside me. It helps me prioritize, as in my mind's eye I see some issues sail to the front while others barely remain afloat. I know, it sounds like Tyler-the-surfer has gotten to me with his water imagery, but trust me, I was doing this long before he showed up.

Today, Gramma's relocation issue was the strong swimmer, the Townes family and Mia drifted far behind. So I made a vow not to mention the other issues again this weekend and to try to keep them out of my mind. After that, I cleared my mind and enjoyed the trail as we wound back and forth crossing the creek on wooden bridges, and climbing through fir, spruce and colorful aspen groves to the majestic falls. We stood quietly holding hands for a while at the top, letting the roar of the falls surround us as we stared at the water rushing over huge rocks into the creek below.

A relaxed peaceful feeling came over me until a bright sunbeam reflecting off a shiny part of a rock drew my attention. I turned toward it and out of the corner of my eye I saw a blond surfer in black shorts riding his board over the falls. Arms wide, knees slightly bent, perfectly balanced on his board and looking directly at me. No way! I jumped, pulled my hand free from Pablo's and ran closer. Pablo looked startled, but neither he nor anyone else seemed to notice anything out of the ordinary in the falls. Tyler! It must be him and I was the only one who could see him. He flickered, then vanished, but I heard him loud and clearly in my head, "Don't blow it, Cleo. You need to hit the surf."

Chapter 7

I kept the Tyler sighting to myself as we hiked back to the car and drove into town. Pablo has not only never seen Tyler, he never wants to see him. And if he believes I see him—which I doubt—he would much rather I didn't. It's one of those tender spots between us that I try not to poke.

Oddly enough, Pablo himself mentioned Tyler as we were checking in to the historic Stanley Hotel in Estes Park. "Hey, Cleo, your buddy Tyler will be right at home here," he said with a smirk. "Ghosts are all over this hotel. I've heard they especially like the billiard room. Does Tyler play?"

Oh so many smart retorts came to mind, but I kept them to myself as I looked around the vast lobby. Leaving aside the sarcasm, Pablo was right. This hotel is one of the top ten haunted hotels in the country, and even gives ghost tours, which are very popular. It was the inspiration for Steven King's "The Shining," half of which he wrote here in room 217. Later the TV miniseries of that book was filmed here.

People say that F. O. Stanley, who built the hotel in 1909, haunts it along with his wife Flora and former servants. Guests report seeing and hearing children playing on the stairs and in the halls when there is no child in the building, smelling strong unexplained lavender scents in some bedrooms, seeing doors open and close by themselves and hearing the piano playing on its own in the music room. Fans of the paranormal come from all over to stay at the Stanley and they're even willing to pay extra to stay in fourth-floor rooms that supposedly have the most ghostly activity, hoping to get pictures or videos of orbs—balls of transparent light sometimes seen in photos taken in haunted places.

Sounds like a perfect fit for me, right? Actually I would have preferred the wedding were somewhere that was less of a ghost magnet. I figured Pablo was right that Tyler would feel right at home here, but I wasn't in the mood for more Tyler counsel about how I needed to help Lacey until I had more time to think about what I wanted to do.

But this majestic white four-story hotel, perched high on the rocks overlooking Estes Park with amazing views in every direction, is a favorite for weddings. The groom is one of Pablo's oldest friends. And the bride is from a rich Boulder family, so I figured it would be a great party.

It was. The wedding and reception were in the MacGregor ballroom off the lobby. It's a grand Victorian room, holds several hundred people, and has a big stage for the wedding and later the band. Round tables draped with white linen filled the main part of the room. Roses and candles were everywhere—all in pale blush tones, mostly soft peach and ivory. Crystal sparkled in the candlelight.

The ceremony was short and sweet, followed by champagne and appetizers, an elegant buffet with wine, an open bar, and dancing to a jazz band. The romantic setting snapped us out of our earlier quarrelsomeness and I was feeling mellow and sentimental. Pablo looked yummy. I love seeing him dressed up. He's great looking—tall and muscular, with black curly hair you want to run your hands through, and adorable brown eyes. In classy clothes he looks even sexier than usual.

As we danced, he held me tightly and I nuzzled into his shoulder. The champagne and the glow of the evening worked their magic to break down the walls I have so carefully constructed to keep Pablo in the not-a-serious-relationship category. I even forgot about Mia and started having fantasies of Pablo and me having a wedding like this, surrounded by our friends and family. Hmm. Maybe I do want commitment.

When the band took a break, Pablo and I headed for the bar, holding hands softly. But our way was blocked by a distinguished-looking elderly man swaying from side to side as he shouted in the face of a much younger man. The young guy was wearing a slender beautifully tailored pinstriped suit and his medium-length dark hair was cut in a shaggy retro style reminiscent of sixties Brit-rock bands. Both men looked rich and both looked angry.

"Is it your job to tell me how much I can drink now, Shane?" the old man boomed. "Where do you get off telling your grandfather how to suck eggs? I was drinking before you were born, you little snot!"

"Don't be an ass, Grandfather. You're drunk and you're spoiling this party. Why don't you go up to your room and sleep it off?" The young man—apparently his name was Shane—took his grandfather's arm and tried to pull him in the direction of the door.

It took me a minute, but I recognized the older man as my grandparents' attorney, Vernon Evers. He's in his late seventies now and he's kept only a few clients, but in his day he was one of Boulder's most prominent attorneys. I was mortified for him and his grandson. And I worried that the ugly behavior might ruin the wedding reception for the bride and groom. Already a ring of curious guests had formed in front of the two men. Pablo moved forward as if to intervene. I grabbed his arm to stop him before he ended up with both men turning on him.

Before we could argue about whether Pablo should break in, a gorgeous long-legged young woman ran up to the men. "Shane, what's going on? I leave for the ladies room for two minutes and when I get back you've created a scene." Her thick shoulder-length auburn hair looked more tousled than I would have expected if she had indeed been in the ladies room, but I figured she must have one of those intentionally messy hairstyles.

Shane didn't answer. Just gave her a disgusted look and walked off. She turned her attention to Mr. Evers. "Calm down, Vern," she said in a velvety-soft voice as she leaned toward him, almost freeing her super-sized breasts from the top of her classic black cocktail dress.

"Let me help you back to our table." She gave him a charming smile and a quick kiss and took his arm to guide him away from the bar.

"Dammit, Glenna, you can't smooth this over that easily." He wasn't shouting anymore though, so she had accomplished something. Not too surprising. This woman was stunning, looked like a European model with huge brown eyes, full lips and high cheekbones. And, although she looked to be about forty years his junior, she gazed at him sweetly like a lover.

But he stood his ground. "I still haven't gotten the drink I came up to get while you were out. I was just about to order another Chivas Regal when along comes my slacker grandson trying to tell me how to live. He can't even manage his own life. What makes him think he's in charge of mine?"

Glenna put her arm around his shoulders—easy because she was as tall as he was—and gave him another dazzling smile. "Shane's gone off now, so how about we go back to our table and then I'll bring you your drink." This time he let her guide him away.

All of us bystanders breathed a combined sigh of relief and turned back to the party. "Wow, do you realize who that old guy is?" I asked Pablo quietly as we walked back to our table with refilled wine glasses.

"Oh yes. That's Vernon Evers. Boulder lawyer and former city commissioner," Pablo said.

"Right. He was my grandparents' lawyer," I said as I set my wine glass on the table next to his. "He handled some copyright stuff when some of Gramma's paintings were included in a photography book. It was kind of a messy thing and he did a great job. But he seems a lot different than I remember him."

We sat down at the table and sipped our wine for a few minutes, still slightly dazed by the episode. "Maybe you just didn't see that side of him," Pablo said. "Evers has always been a character—never one to stay in the background. He was a major player in PLAN Boulder County—that citizens' group that's always pushing for more open space—and he was known for telling people who didn't want to pay taxes for open space that if what they like is urban sprawl they should move to Denver or L.A. Not well-liked by local developers."

"Well it looks like women like him," I said. "That babe he's with is hot. I wonder what she sees in someone so much older."

Pablo laughed. "Money and power are big aphrodisiacs. I've seen it before. Usually when a woman like her is hanging out with an old guy, there's more to it then love. She's probably getting what she wants."

"What about his wife?"

"I think she died a couple of years ago. And then his only daughter died. He probably needs some cheering up. But, hey—his daughter who died was Mirabel Townes, the woman who drowned that you were talking about today."

"Really!!! His daughter! So his grandson Shane must be Lacey and Angelica's brother." The way Mirabel's family kept showing up was getting spooky. Was Tyler finding ways to push this family in my face until I took on the case? In two days I'd met—or at least seen—Mirabel's two daughters Lacey and Angelica, her son Shane, her husband Derrick and now her father Vernon Evers. And in this haunted hotel I might well meet Mirabel herself before the night was over.

Chapter 8

After the party, Pablo and I carried the romantic wedding atmosphere up to our room along with half a bottle of champagne. We slipped out of our clothes and lounged on the bed in each other's arms, sloppily sipping champagne and dripping it on each other—which led to earth-shaking sex.

Afterward, Pablo rolled over and cradled me softly in his arms. "That was amazing!" he said softly as he stroked my face. I snuggled into him, loving the tingly totally relaxed feeling. I felt connected to him at such a deep level that I had no need to say anything. I just knew we were in complete synch. Maybe he was having wedding fantasies that matched my earlier ones.

Well, not exactly. Pablo cradled my face, looked deeply into my eyes, and said, "You know, I was thinking when we were dancing tonight that we're so lucky that we enjoy each other so much without feeling any pressure to get married. That we both agree about that." He hugged me close.

My heart sank. This is how it always is with him, I thought. Close but not too close. How could I forget? At that point I realized he was right—we do best when we enjoy what we have, without a long-term commitment. And I didn't want marriage either. I had gotten caught up in the romantic wedding atmosphere, but was now back to reality. "I know what you mean," I said. "What we have is perfect for me. I don't want to think about forever."

We curled up and slept spoon-style until 3:00 a.m., when I startled awake. The room was dark but enough light shone under the room door from the hall that I could see the shapes of the furniture. I had that momentary disoriented feeling you get when you wake up in a hotel room not knowing at first where you are. The room was quiet except for Pablo's snoring. I felt a prickly sensation at the back of my neck, a strong impression that someone was in the room, and that odd lightheadedness I often get when Tyler shows up.

I sat up and turned my head slowly from side to side, casing the room, expecting Tyler to pop up. But he didn't. Then I found myself looking into a large mirror hanging over the antique dresser across from me. A bit of light crept in around the window curtains and reflected in the mirror like a tiny lamp. As I stared at that light, I saw a beautiful teen-aged girl with dark hair, blue eyes and fair skin looking longingly in my direction. "Please," she said. "Please. They need you." Then she vanished.

I sat quietly and waited for more, but I knew she was gone. The feeling of an otherworldly presence wasn't there any longer. Who was she? And who needed me? The Townes family? Someone else? I ran questions and possibilities through my mind as I snuggled back into Pablo, and the next thing I knew it was 9:00 a.m. Sunday morning.

We grabbed a quick breakfast and set off down the canyon because Pablo needed to get back to Boulder by early afternoon. He was leaving that night for a weeklong training course in Atlanta. Something about crisis intervention where officers get trained to deal with people who are having a mental health crisis or are on a mood-altering substance. I wondered briefly whether training like that would make him more understanding of my occasional emotional outbursts or whether he'd just try to "handle" me in some new professional way.

When we got down as far as Lyons, I turned on my phone to check for messages. The mountains are iffy for cell phone reception, so I hadn't even bothered to keep my phone on while I was up there. There was one from Tim Grosso in his volunteer ombudsman role letting me know about a family meeting set for Sunday afternoon at Shady Terrace. Then six from Lacey Townes, each more urgent than the last, going on and on about how she absolutely had to meet with me. I skipped to the end of most of those, saving them to listen to later.

"Looks like you missed a bunch of messages," Pablo said. "Do you have some desperate grief-therapy clients?"

"Sort of," I said, not wanting to get into the Lacey thing with him again. "But it was also Tim Grosso about a family meeting at Shady Terrace at 4:00 today. I feel like I'm sinking in the quicksand with this relocation thing, so I hope he has some good news for us."

"Seems odd that he's doing this ombudsman thing." Pablo gave me a strange sideways look. "How well do you know Tim Grosso?"

"Not well. Why?"

"I wouldn't think he'd like dealing with rules and regulations much. He's kind of an old Boulder hippie type, don't you think?"

"What do you mean?" I asked. "No long hair—he's bald. And he has a traditional job. He's the head of the university Psych Department. He hired me to teach that paranormal class and he seemed concerned the class might not be respectable enough. Warned me it was on a trial basis. Why do you think he's a hippie type?"

"He's one of those don't-trust-the-cops guys. The word is that he grows a lot of pot—not at home, probably at various places in the mountains. No one has been able to find where it is or to catch him at it yet, though."

That was a surprisingly different take on Tim. I hadn't thought of him that way at all, especially because he's my boss at the university. Still, he is a mellow guy and drugs aren't that unusual in Boulder. Plus Pablo isn't often wrong about this sort of thing. "So how do you know he's doing it?" I asked.

He brushed me off. "I don't. In fact you should probably forget I mentioned it. It's not important to what he's doing for you. I'm not even sure why I brought it up."

Before I could probe further, he changed the subject. "Hey, do you mind stopping at Faye's when we get to town so I can see if any more of my stuff sold since the opening?"

I decided to let the Tim thing go until another time. "Sure. Let's stop."

We were on North Broadway by then so it was only a few minutes to the gallery. Once there, we went straight to Pablo's work to look for red "sold" stickers and to our delight found two new ones—one on a steel dog with big round eyes and pointy ears, and the other on a rusty bird with long spindly legs. We were hugging each other and laughing when a stocky broad-shouldered guy with large muscled arms and legs came along and stood right next to us, staring at me intently from under dark bushy eyebrows.

"Cleo?" he asked. "You look great! How have you been?"

Whoa! I recognized those muscles and the eyebrows and the cowlick in his straight dark hair. Back about ten years ago I'd been on intimate terms with every part of this guy's body. But I hadn't seen or heard from him since we broke up and he moved to California.

"Ohmigod! Brian?? What are you doing back in Boulder?" Shock and awe hit me full in the face. And it didn't help any that Pablo was standing right next to me. Brian and I were together during the years Pablo was away finding his inner muse, so Pablo had never met him, although I had mentioned him occasionally. Now I'd have to introduce them.

"It's a long story," Brian said slowly. "A lot of things have changed in my life. I've actually been back here about a year." He paused briefly as if collecting his thoughts, then continued in a cheerful tone that rang a little false. "I thought about looking you up, but it's been so long and I felt embarrassed that I hadn't called. So I was waiting for the right moment to come along, and here it is."

Wow! What were the odds that Pablo and I would both reconnect in the same week with former lovers from years ago? Not that I felt any connection to Brian—but anyway, here he was.

If there's any good way to introduce a former boyfriend to a current one, I don't know what it is. So I sucked it up and forged ahead. "Um, Brian, this is my boyfriend Pablo. This is his work here that we're looking at. Pablo, this is Brian. He's an old friend." Just like Mia is your old friend, I thought.

They shook hands and muttered polite, not very sincere nice-to-meet-yous. To break the tension, I turned to Brian and asked, "Do you come to Faye's gallery often?"

"Sometimes. Not often. But today I came to see Angelica Townes' paintings," Brian said motioning toward the back of the gallery where her work was hung.

"So you know Angelica?" I asked.

"Not well, but I knew her mother and I know how proud she was of Angelica's art, so I wanted to see her show. I'd say she's talented for a ten-year-old. But you're the artist. What do you think?"

Brian looked genuinely interested in my opinion, but I didn't want to engage him in conversation. "We were here for the opening, but it was crowded and I didn't get much chance to look at her work," I said.

"Sure. Well, I have to go right now anyway. But maybe we can get together next week and catch up. Give me a call when you have some time." He stuck a card in my hand, waved and headed out the front door.

"Okay. See you. Bye." I stuttered, still in a daze. I glanced down at his card. "Brian Alavi, Creative Graphic Design." A phone number and a web address followed. Did he really expect me to call? Especially after he'd been in town for a year but hadn't called me? That was so Brian. Always needing to be in control, looking for the perfect way to present himself. Thinking he could design his life as if it were a book cover or a brochure.

I noticed that Pablo wasn't standing next to me anymore, looked around and found him talking to Faye over at the counter in the middle of the gallery. When I walked up, their conversation seemed to take a sudden turn as if I'd interrupted a confidential talk.

"What's up?" I asked.

"Faye was filling me in on who bought my work," Pablo said.

"And dishing the dirt on your old boyfriend," Faye leaned back against the counter and gave me a big smirk.

"What dirt?" I asked.

"Was he a Scientologist when you were together?" Faye asked.

I laughed. "A Scientologist? No way! Brian? He was so conventional he thought vegetarians were weird. You're not saying he's a Scientologist now, are you?"

Faye nodded vigorously. "Oh yes. He's a Scientologist all right. Very involved. He came in here one day with Mirabel Townes—you know she was the silent partner in this gallery, so she was here quite a bit. Anyway he gave me a bunch of literature about the way to happiness and invited me to a free lecture."

"Yes, I heard that Mirabel became a Scientologist after her daughter died," I said, remembering what Elisa had told me.

"True," Faye said, "but one thing I have to say for Mirabel, after she got into Scientology she never tried to convert me. But this guy Brian is quite the evangelist."

"Sounds like you and Brian have a lot to catch up with," Pablo said.

"At least as much as you and Mia," I shot back.

"Touché," Pablo said with a grin. "How about we drop the former-relationships argument and head home. I have a plane to catch tonight."

"Deal," I said. But I didn't need to be psychic to know that we'd be revisiting the Mia and Brian part of our relationship in the weeks to come.

Chapter 9

Right after Pablo dropped me off at home, I drove over to Shady Terrace so I'd have time to visit Gramma before Tim Grosso's relocation meeting for the residents' families. She was in her room just waking up from an after-lunch nap. I sat down on the side of her bed and gave her a slow, gentle hug. She doesn't always recognize me, and when she's waking up she's more confused than usual, so I wanted to be careful not to startle her.

"Hi, Gramma," I said. "I've been missing you."

"Where was I?" she sounded worried.

"It's okay. You were right here. But I wasn't. I went to a wedding in Estes Park and then Pablo and I stopped by Faye's gallery."

She squirmed, got to her feet, and started toward the door, looking troubled. "Faye's gallery. I need to finish my paintings." These days Gramma lives more in the past than the present, so she sometimes thinks she has a deadline to meet getting paintings ready for a show. Back in the day she was usually more excited than anxious about an upcoming show, but now the agitation and confusion that accompany Alzheimer's throw her into a panic at the idea.

I put my arm around her shoulders. "Don't worry. Everything's fine. Faye has plenty of your paintings at the gallery. Would you like to get some ice cream?"

"Chocolate?" she asked.

We walked together to the activity room where they have ice cream, juice and other snacks available for the residents any time. Several other residents were watching a travelogue on the large-screen

TV. I told her I had to go to a meeting and left her there eating her ice cream with them, while I went off to find out what Tim had come up with to help us deal with Shady Terrace's closing.

Twenty or so family members were already gathered in the faux-town-square lobby when I walked in. To my surprise, one of them was Derrick Townes. I took a chair next to him, reminded him that we'd met Friday night at Faye's gallery, and told him how worried I was about having to move Gramma.

"I know," he commiserated. "My dad's been here ever since his stroke last year. He's on Medicaid so we were lucky to find this place. It wasn't easy. I don't know what we'll do now."

I thought the Townes family was rich. Why would he be so short of money that his father had to go on Medicaid? At least Gramma has money to pay for her care, which gives her more choices. I silently thanked Grampa's financial management skills.

The room had filled up by then and Tim was passing out copies of a *Boulder County Senior Housing Guide* that had information about all the long-term-care facilities in the county. I opened the booklet and began reading through a list of things to look for when touring a facility, like whether there are unpleasant odors, whether the residents are appropriately dressed and so on. My heart sank. Where was I going to find a place that measured up to all these criteria? And if I did find such a place, would it have openings? I was getting more and more scared for Gramma.

Tim got the meeting started by directing our attention to charts in the booklet that listed various living facilities, showed their locations on a map, and gave information about costs, services, levels of care and such for each place. "I would recommend that you decide on some places to visit," he said. "If you call our office we can give you information on how various places did on their health department surveys and whether there have been complaints against them."

"But we aren't in a position to be picky are we?" a plump blonde woman asked. "Aren't most of the places full?"

"Some are," Tim admitted. "But quite a few have vacancies."

"I need to have my husband in a place I can visit easily," a gaunt gray-haired woman said. "Doesn't Shady Terrace have some obligation to help me find a good place for him?" She sounded close to tears.

"They do, and they will help. But it's best if you can check out the places yourself so you can choose the one you like best."

"This is all bogus." Derrick had jumped to his feet to confront Tim. "You're not here to help us. You're supposed to be neutral but it looks like you're just trying to help Shady Terrace look good. If this was happening to your own father, you wouldn't be so calm. We need to stick together and make them keep Shady Terrace open. Why don't you help us with that?" His face was as red as his crimson sweater, and sweat trickled down his face.

Tim stayed cool as he answered slowly. "Actually as a long-term-care ombudsman I'm not supposed to be neutral. My job is to advocate for the rights of the residents. But I don't know any way to keep Shady Terrace from closing and if I pretended I did, I'd be leading you on a path away from what you need to be doing, and I certainly wouldn't be helping you."

"Forget it! I'm not going to waste any more of my time here," Derrick said, stalking off to the front door. His dramatic exit was spoiled when he had to stop and find a staff member to put in the door code to let him out, but he'd made his point. And although I personally did believe Tim was trying his best to help us, I was beginning to realize that there wasn't much he could do.

My mood was dragging bottom when I left the meeting, so when I stopped at Wild Oats to get groceries I picked up roasted salmon and asparagus for dinner to cheer myself up. At home I put on one of my favorite *Sex and the City* DVDs, had a couple of glasses of wine and ate my meal. Then, feeling a bit more mellow, I got out my cell phone and listened again to Lacey's messages.

The first message came in Saturday afternoon at 2:30. "Cleo, it's Lacey Townes. We talked after class on Friday. About my mom and how my sister and I need to reach her. It's urgent!" Her voice rose in pitch and volume. "I can't believe I didn't get you. We have to meet with you. I don't know if you meet clients on weekends, but you must have some sort of emergency coverage. And this is one. An emergency! This is a huge emergency! So call me at 303-819-8203 as soon as you get this message."

Whew. She definitely sounded frantic, but I didn't share her sense of urgency at that point. Even if I'd gotten that message on Saturday, I wouldn't have responded. My emergency weekend coverage doesn't extend to wanna-be clients.

She left another hysterical message Saturday at 4:30. "Cleo, Lacey again. Where are you? You have to help me! I have no one else to turn to. How can I ever live with myself if I don't find out what happened to Mom? You have this gift. How can you refuse to help us? I told Angelica you'd be sure to call today. So don't make a liar out of me, okay. Call me at 303-819-8203. Please!!"

The desperation in her voice made me cautious. Is everything she wants an emergency for her? Clients like that can be a therapist's nightmare.

Saturday at 6:30 she had called again. She'd gotten into a two-hour pattern. Her voice was shriller and even more frenzied this time. "Cleo, this is the worst day of my life. My dad overheard us saying that we think someone drowned Mom, and he threw a fit and yelled at us that we were desecrating Mom's memory, looking to create a scandal and on and on. But we're not giving up. I promised Angelica I'd get you to help us. If my mom was murdered, don't you think she deserves justice? We have to find out if Angelica is right that someone actually drowned Mom. After all my mom did for this community, she deserves better than to have someone drown her and get away with it. Please call me!"

Looking past the hysterics, I could relate to having a difficult, demanding father. My dad never likes the choices I make in life and is fond of letting me know how I could do better. After the behavior I'd seen from Derrick Townes this morning, I sympathized with Lacey and Angelica. Lacey's argument about Mirabel deserving justice also hit home. In fact I'd made that exact argument to Elisa on Friday. If there was any chance that Mirabel's death wasn't accidental, someone should take another look.

Lacey's next message came in Saturday evening at 10:00 pm.

She sounded sullen and angry. "Cleo, it's me again. Where are you? I can't imagine you've gone to bed so early. Maybe you went out and didn't take your phone? By the way, the message you have on your phone has a cold feeling to it. I wouldn't think you'd want to sound that way to your clients. It could hurt your business. But maybe you don't want business. At least I'm beginning to wonder. Because you still haven't called me back after all these messages. My number is 303-819-8203."

That message was a definite turn-off. I don't like it when people try to manipulate me. And her messages were moving beyond manipulation to practically stalking me. Elisa and Pablo's warnings rang in my ears. But I also remembered Tyler telling me I needed to help Angelica because "she's out there alone, body surfing in those mean waves."

Lacey's last Saturday message was at 11:30 pm. This time she sounded despondent and weepy. "Cleo, I sure hope you get my messages tonight. I desperately need to talk to you right now. Give me a call no matter how late it is. I'll keep my phone on all night right next to my bed. It's 303-819-8203. Okay, I'll be waiting."

The next message was early Sunday morning. She was back to loud and desperate. "Cleo, how many ways can I say this is a terrible crisis? You're our only hope! My dad is such a jerk—you have no idea. He hasn't cared about Mom for a long time. Angelica has a bad feeling about him. We can't let him keep us quiet. I'll do anything, pay whatever you want. Please can't we at least meet and talk about this?"

No question Lacey was a drama queen. Her emotions were all over the place. If I took her on, she would be a challenging client, who I might regret ever having gotten involved with. But she needed help and her story was compelling, and her desperation was starting to haunt me. I knew very well what it felt like to have your father dismiss as nonsense what seems important to you.

I was also intrigued by what I'd seen of Angelica. She was an oddly remarkable child. My heart and my gut were telling me to sign on to help Mirabel's daughters investigate her death. And Tyler was sure pushing me in that direction.

Bottom line, I like to help people. I feel all warm and tingly inside when I do it. All my life my friends and family have been telling me to step back and stop getting drawn in to other people's problems. I've made some progress. I used to be a sucker for anyone in despair who wanted my help, but I've learned to set some limits. Unfortunately, I'm also on the high end of the scale when it comes to curiosity. If a problem involves mysterious circumstances—like last summer when I helped a young widow find out who pushed her husband off the rim of the Grand Canyon—I can be all over it before I take time to consider the risks.

Listening to those phone messages, I was well aware that I needed to be cautious about what I was getting myself involved in. Even so, I thought, it can't hurt to just talk to Lacey. So I called her back and made an appointment to meet her and Angelica at my office on Wednesday.

Chapter 10

After all that fuss about meeting with me, Lacey and Angelica were fifteen minutes late for their appointment. Not a good start. Lacey was panting and sweating as she dashed in to the pinkish flat-roofed stucco former house that now serves as my office. Angelica walked calmly at her side. I was amazed at how much alike they looked—same fair skin, dark hair, wide blue eyes—and yet how different they were. Lacey rolled her eyes, frowned and waved her arms as they followed me through the waiting room into my counseling room. "I thought we'd never get here," she said breathlessly. "I couldn't find my keys, then we got stuck in traffic, couldn't find a parking place. It's like the universe is trying to put barriers in our way. But here we are, finally." She pushed past me into the room as if she could barely last another second.

Angelica walked quietly behind me into the counseling room, waiting until Lacey's tirade was over before she spoke. She looked slowly around, taking in the southwestern décor and gazing intently at my Gramma's colorful paintings on the far wall. Then she turned to me with a welcoming smile. "Hi. I'm Angelica. Thank you for letting us come," she said quietly.

"We asked my brother Shane to come too, but he's obviously later than we are," Lacey said, throwing up her hands.

I wasn't happy that they had invited Shane without discussing it with me first, but decided to let it go so as not to start our talk with a confrontation. There was enough going on without that. "It's good to meet you Angelica, and to see you again, Lacey," I said. "We don't have a lot of time, so let's go ahead and start without him, and we can catch him up when he gets here." I motioned them toward chairs in my office. Lacey plopped down on the brown sofa and Angelica sat next to her, leaving the tan leather armchair for Shane. I sat in my usual cream-colored wing chair and started with a question.

"Lacey, you said in your phone messages that this is an emergency situation. Of course I understand the idea that your mother was murdered is horrifying to you and Angelica. But your mom died several months ago, so I need you to tell me why it's an emergency today."

"Someone is out there getting away with murdering my mother! Maybe you don't see that as an emergency, but I do. We have to find out who killed her and put that person in jail." Lacey sat rigidly, leaning forward and clasping and unclasping her hands.

"I need to back up a little. What makes you so sure your mother was murdered? Don't you think the police would have seen the signs?"

"Yes I'd think so—but apparently they didn't. We've tried to tell them, but they ignore what Angelica knows."

I turned to Angelica, who was sitting very quietly with none of the fidgeting usual for a ten-year-old. "Angelica, can you tell me more about what you know about your mother's death and how you know it?"

She looked intently into my eyes and nodded slowly. "I know she was murdered. I have a strong sense of her being pushed under the water and held there. But I don't know who did the pushing. I've tried to reach her to ask her who it was, but I can't get close enough to her. That's why we need your help."

This child had such a presence, such self-confidence that I found myself believing her at a gut level. I'd done a little internet research and found that some people believe Indigo children are unusually spiritually aware from birth and can see and hear things most of us cannot. But she could also be a depressed grieving child who had convinced herself she had special powers. I knew I needed more detail from Angelica. "That must be very upsetting for you. Can you tell me more about the sense you have of her being pushed under? Is it mainly a feeling or do you see it happening?"

Angelica squinted off to her left as if trying to make out a distant image. Then she turned back to me. "No it's not like that," she said. "It's a feeling, a way I have of knowing. It's very strong, but no clear details." She sat there smiling softly like a Buddha, waiting for my response.

In contrast to Angelica's calm demeanor, my thoughts were racing. She was persuasive, but she was also ten years old. And the police hadn't thought her mother was murdered. And in the clear light of day this situation looked like trouble. Even though my gut was telling me to do what they wanted, my head and my sensible friends were warning me to stay away—especially from Lacey, who anyone would agree was a loose cannon. Some of my most difficult clients have been people like her, who thrived on drama.

Finally I said, "I'd like to help you, but I'm not sure the Contact Project is right for this situation. It's about resolving grief, not solving murders. Also, like I told you the other day, I can't do private work with one of my students."

Lacey flew out of her chair and began pacing the room, waving her arms. "I can't stand any more of this," she screeched. "You don't want to help us. If you did, you would. We have nowhere else to turn. My dad and Judith think we're crazy. They don't believe Angelica is an Indigo child—they don't even believe there is such a thing as Indigo children. Instead of respecting Angelica as a highly evolved spiritual being, they accuse her of being fanciful and not knowing the difference between what's real and what she makes up." Lacey was standing right in front of me by then and I felt like covering my ears to mute her yelling.

Instead, I stood up and faced her. "Enough, Lacey," I said, managing to keep my voice calm. "You're not going to bully me into helping you. So please sit down."

Lacey deflated as quickly as she had blown up. "Sorry," she mumbled, heading back to the couch. She sat down, scooted closer to Angelica, and gave her a big hug. Then she turned to me, tears streaming down her face, hands clasping and unclasping rapidly. "I told you that we had another sister Kari who died two years ago of anorexia. That almost killed Mom, but she finally managed to get through it. No thanks to Dad and his girlfriend, Judith. Then just when Mom was getting her life back together, someone drowned her. It's so unfair. All we want is justice for her."

Angelica remained calm, quietly stroking Lacey's arm. "I feel what you're feeling, Lacey," she said. "But I know in my heart we will find out what happened to Mom." Angelica seemed surprisingly centered and calm, especially for a ten-year-old who had recently lost both a sister and her mother. The more extreme Lacey was, the calmer Angelica became. I worried that she was comforting Lacey instead of the other way around. Apparently this was their typical behavior pattern.

Lacey's genuine expression of grief spoke to the therapist in me. Yes she was difficult, but she was hurting and at some level I wanted to help her. Then I mentally flashed on the girl I had seen in the mirror at The Stanley. Was she the dead sister Kari?

I continued to watch Angelica. Despite her calm demeanor, I noticed three tiny tears trickling down her cheek. She said nothing, nor did she move her hand from Lacey's arm to wipe the tears away. I felt tears welling up in my own eyes. I could make myself stand firm against Lacey's histrionics but this little girl reached deep into my heart. Only ten years old and she'd already lost two of the most important people in her life. And the others weren't doing much to help. Her father was more interested in his mistress than his daughter. And her older sister went off the deep end every other minute.

It looked like Tyler was right about Angelica being out there alone and needing my help. How could I walk away from this child?

"Yes," I heard myself saying, "I'll do what I can to help you contact your mother. But Lacey, you'll have to drop my class. You'll also have to restrain yourself when we're working together. The contact process requires focus. Also, you both need to know that the contact process doesn't always work and sometimes you reach someone other than the person you're trying for. There are no guarantees."

"No problem dropping the class. I'll do it tomorrow." Lacey jumped up, clapping. "Thank you, thank you. You won't be sorry. And we understand. No guarantees. But I know it's going to work! I feel it!"

Before Angelica could add anything, we were interrupted by a knock on the front door. I jumped up to answer it and found Shane—wearing torn jeans, a black Lord-of-the-Rings tee shirt and a charming smile.

Chapter 11

I'm Shane. Are my sisters here? Sorry to be late." He didn't look sorry, but he did look agreeable so I took him at his word and showed him into the counseling room.

"Shane, what took you so long? I was about to give up on you," Lacey said in an accusing tone.

"Chill, Lacey. I'm here. So what's the big emergency?" Shane stood in front of the couch where Lacey and Angelica sat. Fortunately he sounded much more mellow than he had been when Pablo and I saw him at the wedding last weekend.

"Shane, why don't you sit over there," I said pointing to the tan chair between my chair and the couch. "Then we can fill you in."

He sat and looked inquiringly at Lacey. "So this is more about you thinking Mom was murdered? You must know Dad thinks you're crazy the way you keep bringing this up. What do you hope to gain by pushing this? Don't we have enough trouble with Dad being disagreeable already?"

"Shane," Lacey shrieked. "You need to quit being so lazy and pay attention to what's happening. I'm the one who moved home after Mom died so Angelica isn't alone there with Dad and Judith. I'm twenty-three years old and living at home to help out while you sit on your ass in your apartment playing that online game night and day, letting the real world go on around you like nothing matters."

I noticed that Angelica was sitting quietly, not trying to calm Lacey like she often does. It was almost as if she had tuned them both out. Probably after years of practice.

But Shane was fully engaged and defensive. He took the bait. "Whatever, Lacey. Look, I did you a favor coming here today. And as usual, you fly off the handle without any reason."

"No reason? To start with you're twenty-five minutes late. Then you accuse me of being crazy."

"I had to get to a good stopping place before I could leave. I was right in the middle of a major update for Gyaki-Birquit—or as you call it, that online game. And by the way, I don't just play the game all day. I'm the community developer and they actually pay me for that."

"Everything isn't about money, Shane," Lacey said dismissively. "Just look at Dad for a bad example of letting money run you."

"At least I have a job, not hanging around the university like you taking extra classes after you've already graduated. Anyway, as I was saying before you interrupted, Gyaki-Birquit is a very complex game and I have to play at least several hours a day to stay in touch with the player base and with what's going on in the game. I also manage a huge Gyaki-Birquit fan site, so I actually need to be sitting on my ass in front of my computer most of the time."

I had been letting them go on to get a sense of how they interacted, but at this point I'd had enough of their bickering. The dynamics of this family posed a challenge for sure. I was expecting more enthusiasm and less hostility. I decided to bring Angelica in to get the discussion back on track. "Shane, we've been talking about Angelica's belief about what happened to your mom," I said, turning toward the young girl. "Angelica, why don't you fill Shane in on why you and Lacey came here today."

Angelica perked up and turned to face Shane. "Shane, you know I'm an Indigo and I see things differently than most people do. So when I tell you I know someone pushed Mom under the water, you have to believe that."

Shane closed his eyes briefly, then opened them and looked at Angelica. "Who do you think pushed her under?" he asked.

"I don't know. It might have been Dad and that horrible Judith. She has the worst muddy dark red aura. She's a mean-spirited person, but Dad can't see that at all. She has no respect for me, doesn't believe I'm Indigo. Like the other day when my teacher called Dad complaining that I hadn't turned in some stupid math homework. I told him that the homework was a waste of time and I didn't want to waste my time, so I refused to do it. Judith was listening and she started yelling at me that it wasn't up to me to decide what is or isn't a waste of time at school. She called me a spoiled brat who thinks I'm better than anyone else."

Hmm…she did sound a little arrogant about the whole homework thing. I could see where Judith's spoiled brat comment probably came from. Was Angelica indeed a highly evolved Indigo child or was she a stubborn little girl who had found a rationale to get her own way? And if she was special, did that give her license to refuse to do schoolwork?

Shane scowled. "I can see why you don't like her," he said. "And she's not one of my favorite people either. But would she kill Mom? And would Dad be involved? That's a huge leap. And how are you going to know if it was her—or them? You can't just accuse them."

"I know that," Angelica said leaning forward in Shane's direction. "I've tried to reach Mom and ask her about it, but I haven't been able to. Lacey found out about Dr. Sims' project that helps people contact spirits who have passed on. We came here to ask her to help us contact Mom and she's agreed to do that."

Shane leaned back in his chair and closed his eyes in thought for a minute. Thankfully Lacey stayed silent as we waited to see what he would say. So far he didn't seem all that open to Angelica and Lacey's theory, which admittedly didn't have any basis in fact so far. His answer definitely surprised me.

"Okay, Angelica," he said. "Let's say for a minute that I accept your belief and agree that someone pushed Mom under the water. I don't think it would have been Dad and Judith. Why would they kill her when Dad could easily get a divorce?"

Lacey jumped in. "If she died, he'd inherit a lot of her money. With a divorce, he probably wouldn't get any of it. His business has been a sinkhole in the last few years. He was desperate for money. Maybe couldn't see any other way out."

Shane shook his head. "No, if you think someone killed her for money, I'd look at the Scientologists. You know Mom left them a lot of money in her will. Dad said he argued with her about it and he thought she was going to make a new will that left them out. Grandad is the one who did her will, and he says he didn't draw up a new one for her. Still, if they thought she was going to cut them out, they probably would have wanted her to die before she did it."

Angelica looked interested. "Two Scientologists used to visit Mom at home just about every week. A guy named Brian and a woman named India. Dad hated them," she said. "He said they were just after her money."

Uh-oh. A Scientologist named Brian? Could that be my ex-boyfriend Brian? He did say he knew Mirabel and he came to the gallery to see Angelica's show. I put that thought out of my mind to listen to Lacey, who was speaking to Shane in a civil, almost friendly, tone.

"You might be right, Shane," Lacey said. "For such a smart woman, Mom could be very naïve. I warned her that once the Scientologists get their hands in your pockets, you never get rid of them. But she was so gullible. She was paying them a fortune to help her with her grief. She said they were getting her to recover buried memories and erase the trauma from them, which brought her amazing relief. We argued about it over and over. Mom remembered incidents with Kari that I'm pretty sure never happened, but I couldn't get her to admit that. In some way the process made her feel better and that's all she cared about. She was addicted to those auditing sessions."

I didn't know much about Scientology, but some of this sounded ominous. Maybe I'd reconsider meeting Brian for coffee. He wouldn't know I was involved with the Townes family and maybe I could pump him for information.

Angelica looked intently at Lacey. "But, Lacey," she said. "To be fair, you didn't give Mom much chance to tell you what she thought was good about the Scientologists. She told me they do a lot to help other people and they live ethical lives. They also believe in reincarnation like Mom and I do."

"Maybe that's how she saw them," Lacey said shrilly. "But she was wrong. They're vultures who milk human tragedy to build their organization. They were using Mom, but she couldn't see it."

"I have to agree with Lacey there," Shane said. "When I was in California, studying game design at USC, I heard stories. Apparently Scientologists work really hard to recruit rich people and celebrities to promote their agenda and they get quite a few of the Hollywood types. I knew one guy whose uncle gave them over $500,000 before he figured out it was a cult that was using him."

Shane's view of Scientology sounded accurate. It was pretty much my understanding of Scientology tactics. I sat back to see where the discussion would go.

Lacey looked quizzically at Shane. "So if you thought they were using Mom too, Shane, why didn't you try to get her out of it like I did?" she asked.

"I figured she was a grown-up who could make her own choices. And I don't have your taste for turmoil, Lacey. Anyway, I figured she'd get tired of them and quit pretty soon. Actually, I think she was already beginning to feel that Scientology wasn't for her."

"What makes you think that?" Lacey asked.

"She told me they were visiting too often and demanding too much of her time. It was getting in the way of all those causes she was always working for."

"So is that why you think she was going to change her will and write Scientology out of it?" Lacey asked.

Shane shook his head. "No, Dad told me that. He seemed sure that she'd done it, too. If Dad can't find the new will, I think he's going to contest the Scientology bequest as having been made under undue influence. But Scientologists are good at winning those suits so they'll probably still get the money."

"But ..." Lacey tried to interrupt.

"Let me finish, Lacey," Shane said firmly. "This is why Dad's crazy to find the new will. But it's tough because Grandad's always been her lawyer and he told Dad he never helped Mom make a different will. The thing is, we all know Grandad drinks a lot and his memory's not as good as it used to be, so he might have forgotten. I've been trying to talk to him about it to see if he might say something different, but

I haven't gotten anywhere."

As I thought back on Shane's interaction with his grandfather at the wedding last weekend, I wasn't surprised that he hadn't gotten anywhere with Vernon Evers. But Shane didn't know I'd been there and seen him and his grandfather, and I couldn't see any reason to bring it up. Besides, I needed to bring the session to a close.

"We're running out of time today," I said. "I'm willing to have one of you be in the Contact Project to try to reach your mom," but it can't be you Angelica because you're a minor child. So it will have to be Lacey or Shane."

Angelica's face fell. "But I'm the one who was closest to her," she said. "I'm the one she'd want to talk to."

"I understand," I said. "But it wouldn't be ethical or legal for me to have a minor in the project. Even if your dad agreed, which isn't very likely, I wouldn't do it."

Lacey spoke up. "Can't you do it without telling him? We'd keep it quiet."

What is it about that being illegal and unethical that's hard for her to understand? "No, Lacey," I said. "I'm a licensed therapist and I have to operate within the rules if I want to keep doing this work—which I do. We're going to do this legally or not at all. So it will have to be you or Shane."

Lacey sagged and began her hand-clasping thing. "This is the worst news," she said glumly. "I thought it would be Angelica doing it. Mom and I weren't getting along well at all, so I don't know if she'd want to talk to me. I guess there's no chance you'd do it Shane?"

Shane shrugged his shoulders. "I'm not sure I believe in this or that it's a good idea. I'll think about it," he said.

But Lacey was in no mood for delay. "Oh never mind, Shane," she said exasperatedly. "I'll do it. But if I can't reach her, you'd better be ready to be the backup."

I was totally ready to see them go as I ushered them out of my office. Lacey and Shane's lukewarm enthusiasm was a real turnoff. I had hoped for more, given that I was getting myself involved in a messy situation that both Pablo and Elisa had warned me to stay away from.

Chapter 12

After they left, I headed straight to my tiny under-counter refrigerator and poured myself a glass of sun tea to fortify me while I did some hard thinking. I took it into my office where my desk faces the window. As I sipped my tea I took a few minutes to enjoy my gigantic maple tree's colorful display of red and orange leaves.

In my weekly meditation class I've learned to sit quietly, breathe deeply and fix my attention on a plant or flower to center myself and clear my mind of upsetting thoughts. At my desk, the maple tree is my focus. I learned the centering technique to help me cope with the helpless feeling I had about Gramma's deteriorating mind. But I've found it useful to get clarity in any tough situation. Like today's decision to help Mirabel Townes' children try to contact her.

I gazed out at the fiery leaves fluttering in the afternoon breeze, and considered the choice I'd made. I wanted to believe I had solid reasons that supported my decision. I wanted clarity. I wanted to be sure I was doing the right thing. I had almost lost my license to practice as a psychologist in the state of Colorado the last time I helped someone go after a murderer. And my teaching at the university was on a trial basis because so many faculty saw me as being on the fringe.

But instead of clarity and solid reasons, I had my intuition—a gut feeling that I was supposed to help—and of course Tyler's encouragement. I knew I had to go forward. The times in the past that I've let fear overcome my intuition or stop me from following a spirit's advice hadn't worked out well.

My thoughts drifted back to a time when I was fourteen and had gone with some friends to see a psychic. My friends had asked about their futures—would they marry, have careers, have children? But when my time came to go inside the curtain, I had something much different on my mind. "Sometimes when I wake up in the night, I see someone," I said. "She's always the same—a woman, very beautiful wearing amazing jewelry. I think she's Cleopatra. I was named for her and I've watched that Elizabeth Taylor movie about her over and over. She tells me that I have a gift that I should use to help people. I don't know what this means. Maybe it's a dream, but I don't think so."

I've never forgotten the psychic's answer to me because her advice turned out to be so accurate. "You are closer to the curtain than most people," she said. "Trust your feelings." That may sound confusing, but I took her meaning because deep down I already knew that my visitor was a spirit. I didn't talk about my Cleopatra visions to other people—certainly not my family—because I didn't want them to think I was strange. But I did take the visits seriously.

As it was, I got into huge trouble with my father a couple of days later when he found out about our visit to the psychic. "Cleo, what did you think you were doing going into that part of town at night to see a psychic? They're all fakes who are after your money. You need to learn to think before you act." To reinforce that point, Dad had grounded me for two weeks—overreacting in the harsh direction as usual.

The next week the spirit visited me just after midnight, waking me out of a sound sleep. "Your friend Emil needs you," she said. "You need to go to him now." I knew Emil had been seriously unhappy ever since the school bitch had dumped him two months ago. I'd listened and tried to be supportive as he grieved the breakup, but nothing I said broke though his wall of misery.

"I'm grounded," I said to the spirit. "I can't go out or even use the phone. My father would kill me."

"Emil's needs are greater," she said. "You will survive. He may not." Then she faded away.

Dad was still up. I could see the light from the living room where he read at night. I knew I couldn't get past him. I wanted to help

Emil but I was afraid, so I didn't go. I didn't see Emil that night or ever again. He killed himself at 2:00 a.m. And that was the last time I saw the beautiful spirit.

Even worse than my grief over losing Emil was my guilt that I had let fear win over what I knew I should do. I was torn between hoping I'd never see another spirit and hoping the Cleopatra spirit would return and give me another chance. Mostly I vowed that in the future if any spirits did show up, I would do what they asked even if it seemed risky to me personally.

But my life was spirit-free until Tyler showed up a few years ago when I was trying to contact my Grampa, who had been dead for five years. By that time I had gotten so interested in finding a way to contact Grampa that I had built my first apparition chamber in a spare room in my house. I was astonished when instead of Grampa I got Tyler—a surfer I'd never heard of or known.

At first I wondered whether he was real or a figment of my imagination. Then I asked myself which way made me crazier. Inventing an imaginary surfer-dude friend who tells me what to do, or seeing and talking to a surfer-dude spirit who no one else can see or hear? I figured I'd come off as kind of nutty either way.

But I couldn't make up the strange way he talks in surfer language. I've spent most of my life in Kansas and Colorado. I've never been surfing, never known a surfer. After the first time he spoke to me I had to look up surfer lingo on the internet to make sense out of what he said. So why and how could I have invented Tyler? I decided he must be real. And I resolved to take his advice seriously.

By then the sun had gone down behind the foothills so my tree-gazing was over. But I had my answer. Go with my gut and help Lacey and Angelica, like Tyler had been telling me to do.

I left the office at 6:00 to meet Elisa for an early dinner. Since Sunday I had managed to squeeze in a few more trips to check out nursing homes and she had offered to help me sort out my impressions. We met at our favorite Mexican restaurant, The Rio Grande, famous for its strong and tasty margaritas—on-the-rocks, frozen, strawberry, they're all delicious.

We got a table in my favorite part of the restaurant. It's called "the garage" because of its huge garage-door-style windows that open to the street on two sides. I love the porch-like feeling of eating outside while being inside out of the chilly evening air. A young guy in jeans and a dark blue tee shirt showed up right away with water, homemade chips and fresh salsa. Our server took our drink order and promptly grabbed us a couple of salt-rimmed margaritas from the bar.

"Whew! I've been tasting this drink in my mind all day," Elisa said after taking a mega-swallow.

"Like I always say, their margaritas are the best I've had any-where, including Mexico," I said. "I wish I could get hold of their secret recipe."

Our server came back for our order—a chicken tostada for Elisa, and mahi-mahi tacos for me. Some people say the drinks are the only reason to go to the Rio, but I love their fresh, healthy tex-mex food as much as the margs.

While we waited for our food, I filled Elisa in on the nursing homes I'd visited and we discussed pros and cons of various ones. As usual she helped me see through my confusion. "I'm not hearing any enthusiasm from you about any of those nursing homes," she said.

"Okay, bottom line—I don't have a good feeling about any of the places I've seen, and there are only two left to visit," I said. "I'm starting to think bringing her home and hiring a round-the-clock caregiver might be the way to go."

"Can you and she afford that?" Elisa asked. "The agencies charge a fortune for twenty-four-hour care."

"I know. I'm hoping I can hire someone privately, so I won't have to pay the agency fees. But it can be hard to find someone good. I think I'll talk to Tim Grosso about that. He said something the other night about some bad experience he had with his father's housekeeper. I need to know what to look out for."

Our food arrived and we took a break from conversation while we poured salsa over everything and dug in. After her second bite,

Elisa looked up and said, "Between the Psych Department and the ombudsman thing, you're getting to know Tim pretty well. What do you think of him?"

"He's helping me and he seems nice enough. I'm amazed that he gives so much time to a volunteer job when he's also the chair of the Psych Department. But it's hard for me to picture him with Faye. She's so fiery and he's so laid back. She's an elegant dresser and he's mostly a jeans-and-tee-shirt kind of guy."

Then I flashed on what Pablo had said about Tim. "In fact Pablo says Tim's an old hippie. Do you know anything about him growing marijuana?"

Elisa laughed. "I think Pablo's got that right. Tim's laid-back style probably owes something to his favorite herb. I know he's a smoker, but I have no idea where he gets his supply. If he's a grower, he's a very careful one."

We were distracted by a toddler at the table next to us who was happily eating black beans with his hands, smearing them all over his face in the process. His bemused parents watched but didn't interrupt his fun—probably content to enjoy their own dinner and drinks in peace.

My thoughts kept drifting back to the decision I'd made about Lacey. I knew Elisa would disapprove, but I decided to bite the bullet. I didn't really want to hear what Elisa had to say about it, but she'd find out eventually so we might as well get it over with. "I met with the Townes kids today—Lacey, Angelica and Shane—and I agreed to bring Lacey into the Contact Project so she can try to reach Mirabel."

Elisa slammed her glass down on the table so hard that some margarita slopped over the side. "Cleo you need to think before you jump into a hornet's nest. This business with the Townes family has trouble written all over it. I thought you were trying to lay low for a while."

I watched the small lime-tequila pool that had spilled from her drink dribble along the smooth black table toward its lowest corner. I told myself that if she stopped talking before it flowed over onto the brick floor, she wasn't as upset as she seemed. But it dripped over, and she continued.

"Here you've finally gotten yourself a sweet spot at the university teaching this paranormal class, which can help you build some credibility for what you do in your Contact Project. If you remember, I put myself out there in the department supporting you for that. But now you want to blow it to get involved with a drama queen, an Indigo child and a slacker! Sounds like a death-to-your-career wish to me!"

I sighed. "Give me a break, Elisa. I can't operate out of fear when someone needs my help, especially when the main victim is a ten-year-old child. It's not easy to refuse a little girl who has lost both her sister and her mother and whose father is more interested in his mistress than in her. I don't think you'd turn her down either."

"Honey, you know I'm not one to back off to save my own ass. But I always say pick your battles, and I say this is a bad pick."

"Well, it's my pick. So I'll have to live with it."

Our server came by to see if we wanted seconds on drinks. I was sorely tempted to drown my annoyance in more tequila, but I resisted and asked for the check instead. As the server went off to get our bill, I continued pleading my case to Elisa. "Look, I'll get plenty of grief from Pablo when he gets back from his conference on Saturday and finds out what I'm doing. It would help a lot not to have you on my case along with him. How about I agree to be extra careful and you agree to trust that I'm not going to do anything stupid?"

She sighed and gave me a penetrating no-nonsense look. "Okay but you have to promise to keep me in the loop, so I have a clue what's coming before it blows up in your face."

I smiled. "That request wouldn't have anything to do with satisfying your love of gossip and your insatiable curiosity about scandals, would it?"

"Touché. I admit I'm curious and I like to know what's up. But I also care about you and I don't want to see you get sucked under."

"That's fair. I agree," I said, "and now I have to go." We settled the bill and made our way to the door. Once we were outside we gave each other a big hug. Although I was nowhere near as comfortable with my decision as I pretended to be, I felt much better having Elisa's support.

Chapter 13

I walked home along Pearl Street enjoying the view of the foothills and basking in my margarita-induced glow. I decided to take my new energy into my studio to work on a painting. I live in my grandparents' old historic house and my studio is the stone carriage house behind it, which my grandmother remodeled years ago and where I spent so many sweet summer mornings painting with her during my childhood and teenage years. The room is full of stacked paintings—both mine and Gramma's—and happy memories of our time together.

I hadn't had any time for painting since the Shady Terrace bombshell, so I was eager to jump in. I was deeply absorbed when my cell phone rang. Without thinking, I answered without checking the caller ID, which I later noticed said "unavailable."

"Am I speaking to Cleo Sims?" the female voice asked.

I already regretted answering. It was probably someone trying to sell me something, but—since I use my cell for both business and personal calls—it could be a new client. "Who's calling please?" I asked in my business voice.

"This is Judith Demar," she said brusquely. "I'm a friend of Derrick Townes. You met me at the West End Gallery last Friday. Faye introduced us."

Oh yes, Angelica's horrible Judith with the dark-red aura. Now I definitely regretted answering. So I cut to the chase. "What can I do for you, Judith?"

"I'm calling on behalf of Derrick. We have to meet with you

right away." Her voice sounded like a no-nonsense drill sergeant. "Tomorrow. We're both tied up in the morning so it will have to be afternoon. Can we say two o'clock?"

Whoa! This woman is a steamroller. And why was she calling on behalf of Derrick? My first inclination was to tell her I had no openings for the next month, if ever. But I decided to stay more civil. If I was going to work with the Townes children, I didn't want her standing in the way. "My schedule is very busy tomorrow, Judith. I don't have my appointment book with me right now, but I could call you in the morning and set up a time for next week."

"Didn't you hear me say I'm tied up in the morning?" She sounded like she was lecturing a small child. I could see why Angelica disliked her.

I stayed cool. "No problem. I'll call in the morning and leave a message with a few available times. You can pick one and call me back."

"Actually you're wrong. There is a problem. And it's your problem. Derrick's daughter Lacey brought her sister Angelica to your office today without his permission. I'm sure you know that treating a minor requires parental permission."

"Of course. But I wasn't treating her. She and Lacey and Shane and I were just having a conversation."

"Well now you and Derrick and I need to have a conversation about that conversation. And we need to have it tomorrow."

Uh-oh. Elisa's prediction of trouble was already coming true. I realized that I shouldn't have let Lacey bring Angelica to my office. We should have met somewhere else to talk where it wouldn't have looked like a therapy session. I could see how Derrick and Judith could make trouble for me, since it could be hard to prove I wasn't treating a minor without permission.

So I agreed to a meeting. "Okay. I left my 4:00 time open tomorrow to catch up on my clients' insurance forms. You can come then," I said grudgingly. "That's the only time I can offer you right now."

Judith and Derrick breezed into my office like they owned the place at 4:00 on Thursday. They were both dressed in tennis clothes. Judith wore a tiny short black tennis dress that had white side inserts and a sporty racer back. Derrick matched her with sleek black shorts and a black tee that had a white stripe running down the right side and underarm mesh venting panels. Their shoes looked like the expensive kind that you see in pro tournaments or at Wimbleton.

"Excuse the tennis clothes," Derrick said with a smile as I showed them in to my counseling room. "Since you couldn't meet us at two, we took advantage of our free time to get in some extra practice. We're playing in a tournament this weekend and we don't like to lose."

"Not that we lose very often," Judith said. "But we never pass up a chance to play."

They sat together on the couch and I took the chair across from them. Might as well start things off on a pleasant note, I thought. So I followed up on the tennis thing. "It sounds like you're both serious tennis players," I said. "Is your tournament here in Boulder?"

"It's here at the university tennis complex," Derrick said. "I used to play professionally and if I had my wish, I still would. In fact I'd love to spend most of my time playing tennis. But I have to balance my tennis life and my business life." I nodded. With his black curly hair, blue eyes, fit body and tanned skin, I could easily picture him as a tennis coach hanging out at the courts helping cute young girls improve their backhand.

"Derrick could still be a pro," Judith said imperiously. "In fact we both could. But with all my books and academic articles, plus my grants and national committees, not to mention teaching two graduate seminars, I don't have that kind of time."

Whew! This woman sounded like the president of her own fan club. I didn't want to hear any more of her resume, so I said, "Thinking of time, I know you're both busy—and this meeting is an extra for my schedule too—so let's talk about why you wanted to see me today.

"We don't want you seeing Angelica again," Judith said. "Just to be perfectly clear, neither Lacey nor Shane has legal authority to make decisions regarding Angelica, so they can't bring her here without Derrick's permission. We're willing to overlook your seeing her without our permission yesterday if you promise to stay strictly away from her from now on."

Derrick didn't look quite as sure as Judith did and he, not Judith, was Angelica's parent, so I waited to see what he would say. He stayed silent, so I turned to him and said, "How do you feel about this Derrick?"

He leaned forward in my direction. "Actually Angelica is a very disturbed child. I don't know if she told you that she thinks she's some kind of special child—Indigo—who doesn't have to do things the way other children do. Unfortunately Mirabel supported her in that. In fact she's the one who came up with it. I tried to get her to see reason, but I never got anywhere. Now Angelica refuses to do half her schoolwork because she says it's irrelevant. I know she needs therapy and I'm sure you're a good therapist, but Judith has found another therapist for her."

"Yes, she'll be starting therapy tomorrow and her pediatrician will be starting her on Ritalin," Judith said. "Angelica needs to learn to focus and do her schoolwork. She may be gifted in some areas but she's out of control and she needs stability."

I hadn't seen any evidence of Angelica being out of control, but I had seen that she was grieving the loss of her mother and her sister. I doubted that Ritalin was a good choice for her. I wasn't her therapist and they weren't asking my advice, but I still felt a need to remind Derrick that he had some responsibility as a father.

"I can see you're concerned about Angelica," I said, addressing Derrick. "She's been through a lot losing her sister and her mother. She's going to need a lot of your attention while she's dealing with all that."

Derrick's face sagged. "I know that," he said softly, "but I've never had that kind of relationship with her. I've tried everything, but she won't talk to me about how she's feeling."

"Does she talk to anyone about how she's feeling?" I asked.

Derrick sighed. "Just Lacey," he said. "And now she and Lacey have come up with this notion that Mirabel was murdered. I don't blame Angelica. She's young, and as you say, she's been through a lot."

He frowned and his voice took on an angry tone as he went on. "But Lacey should know better than to encourage Angelica's crazy ideas."

Judith put her arm around his shoulders and looked him directly in the face. "Derrick, you know Lacey likes to stir the pot. She thrives on conflict. You need to keep her away from Angelica as much as you can."

Judith did have a point about Lacey loving drama, but the idea of keeping her away from Angelica was cruel. Fortunately Derrick stood up for Lacey and Angelica. He shook his head and nixed Judith's demand. "No, I can't do that, Judith. Angelica needs someone to talk to and Lacey is the only one she feels close to right now."

"That's why we're starting Angelica in therapy," Judith said. "But we can discuss this later. There's no reason for Dr. Sims to be involved." She turned toward me, "So I assume we're clear here. We'd prefer you to stay out of our family business. Unfortunately, we can't stop Lacey or Shane from coming to you. But they do not have our permission to bring Angelica and you do not have our permission to treat her."

I had certainly gotten the message by then and I was more than ready to see the last of Judith. "You've made you point," I said. "Now I have phone calls to return and paperwork to catch up on." I stood up and headed toward the door to the waiting room. They followed.

Derrick made a half-hearted attempt to make nice. "Thanks for seeing us on such short notice," he said. He smiled, shook my hand, and added, "I'll probably be seeing you over at Shady Terrace dealing with that mess. I still haven't figured out where my dad will live now that the place is closing."

As I closed the door behind them, I wondered what Derrick saw in Judith. Was her tennis game so strong that he was willing to overlook her nasty disposition? Or did she have some other hold over him?

I sat in my office for a while contemplating the issues Judith and Derrick had raised. Was Angelica making up or imagining her Indigo-child status as a way to get out of doing stuff she didn't want to do? I certainly wasn't any expert on Indigo children. Had Angelica's sense of what had happened to Mirabel come from an over-active imagination rather than a spiritual connection?

I felt a need for more information so I typed "indigo child" into my Google search engine. Over a million hits. I started with Wikipedia. Their entry described Indigo children as a controversial New Age concept with no scientific evidence to back it up. Believers describe Indigo children as bright, empathetic, highly intuitive kids who are here on earth to remake the world into a place of peace, but who function poorly in conventional schools due to their rejection of authority, being smarter than their teachers and a lack of response to guilt-, fear- or manipulation-based discipline. Okay, that sounded like Angelica.

Skeptics say that the traits attributed to Indigos are so vague they could describe anyone and that applying the Indigo label to a disruptive child may delay proper diagnosis and treatment the child needs. A good summary of Judith's point of view.

Wikpedia continued with a paragraph about how some children whose parents believe they are Indigos are diagnosed with attention-deficit hyperactivity disorder by the school system because they are impatient and easily bored at school. When school psychologists suggest a drug like Ritalin to treat the ADHD, these parents refuse. They insist that Indigos are a new stage of evolution who require special treatment, not medications.

Angelica didn't strike me as a hyperactive child, but that diagnosis was outside my areas of expertise. Also, I had only seen Angelica in a few limited settings. I didn't feel competent to judge whether Judith was right about Angelica.

Next I went to the Indigo Childern website, where I read a long warning about how the Wikipedia entry is a page filled with misinformation and bias. The writer admitted there is no scientific evidence of the Indigo phenomena but insisted that these children are the beginning of a change in human nature described by many around the world as a new consciousness.

Another site had a list of questions to help a person know whether they are an Indigo. Do you sometimes feel wise beyond your years?

Does your family misunderstand you? Do you have strong intuition about certain things that most others do not? Do you have trouble conforming to the ways of society? Do you often feel misunderstood when you try to talk to people about what's real? If you answer yes to such questions, you are most likely an Indigo who has come to earth to build a new society.

Or, I thought, maybe you're a child who feels lost after the deaths of both her sister and her mother, and who feels misunderstood by her father and his bossy live-in mistress.

I turned off my computer. More information wouldn't help. I needed to clarify my thoughts. Was Angelica Indigo? For that matter are Indigos real or are they merely wishful thinking on the part of their parents? Had Mirabel encouraged Angelica's oddness and given her this special label as a way for them both to overcome their grief over Kari's death? Was Angelica's strong intuition that Mirabel had been murdered an important insight by a child with special abilities? Or was it a cry for help from a grief-stricken child who felt misunderstood? If I encouraged her to pursue her intuition would I be making it harder for her to accept the loss of her mother and move on? Should I reconsider my involvement?

The sun slipped behind the mountains, leaving me in the dusk as I tried to resolve these stubborn questions. Suddenly a familiar voice came from a far corner of the room.

"Yo, Cleo. You can't bail in two feet of water. You're heading for a nose-dive."

Tyler! I couldn't see him in the dim light, but there was no mistaking that voice or that surfer slang. This time I was going to get some answers. "Tyler, can you come closer so I can see you? I really need to talk to you."

Usually he ignores my requests, but to my surprise he did what I asked. Suddenly I could see him perched cross-legged on the windowsill, wearing his usual "Never Stop Surfing" tee shirt and rubber sandals. I was encouraged that he had responded to my request. Maybe he was in an unusually helpful mood.

"Tyler, I feel like I'm already in a nose-dive. I want to help Angelica and Lacey, but this is a messy situation. I don't know who to believe."

"Believe in yourself. Don't sit in the channel and watch. Get into the lineup. Don't back down. You'll blow it if you miss the good wave."

I groaned in frustration. "Argggh! Tyler, if you know so much you must know that what you're saying doesn't mean anything to me!"

I should have known better. Tyler never hangs around when I get confrontational with him. He bounced off the windowsill and floated off toward the corner, where he melted into the wall and vanished. But his words trailed behind him like a gusty tailwind. "Forget about meaning, Cleo. It's time to hit the surf. Angelica's in the impact zone."

Chapter 14

After Tyler left, I went through the rest of my phone messages. Surprisingly one of them was from Shane Townes. He'd left a cryptic voice mail. "Hey, Cleo. Could I buy you a drink after work? There's some stuff I'd like to run by you."

Buy me a drink? The image of Shane yesterday in his torn jeans and Lord of the Rings tee-shirt talking about online games brought to mind a high-school age geek—someone who'd be more at home in a coffee house than a bar. But then I remembered the Shane from the wedding dressed in the pricey pinstriped suit. He definitely had his sophisticated side. And he was twenty-four and he'd gone to USC, so he was probably no stranger to trendy bars.

Anyway, I didn't have any plans for the evening, and a drink could be just what I needed to defuse the lingering tension I felt from tangling with Judith. Also, my curiosity got the better of me, like it always does.

He was old enough for me to talk to without permission. So why not give him a call and see if he was free. I did. He was. We agreed to meet at The Med at 5:30 for their happy-hour drinks and tapas.

The Med is on Walnut not far from my office, so I walked over. I didn't feel like waiting so I was happy to see Shane walking up when I arrived and even happier when we managed to get a table in the bar right away. In keeping with its name, the Med's décor is Mediterranean—terra-cotta floors, white stucco walls accented with colorful tiles, plants and fresh flowers everywhere. We ordered the red Sangria and a selection of small plates—tapas—which are their specialty and a great deal at happy hour. We chose skewers of Moroccan spiced shrimp, fried garlic calamari with Spanish sauce, hummus with black beans and cilantro, and roasted mushrooms in garlic herb butter sauce.

I wanted to get to know Shane a little before we started in on the family issues, so I indulged my curiosity and asked him about his work. "You said you have a job working on an online game. What's it like? I've heard about games like Second Life but I've never played one."

Shane speared a roasted mushroom, swirled it around in its garlic butter sauce and popped it in his mouth without dripping even a tiny bit of the sauce. Then he leaned forward and spoke with an intensity that reminded me of one of my students trying to convince the class of a favorite theory. "Gyaki-Birquit is a virtual world on another planet in the future. Like on Second Life, everyone who plays is represented by an avatar—a computer-generated character that can walk around, interact with other characters, teleport to other parts of the planet, and that's just a start. You can customize your avatar's looks, clothes, skills, personality and more. But because it's all in the future everyone has super abilities like being able to teleport or send out shock waves that stun people near them. When you're in Gyaki-Birquit your avatar is you, and you can make yourself anyone you want to be. You could be a person a lot like who you are now or someone totally different."

I was beginning to see the attraction. Who wouldn't want to try on some totally different identities? "So I could be a big muscle-bound guy or a cute sex kitten?"

He laughed. "If that's who you want to be. You might want to add some brainpower too, though. In Gyaki-Birquit getting ahead is based on winning challenges that require thinking."

I tore off a piece of pita bread and spread some hummus on it. "So I'd have to work there, try to get ahead?" I paused to enjoy the hummus and then added, "I thought this game was supposed to be recreation. Sounds kind of stressful."

"No, it's all your choice. You can make friends, join groups, start a business, compete in games, learn new skills, run for political office—just about anything you can do here. But because the characters all have super powers, everything moves way faster there. For example, my mom spent years trying to find more land the city and county could buy for open space—and working out details to get the land. But in Gyaki-Birquit a powerful advanced character can create additional land in an instant, choose what it will look like and what it will be used for. It's the world like you ideally want it to be." Shane stopped his explanation to motion our server over and order more Sangria

I was genuinely captivated. "It sounds amazing. Does everyone get along and have the same ideas of what will make the world better?"

He laughed again. "No. That would make for a very dull game. There are rival factions always competing with each other to win more power—not so different from this world. But in Gyaki-Birquit, unlike here, the smartest and most skillful characters rule. You can't just run a bunch of stupid political ads and win power. You can't buy your way to the top. You have to work your way up through the skill levels by playing masterfully, completing missions and defeating enemies. I respect the integrity of the process."

"What do you get paid to do there?"

"I'm a community developer so I set up greeters to help new players get oriented and find friends. I provide customer service, and I also monitor forums and clubs for harassment or any rude or insulting behavior." So he wasn't the slacker Lacey painted him as.

I was about to ask him to elaborate on that job when I suddenly realized that I was letting my curiosity run the conversation instead of finding out what Shane wanted to talk to me about.

"I'd love to hear more about Gyaki-Birquit," I said. "But you had something you wanted to talk about, so we should probably move on to that." I dipped a piece of calamari in sauce and munched it while I waited for his response.

Shane leaned back and closed his eyes for a minute as if mentally changing channels. "Sure. Here's the thing. I've been thinking about how Angelica is so convinced that someone pushed Mom under the water. I'm not saying she's right, but she does have a kind of spooky way of knowing things. And Mom wasn't so popular with some people. She had a habit of going after people she didn't agree with, and she either didn't see or didn't care when she'd gone too far. She could be pretty pushy, so she had her enemies. "

"What do you mean?"

"Well there's that prairie dog fight she got into with that developer Hugh Symes. She was bringing a suit against him for killing prairie dogs on some property he was developing. I think Mom was a little over the top on the subject, but she had the law on her side. From what she said, he didn't even try to relocate the prairie dogs like the law requires and he didn't have a permit to kill them. He slaughtered the whole colony and somehow got away with calling it an accident. She couldn't accept what happened and move on—was insistent that he be held accountable and his development stopped."

It was tempting to settle on Hugh Symes as the bad guy since I already disliked him for his role in the closing of Shady Terrace. But Shane had mentioned "people" who didn't like Mirabel, so I wanted to know who else was on his list. "Symes sounds like he had reason to dislike your mother for sure. Who else were you thinking of?"

"Another person she didn't get along with was Grandad's dishy young girlfriend Glenna Corn. She thought Glenna was after his money, so she was trying hard to get Grandad to dump her. And I think Mom was investigating Glenna's background."

He stopped to eat a shrimp. I waited silently to see who else he would come up with.

"Of course there's Dad and Judith. Like Angelica and Lacey said, Mom knew they had been having an affair forever. And she'd been pushing Dad to break it off." He took a gulp of sangria and then went on. "I don't think they'd kill her, though."

He thought for a minute and then continued. "Like I said yesterday, I think she was backing off of the Scientologists and they weren't too happy about that because they were counting on her for big donations. Right now they're getting a huge bequest from her estate. If Lacey can reach Mom through your project, she definitely needs to ask her if she made a new will. If she did disinherit the Scientologists, the rest of us will get a whole lot more."

I took a drink of my sangria and considered what to say next.

Yesterday Shane said he wasn't sure he believed in the possibility of reaching Mirabel, and now he was telling me what he wanted to find out if Lacey was able to reach her. "It's not always possible to get specific answers like that from a spirit," I said. "But she can try." Then, just to see what else he had in mind, I asked "Is that your complete list of suspects?"

He thought for a minute as he chewed the last of the calamari. "I don't know all the people and causes she was involved with. She owned half of that art gallery with Faye Whitton. They seemed to get along okay, but that gallery was a sink-hole for money. It was a terrible investment, but I couldn't convince Mom of that."

Interesting and a little scary. Would Faye have the resources to market Gramma's work? Given Shane's negative view of Faye's gallery, I was debating whether to bring up my ties with it. But I didn't have to decide, because he went on with another even more surprising thought.

"One of our neighbors—a guy named Tim—was a friend of hers from working on political campaigns. I happen to know that he sold Mom pot for her arthritis pain. Then they had a falling out and weren't speaking. Who knows, maybe he was afraid she'd rat him out for drug dealing."

My mind was reeling by then, and not from the wine. And the next day was Friday, my teaching day, so I needed to prepare for class. I decided to wrap things up. "I'm wondering since you called me whether you're rethinking whether you want to try to contact your mom."

"No. I don't have the time. I spend about seventy hours a week on Gyaki-Birquit, and even then I can't keep up. Lacey has plenty of time. Let her do it. But I think Lacey and Angelica are way too focused on Dad and Judith. It's all they talk about. I wanted to fill you in on some of Mom's other issues."

I thanked him and we got up to leave. But I couldn't resist one more question. "Why does Gyaki-Birquit take so much time?"

He frowned and answered quickly. "I'm a major investor in Gyaki-Birquit and the game is short of resources. We have to increase the membership and get the current players to spend more time so we can raise enough money to complete the expansion packs for the game."

Just then, a couple being seated at a nearby table called out to Shane. We said our goodbyes, he went off to join them, and I headed out to walk home along Pearl Street. The sun had slipped behind the mountains bringing a chill to the evening air. I hustled along preoccupied by the jumbled thoughts racing through my mind of Mirabel and people who had reasons to bump her off. I was several blocks past Faye's gallery before I even realized I had passed it without checking to see if any more of Pablo's work had sold.

Chapter 15

Lacey didn't show up for my class the next morning, but when class ended at 12:30 she was pacing the hall outside the classroom door. She looked like she'd just come from a yoga class. Her long dark hair was pulled back in a ponytail, and she was wearing lightweight gray yoga pants that sat on her hips, a white tank, and a gray hoodie. But if she'd been to yoga, she'd missed out on its calming effects.

The minute I stepped through the door, she dashed over, stuck her drop slip in my face, and said breathlessly, "Here. Sign it now so I'm not your student anymore and you can help me. Please. I'm desperate." Her eyes were red and swollen and brimming with tears. "We have to talk," she said. "I don't know what to do." She looked so forlorn that I paused even though I wasn't in the mood to get drawn into Lacey's drama of the day.

Not only was I keyed up from teaching for two hours, I was also starving. I'd been looking forward to going home and relaxing on my back porch with a sandwich and a cup of tea before going to the office to meet my afternoon clients. But I knew from her involvement in past class discussions that Lacey was more than a drama queen. She could be bright and thoughtful when she wasn't so stressed out. And then I flashed on the image of the beautiful teen-aged girl I'd seen in the mirror at The Stanley Hotel last weekend. She'd looked so much like Lacey that I was almost sure she was Lacey's deceased younger sister Kari. The same long dark hair, milky white skin, and probing blue eyes. And the same melancholy expression when the apparition had pleaded with me. "Please," she'd said. "They need you."

So I put my own wishes aside and said, "I can see that you're upset, Lacey and I want to talk with you about what's going on. I have to get back to my office soon, but we can talk for a bit. I don't know about you, but I'm starving, so let's grab some lunch while we talk."

She suggested the Burnt Toast restaurant, so we walked over to the commercial area on the edge of campus. It was a warm sunny October day, one of my favorite times to walk on the tree-lined campus. Backpack-toting students with cell phones or iPods plugged into their ears filled the sidewalks and the spacious grassy areas. A group of young guys clad in shorts and tank tops played a fierce game of Frisbee on the quad in front of the library.

"What's happened to upset you so much?" I asked jumping off the walk to dodge a yellow Frisbee headed straight for my head.

Lacey took one graceful sidestep to avoid the Frisbee, but kept her attention focused on me. "Last night was ghastly beyond belief," she said, wiping her eyes with a tissue. "Just when I thought things couldn't get any worse, Dad and Judith stabbed me in the back again." She began sobbing in earnest.

I didn't try to stop her crying. As a therapist I know that crying is an excellent release of physical and emotional tension, which leaves people feeling better. I also knew Lacey had something she wanted to say and she'd get to it when she was ready.

Sure enough her weeping subsided after a few minutes. She blew her nose, wiped her eyes, took a deep breath, and said, "Sorry. It's hard to talk about."

We were in front of the absurdly named Burnt Toast by then. I wanted to give her time to collect her thoughts, so I said, "That's okay. Take your time."

"I'm ready," she said. "Let's go in and sit down."

We got a table next to one of the huge windows. The restaurant is a homey café in an old house with hardwood floors, several rooms, and interesting touches like menus placed in old books, and displays of local art. It's almost like eating at a friend's cozy funky house. We got a pot of tea and ordered some food. The tofu scramble with veggies for Lacey, and an omelet with spinach and mushrooms for me.

The tea and comfy atmosphere seemed to soothe Lacey. She took up her story again in a much calmer voice. "I guess you know that Dad and Judith were totally bent out of shape about me taking Angelica to your office the other day. They told me last night that they'd been to see you and told you not to see her any more. They were acting like you're some witch doctor or something. I don't see what the big deal is. Angelica deals with life a lot better than they do."

"The big deal is that she's a minor and your father has to give permission for her to see a therapist," I said. "We may not like it, but he has the right to say what she can and can't do."

Lacey looked down at the table and began turning her knife over and over. "I know that," she said. "But I never thought about it when I brought her to your office. And anyway I can't see why Dad would refuse to give permission for Angelica to have grief therapy after all she's been through. Unless he knows you can help her contact Mom, and there's something he doesn't want Angelica to find out."

I refilled my teacup while I took a minute to think. Then I said, "That's a big assumption. It could be that he just wants to closely monitor what's going on with Angelica. Judith said they had arranged for her to see a therapist. In fact, I think she's supposed to start today."

The server brought our food and I started right in on my omelet. But Lacey ignored her meal as tears welled up in her eyes once again. "That's what started it all," she said passionately. "They're not sending her to therapy because she's grieving. They're sending her as some kind of attempt to deprogram her. They say they want her to get over thinking she's so special. They don't believe in Indigo children and they say she needs to get her head straightened out and start doing her schoolwork even if she does think it's boring. I'm afraid of what some therapist like that could do to Angelica. If she loses the inner calm and tranquility that is part of her specialness, she might crack from the stress." Lacey stopped, wiped her eyes, took a deep breath, picked up her fork and took a bite of her tofu.

My first impulse was to tell Lacey that no therapist would take on this challenge with a ten-year-old child. But I thought about the huge roster of psychotherapists in Boulder, many of who are unlicensed—

which is perfectly legal in this state. Psychotherapists in Colorado are required to register and provide certain basic information about themselves, their education and their work, but no specific level or type of education is required. This leaves the door open for some rather unusual practitioners, and I had an uneasy feeling that Judith would go the distance to find one who would do what she wanted done.

"How does Angelica feel about this?" I asked quietly.

Lacey had stopped eating and was gazing down sadly at her plate. "That's just it. She absolutely refused to go to their therapist." Lacey teared up again. "So now they're saying either she goes to their therapist or they're going to send her away to a school where she'll learn how to follow directions and get her work done."

"I doubt she wants to go away to school. Did she give in and agree to see the therapist?"

"No. Angelica can be very stubborn. She's very wise and takes responsibility for her own choices, but when people who don't respect her rights try to force her to go in a way that she knows is wrong, she shuts them out."

"How does she do that?"

"Last night she simply turned to them and said, 'You don't understand me, so I'm not going to talk to you anymore.' Then she went into her room and worked on a painting. Judith kept screaming at her that ten-year-olds have to do what their parents decide and that she will do what they decide is best for her. But Angelica ignored her." Lacey had perked up as she described Angelica's resistance. Now she began to do justice to her lunch, devouring big spears of broccoli, slices of carrot and chunks of tofu.

I wondered why Derrick let Judith have this much authority over Angelica. After all, he was the parent. She wasn't even a stepparent. "What about your dad? Does he agree with Judith about all this?"

"Oh yes," Lacey said between bites. "Dad listens to Judith most of the time about Angelica. He acts like she knows more about children than he does—even though she's never had any."

"I know this isn't what you want for Angelica," I said. "But if your dad is on board, there may not be anything you can do to stop them, unless you can persuade them to take a different approach."

Lacey looked briefly off into the distance as she finished chewing. Then she said slowly. "I tried. I reminded Dad that he downplayed Kari's anorexia, and look what happened. I tried to get both Mom and Dad to help Kari before it was too late, but Mom was too busy with her causes and Dad was too involved with his work and tennis. They accused me of exaggerating and making a big deal out of everything like they say I always do. I tried to help Kari myself but got nowhere. By the time they realized how sick she was, it was too late."

"Do you think maybe your father is trying to avoid that mistake by getting Angelica some therapy for what he sees as her problems?"

"That may be what he's thinking, but he's way off base. Angelica is nothing like Kari. Kari was always trying to make it with Mom and Dad. She played tennis, got involved with the environment, was a perfect student. She tried so hard to get the love and approval she wanted from them, but they didn't give it. She thought it was her fault, that she wasn't perfect enough."

"But you don't see Angelica doing this?"

"No, Angelica is very sure of herself, completely steady inside. She's so in touch with her spiritual base that she doesn't need approval from outside. But she does need some support for who she is—any child that age does. And she does need to contact Mom—now more than ever. She has to find out what happened. Right now she hates Dad and Judith because she thinks they killed Mom. If she's right, they need to be arrested. If she's wrong, she needs to move on and make peace with them somehow." Lacey leaned forward and gazed intently into my eyes. "You have to see her again. I don't care what they say."

Apparently I hadn't made the minor-child-needs-parental-permission thing clear to her. My commitment to helping them didn't include giving up my psychologist's license. So I explained again, as clearly and simply as I could. "Lacey, much as I would like to help you and Angelica, there is no way I can work with her without your father's permission. If he won't give it, that's that."

Lacey took the news better than I had expected. "Okay then, if that's what it takes, I'll find a way to get Dad to give permission. He can be totally clueless sometimes, but he's not mean. If I can get him away from Judith, I might be able to get to him."

Before I could reply, an older man walking by our table interrupted us. "Lacey, you look like hell," he said in a deep powerful voice that carried throughout the small room. "Did you lose your best friend or did a boyfriend dump you?"

I looked up to see Gramma's lawyer—and Lacey's grandfather—Vernon Evers, accompanied by his gorgeous girlfriend, Glenna. They had stopped next to our table, both facing Lacey.

"Grandad! No, it's more family stuff. Maybe you can help. Can you and Glenna sit down for a few minutes?"

They hadn't shown any signs of noticing me and I figured he wouldn't remember me anyway after all these years, so I broke in to introduce myself. "Mr. Evers, I'm Martha Donnelly's granddaughter. I don't know whether you remember me."

He turned toward me with a smile. "I forget more than I like to admit these days, but I could never forget Martha. Now there's a painter! I have three of her paintings. Some of my favorite work. So sorry about the Alzheimer's. How's she getting along?"

"She was doing pretty well but now the nursing home where she lives is closing and I'm having a hard time figuring out what to do. I was planning to call you about the trust Grampa had you set up for her before he died."

"It sounds like we should sit with you and Lacey and talk a bit," he said. He turned toward Glenna, put his arm around her shoulder and pulled her close. "How about it, Glenna? You know my grand-daughter Lacey, and this is the granddaughter of an old friend. She'll have to tell you her name, though. You know my memory."

"Cleo," I said. "Cleo Sims. Nice to meet you."

Glenna patted Vernon's arm and turned to me with a smile. "We'd love to join you if we're not interrupting your lunch," she said graciously.

"No, actually I have to go meet some clients," I said. I turned to Vernon Evers. "Thanks for offering to talk now, but I'll have to call you to find another time." I got up, they sat down, and we said hellos and good-byes all around. As I left the restaurant they were deep in conversation with Lacey. I figured there was a good chance that Vernon Evers, sharp lawyer that he was, would come up with a strategy to help Angelica. In his heyday he could crush a bitch like Judith Demar without even working up a sweat. His memory may not be what it used to be, but I had faith that his instincts were still razor sharp.

Chapter 16

Ihad to run all the way to my car to get to my office in time for my 2:30 client—a young man who was in intense grief following a tough breakup with his girlfriend of five years. I like the challenge of using my skills in a variety of situations, so I've worked hard to diversify my grief therapy practice beyond clients who've lost a loved one to death. My clients now include people suffering from all kinds of losses—divorce, job loss, physical disability, and more.

A good chunk of my income comes from the endowment for my Contact Project. My benefactor, Bruce, came to me for grief therapy not long after I first set up the apparition chamber. His only daughter had died from a drug overdose. They'd had a stormy relationship, and after she died he was in profound grief knowing he'd never be able to make peace with her. He was so distraught about not being able to tell her that he loved her that I suggested he might want to try reaching her through the apparition chamber. He had some initial reservations but eventually decided to try it. He reached his daughter, they shared love and forgiveness for each other, and he was able to say goodbye to her in a way that brought him deep peace.

Because his experience in the apparition chamber had changed his life, Bruce wanted other people to have the opportunity to benefit from the process. He created an endowment for the Contact Project, using some of the fortune he'd made in high-tech businesses. While there are some conditions as to who qualifies and what kind of records I keep, it's pretty much my show to run.

The endowment is a dream come true for me. It gives me a way to continue to develop the contact process and to accept clients into it who have the potential for great benefit, but who wouldn't otherwise be able to afford it. Grief is one of life's greatest psychological pains. Loss leaves some people mired in unending misery. These people are desperate for relief. Contacting the dead person can help if the bereaved person is able to get answers to troublesome questions or make peace with the deceased loved one.

My second client that afternoon was a young woman whose brother had died when he crashed his car into a tree at 2:00 a.m. on a rainy night. He was speeding and he'd been drinking. His death was ruled an accident, but my client was tormented by the idea that the crash was suicide. She wanted to reach her brother to get some resolution and to find out if he was at peace. She seemed like a good candidate for the Contact Project, so we set up another appointment for the next week to discuss what she expected and what she might experience.

Because it was Friday afternoon, I had scheduled only those two clients. I was done at 4:30 and started checking my phone messages. The first one was a big surprise. Vernon Evers had called. "Hey, Cleo. I got your number from Lacey. I felt bad that we didn't get to finish that conversation about Martha's trust. How about a TGIF drink at my house? I'm at 560 13th Street. Come by around 5:00 if you can. No need to call back. Glenna and I will be here."

I was going to Elisa's for dinner, but not until 7:00, so I had time to take him up on the offer. And I wanted to find out whether there was a way to use more of the money in Gramma's trust each year in case I couldn't find another good nursing home and needed to bring her home with round-the-clock care.

I'd never been to Vernon Evers house. Not surprisingly, it turned out to be in one of Boulder's best locations, next to the historic Chautauqua Park at the base of the famous foothills known as the Flatirons because their upthrust flat surfaces resemble irons used to press clothes. The house is a stately old two-story on a tree-lined cul-de-sac. I guesstimated the value of his property at several million.

On my way to the massive double front doors, I took a minute to enjoy the terraced garden ablaze with fall color from shrubs and blooming plants. But my reverie was quickly interrupted as one of the doors swung open. "Hey, Cleo. You made it. Come on in." Vernon Evers stood in the doorway beaming, drink in hand. His outfit of brown slacks and shirt, topped with a beige cashmere cardigan blended perfectly with the sandstone steps and patio. I wondered whether this attention to detail was one of the traits that had made him so successful.

"Mr. Evers, your gardens are amazing," I gushed. "Are you the gardener, or is it Glenna?"

He laughed. "Hey, call me Vern. And to answer your question, I have a gardener. I don't have the green thumb your grandfather had. I remember James' impressive herb gardens."

"I'm living in their house, you know," I said. "I try to keep his gardens up, but I don't have the time to do nearly enough."

"Sounds like you have a lot of obligations," he said. "Let's go inside and get you a drink and you can tell me more about what's going on with Martha."

He ushered me into the entry hall, past a stunning curved stairway, and into a living room that could have come from an English country-house. White walls, hardwood floors, pale green accent rugs, and paintings in gold frames. Built-in bookshelves flanking both sides of French doors that led to a backyard garden and patio. Glenna jumped up from the off-white couch, tossed her copy of *Entertainment Weekly* on the coffee table, and came over to greet me.

Once again her beauty struck me. Her slim legs in designer jeans seemed to go on forever, and the cleavage of her full breasts was discreetly evident at the curved neckline of her white ribbed tee. Her tousled auburn hair and understated makeup completed the perfect Friday-afternoon-casual look.

"Cleo, we're glad you could come by on such short notice," she said with a warm smile. "Vern's such an admirer of your grandmother's work. We have three of her paintings hanging here in the house, you know. Vern, you should show her." She pointed off in the direction of the hall.

Vernon had gone over to a side table where a tray held glasses, an ice bucket, bottles of liquor and mixes. "Let's get her a drink first," he said. "What will you have, Cleo?"

"Gin and tonic would be perfect if you have it," I said. "And I'd love to see Gramma's paintings if you don't mind showing me."

He mixed up my drink and brought it over, then led me across the entry hall into an office dominated by a king-size desk that sat in the center of the room. Cherry built-in cabinets and shelves filled one wall, and the opposite wall held two of Gramma's floral paintings—one a vase of white roses against a rust-colored wall, and the other a pewter pitcher full of fiery tiger lilies. "When I'm working and need a break, those flowers restore me," he said. "I never get tired of looking at them. And I have another splendid one upstairs, one of her mountain scenes."

My heart swelled with pride for Gramma. "That's so great to hear," I said. "I worry that people will forget her. I hope her work continues to speak for her now that she…" Before I could finish my thought, the doorbell rang.

I followed Vernon back out to the entry hall, wondering who else he had invited to this Friday afternoon gathering. When he opened the door, he looked as surprised as I was to see Lacey and Angelica standing on the porch. "Hey Lacey, Angelica," he said, "I thought we were getting together tomorrow morning. Did I get my signals crossed again?"

"No, Grandad, you're right," Lacey said hastily. "I'm sorry if we interrupted, but it suddenly hit me that when you asked me for Cleo's phone number, you said you were going to invite her over to talk about her grandmother this afternoon. Dad won't let me take Angelica to Cleo's office anymore, but I figured Angelica could talk to her here."

Uh-oh. Judith had made it quite clear that she and Derrick would have my head if I talked to Angelica anywhere. This technical distinction between my office and her grandfather's house wouldn't cut any ice with them. But it would be awkward to leave now.

"Well, come on in," Vernon said enthusiastically. He seemed to pay no mind to Lacey's comment about Derrick not allowing Angelica to come to my office. "We're having drinks and I think Glenna has some snacks in there." He ushered us into the living room just as Glenna showed up from the kitchen carrying a tray that held a cheese plate, a bowl of purple grapes, and two small dishes of nuts.

"Hi, Lacey, Angelica. I thought I heard your voices," she said putting the tray on the coffee table. "Lacey, help yourself to a drink. Angelica, what can I get you?"

"Do you have Izze?" Angelica asked, speaking of the all-natural fruit juice and sparkling water drink that was created in Boulder.

"I think so. Let's go check in the kitchen," Glenna said, putting her arm around Angelica and leading her off.

Lacey and Vernon went over to the side table to get her a drink and refresh his. I sat down in a chair next to the couch to collect my thoughts. The afternoon was taking a disconcerting turn—no surprise when Lacey was involved. If she knew Vernon planned to invite me over to discuss Gramma's problems, why did she show up with another agenda? And why did she bring Angelica? Visions of Judith Demar's scowling face swam in front of my eyes. "I don't think this is such a good idea, Lacey," I said. "Your father and Judith were insistent about your not having permission to bring Angelica to see me."

Lacey brought her drink over to the couch and sat facing me. "Judith has *nothing* to say about *any* of this," she said shrilly. "And Dad said I couldn't take Angelica to your office. He didn't say we couldn't run into you at Grandad's house." Wow, she hadn't taken more than one sip of her drink and she was already shouting. I had a hunch this conversation wasn't going anywhere I wanted to be. And as it turned out, my concern wasn't misplaced.

Angelica walked back into the living room carrying a bottle of Clementine-flavored Izze and a glass of ice. She sat next to Lacey on the couch, set her bottle and glass on the coffee table, put her hand on Lacey's arm and said, "When you get upset about Judith, you're giving her power over you. Ignore her. She's not worth your energy." Angelica took back her arm, carefully poured her drink into her glass, and took a long swallow.

"What's all this about, Lacey?" Vernon asked, as he sat down in the chair next to me, I couldn't help but notice that he'd almost downed his refreshed drink already.

Glenna joined Lacey and Angelica on the couch. She reached for a bunch of grapes and said, "Yes, Lacey. At lunch you said the big issue was Derrick and Judith wanting to send Angelica away to school. What's Cleo's involvement?"

We all looked at Lacey, who didn't answer right away. Her eyes darted around the room. Her fingers twirled a long strand of hair into a tight coil, in some unconscious mirroring of her inner tension. As we waited, my anxiety grew. I wondered whether she'd told them about the Contact Project and her and Angelica's desire to reach Mirabel or, if not, whether she'd bring it up now. I hoped not. I'm always a bit squeamish about explaining the apparition-chamber thing in a social setting and I was afraid Vernon Evers would think I was a flake. If he did, he might wonder about my ability to make good choices for Gramma.

Lacey took a deep breath and turned toward Vernon. "Grandad, I wasn't going to tell you this until we had more proof," she said. "It's horrible to even think about, but Angelica and I believe Mom was murdered. We're trying to investigate, but Dad and Judith are doing everything they can to shut us up."

True to his legal training, Vernon showed no reaction to Lacey's bombshell. He waited a minute to give her time to go on, then said quietly, "Have you talked to the police about this?"

"Yes, I've talked to them many times and they give me the same answer over and over. The police don't care," Lacey's voice took on that familiar strident quality. "They called it an accident and now they don't want to be bothered with taking another look. It's all on us to find out who killed Mom. We have to have proof before they'll pay any attention."

I noticed that Angelica was sitting quietly nibbling on some cheese and drinking her Izze. She showed no sign of agitation. I expected her to rescue or try to calm Lacey like I'd seen her do in the past, but she didn't.

Vernon got up and walked over to the table that held the liquor. "What makes you think Mirabel was murdered?" he asked casually as he poured himself another drink. He came back to his chair, sipped his bourbon and waited for Lacey's response.

But apparently she wasn't ready to explain Angelica's premonitions. Instead Lacey's face turned sad and she burst into tears. "I'm worn out," she sobbed. "I can't deal with all this by myself anymore."

Glenna put her arm around Lacey's shoulders. "Lacey, God works through people and He has chosen you to help your family. He has opened your mind to the pain and experiences of others," she said. "He will give you the strength to serve. Have you prayed and asked God to help you?"

Lacey stopped crying and pulled away from Glenna's arm. "I'm not much of a churchgoer," she said softly. "God might be a little surprised to hear from me."

"Anyone who is helping someone else is doing God's work, Lacey," Glenna said, handing her a tissue. "God will help you. All you have to do is ask."

Vernon ignored Glenna and interrupted with a more legalistic perspective. "We might be able to get the police to re-open the case," he said. "But I need to know why you believe Mirabel was murdered."

Angelica finally decided to come to Lacey's rescue. She set down her glass and began to speak matter-of-factly. "You know I'm an Indigo. I have ways of knowing that go beyond what most people understand. I know someone pushed Mom under the water and held her there. I can feel it clearly, but I don't know who did the pushing." She paused, quietly gazing at Vernon.

"Let's see if I understand you correctly Angelica," Vernon said gently. "You know someone pushed your mother under water and held her there until she drowned, but you don't know who did it."

"That's right," Angelica replied. She looked and sounded as confident as if she was describing a scene from a movie rather than a supernatural experience of her mother's murder. I wondered what Vernon and Glenna thought of Angelica's Indigo status and whether they believed in her special ways of knowing. Vernon showed no reaction, but Glenna was frowning.

Angelica continued in the same self-assured voice. "Lacey and I knew we had to find out who did it, so we went to Cleo to get her to help us reach Mom. I plan to ask Mom what happened, but Dad and Judith don't want me to talk to her." She stopped speaking, but continued to gaze intently at Vernon, who still showed no reaction other than draining his glass in one long swallow.

Lacey blew her nose and jumped in with the information I was hoping she'd leave to their imaginations. "Cleo has this project where she helps people contact dead people in an apparition chamber," she said. "I heard about it from a friend and told Angelica. We knew it was what we needed, so we went to see Cleo and convinced her to help us contact Mom."

Lacey turned to Angelica, who finished the story in her usual quiet voice. "The problem is that Dad and Judith won't let me see Cleo anymore. And now they're using the excuse of my not doing some stupid schoolwork to send me away. But I know it's so I can't help Lacey try to get in touch with Mom."

My mind was a jumble. Should I jump in and try to explain the Contact Project in a more rational way, talk about how and why I started it? I'm usually very careful how I give out information about it. Lacey's single-sentence description did not fit my criteria.

But before I could reframe my work, Glenna had a complete meltdown. "No. Enough," she screeched, twitching nervously. She jumped up from the couch, stood facing us all, and let loose. "No séances! No apparition chamber! No spiritualism! That's the work of Satan! You can't be both a spiritualist and a Christian. The Bible says mediums are blasphemy against God and that anyone who calls upon spirits shall be put to death by stoning."

She stopped to take a breath and Vernon stood up and walked over to her. He was a little flushed and wobbly from the bourbon, but still in clear command of the room. He put his arm around Glenna and led her away from us. "If you'll excuse us, Cleo, Lacey and Angelica, I think it's time for you to go. You can let yourselves out. Glenna and I need to talk." He led her out of the room and across the entry hall to his office, where—once they were inside—he quietly closed the door.

Chapter 17

After Glenna's attack, I drove carefully up the winding mountain road to my friend Elisa's house in the foothills, feeling as jumpy as a grasshopper in August. The idea of being stoned to death for talking to spirits totally blew me away. Who knew my conversations with Tyler could have such dire consequences? Did Tyler know about this punishment? And, if so, why he was endangering me by appearing?

In an attempt to distract myself, I thought about Vernon and Glenna. What was going on between them behind that closed office door? They make an unusual couple, although it's not hard to get what they each see in the other. He has a gorgeous young woman doting on him, and she has a rich, powerful man taking care of her. A match made in heaven? Given Glenna's religious beliefs, maybe she sees it that way. She probably believes God chose Vernon to be her soulmate. But Vernon didn't look too happy when we left. I wondered whether he was having second thoughts about her, given her nasty behavior this afternoon.

I was disappointed that I hadn't had any chance to talk to Vernon about Gramma's trust account. Since his office is at his house, I figured I'd have to think up a way to see him without running into Glenna and any stones she might have handy for throwing.

I got to my destination before I'd had time to put the afternoon in perspective. Usually I take a few minutes to enjoy the view from the front yard of Elisa and her husband Jack's gorgeous house in the foothills before I ring. But today I was so preoccupied I headed straight for the door and punched the doorbell.

Elisa came to the door wearing a big smile, slim jeans and a honey-colored sweater that matched her hair. The lively strains of Abba's "Super Trouper" drifted out behind her. My mood took an instant uptick. "Cleo, honey, come on in and join me in a glass of wine. Jack got held up with some clients and you're a little late, so I'm in here drinking by myself."

I followed her through her huge living room, barely glancing at the beautiful moss rock fireplace and walls of windows. "I need to be careful with the wine," I said. "I already had a drink and I've had kind of an unsettling afternoon. I want to be able to drive home."

"Sweetie, you do look like you're in a flap," Elisa said. "Have some wine and fill me in on the gory details. Don't worry about driving home. You can always stay over in our guest room."

As we settled in the cozy family room off the kitchen with glasses of a slightly fruity fume´ blanc, I began to relax and describe what happened at Vernon's, ending with Glenna's threatening outburst.

"I've had some negative reactions to my Contact Project, been called a fraud, but never anything like this," I said. "It was scary thinking about having rocks thrown at me with deadly intent."

"Ouch," Elisa said. "I can see why you were in a dither. What's the deal with Vernon Evers and the dishy babe anyway? Do you think she's finding ways to rip him off financially behind his back?"

"Who knows," I said. "Not to be callous, but that's not my problem. I expect Mr. Evers can take care of himself. Although he does drink too much. I saw him drunk at a wedding up in Estes last week, and today while I was at his house he downed at least four drinks. He was definitely wobbly when we left. That probably gives Glenna some opportunities to line her pockets if that's what she's up to."

"I wonder what Mirabel thought about her dad hooking up," Elisa said. "If that were my dad, getting together with a gorgeous young woman, I'd be checking it out. But enough about that. As you say, he's not your problem. My predictions about how much trouble the Townes family can be for you are on the mark though, you'll have to admit."

I sighed. "That family is a mess, it's true. It's worse than you know." I gave her the nasty details of Judith and Derrick's visit, their plan to start Angelica on Ritalin and to send her away to school, and Judith's warnings for me to stay away from Angelica. Once again I was grateful that Elisa is my therapist and clinical supervisor as well as my friend. I can tell her everything and she will keep my confidences.

Elisa listened and then spoke quietly in what I've come to know as her I'm-totally-serious-about-this voice. "Cleo, I'm advising you again to back away from this. I know you like to help people, and I know you believe Angelica needs you, but take my word for it, Judith Demar is not an enemy you want to make."

"She's full of herself and pushy, but I'm not afraid of her," I said dismissively.

"Listen Cleo, I have first-hand knowledge of her nastiness." Elisa said, grimacing. "A couple of years ago she got pissed off at a couple of her graduate students who wanted to be listed as co-authors on a paper she was writing that included some of their research. I knew one of them pretty well from work we were doing together at Democracy for Colorado. Anyway this student told me that Judith planned to give them credit in a footnote, but not to give them author credit. They asked to be co-authors, but she refused, insisted all the original work was hers."

Elisa leaned forward, the pitch of her voice rising to incredulity. "I couldn't believe it. They took their case to the chair of the Sociology department, but Judith managed to turn the whole thing around, and the students wound up getting kicked out of the program. I tried to talk to the department chair myself in their behalf, but he'd closed his mind against them. That Judith is one powerful bitch."

"I'd agree with that," I said. "I've seen her in action. She can be cruel and controlling. Thinks the world revolves around her, and if you don't agree, she'll make your life miserable. But, like I said, I'm not afraid of her. I can push as hard as she can if I need to."

Elisa refilled my glass and hers, then said, "Let's move this conversation out to the kitchen. We need to eat if we're going to keep guzzling this wine. Jack said we should go on and eat and keep him some for later." She stood up and went over to the refrigerator where she began getting food out and tossing it on the counter.

I followed her and sat on one of the high stools at the center island. Her kitchen is sleek with granite counters and stainless steel appliances, but also has warm touches like custom cabinets with glass fronts and open shelving. Elisa loves to cook and she does it with such ease that watching her is like poetry. That night she was fixing a dish of spicy rice with shrimp and peppers, and a spinach salad with oranges and almonds.

As she chopped and sautéed the peppers, and I peeled and separated the segments of the oranges, we talked more about Judith. "You'd think she'd be a little more in the background, since it's been only a few months since Mirabel died," I said. "But she's front and center, taking over the family, trying to run their lives. Plus, her overall attitude to Lacey and Angelica is just plain rude."

"I think she's marking her territory," Elisa said. "She plans to marry Derrick and she wants her claim to be clear. So she's asserting her authority as a substitute parent."

"I suppose Derrick's an especially good catch now that he's inherited Mirabel's money," I said. "Although from what Shane told me, a lot of her money will be going to the Church of Scientology." I dumped the pre-washed baby spinach leaves out of their plastic bag into Elisa's bamboo salad bowl and added the orange segments.

"I know Mirabel was pretty deeply involved with Scientology," Elisa said as she dropped shrimp into oil sizzling in a wok. She tossed the shrimp expertly, adding garlic and spices as they browned. She continued talking as she cooked, raising her voice a bit so I could hear over the spitting oil. "After Kari died, Mirabel used to talk to me about how awful she felt about missing the seriousness of Kari's anorexia until it was too late. But once she joined Scientology, she stopped talking about Kari. When I brought her up once, she said Scientologists aren't supposed to talk about any of their problems to anyone except their Scientology auditor. Good grief! Not only do people who join that cult cut off their friends, but I've heard they pay huge amounts of money to discuss their problems with the auditors."

"I guess she thought they were worth it," I said as I added nuts and dressing to the spinach and tossed the salad. "Shane thought Derrick had convinced her to make a new will that left the Scientologists out, but apparently no one can find a new will so it looks like she chose the Scientologists over him."

Elisa stirred the sautéed peppers into the spicy shrimp along with cooked rice, cilantro and chopped green onions. We filled our plates with the shrimp dish and salad, refilled our wine glasses and took it all over to a small table in the family room overlooking the city below. Great view. Great food. Great wine. I felt pampered and snug. So I took a risk and threw out another tricky topic.

"Thinking of Scientology," I said tentatively, "you'll never guess who I ran into the other day who is now a Scientologist. Totally blew me away."

"I don't even have a hunch," Elisa said. "So spill it. Who?"

"Remember Brian—the guy I was involved with about ten years ago, after Pablo took off for Mexico? Pablo and I ran into him last weekend at Faye's gallery. Turns out he's been back in Boulder for a year. He said he'd been planning to call me to let me know he was back, but he hadn't gotten around to doing it. Anyway, according to Faye, he's a Scientologist now."

"Whoa, whoa! Hold on a minute." Elisa put down her fork and waved her hands in front of my face. "I remember Brian. Short, stocky, dark-haired guy. Right? I always thought of him as super stud. His default was set at schmooze. Hard to picture him as a Scientologist, but I guess if it works for Tom Cruise, it can work for Brian."

"I agree that he came off as a stud. But no false advertising there. He was great in bed. Just what I needed at the time. Totally took my mind off Pablo. But if you remember, Brian had a wandering eye that led him off to be great in beds all over town. As I recall, you got good and sick of listening to me complain about his bed-hopping before I finally broke it off with him."

Elisa laughed. "Right. I was cheering you on to get rid of him. So where's he been all these years?"

"California as far as I know. At least that's where he said he was going after we broke up. He's a graphic artist, so L.A. looked like the land of opportunity. Now he has his own graphic design business here in Boulder. He gave me his card so I could call him."

"Are you going to?"

"I wasn't, especially after Faye told me he's been trying to convert her to Scientology. But there's more. He knew Mirabel Townes. In fact, he came to the gallery to see Angelica's work. And later I found out from Angelica that a Scientologist named Brain used to visit Mirabel at home. So I'm thinking I might call him and get together to see if I can pump him for some information about how she was getting along with the Scientologists before she died."

Before Elisa could start in telling me what a mistake it would be to talk to Brian about Mirabel, we heard Elisa's husband Jack from the front hall. "Hi, I'm home," he yelled. "And whatever you're eating smells amazing." He headed out to us, gave Elisa a big kiss, me a big hug, and went straight to the kitchen to fill a plate with food.

Jack is a lanky, sandy-haired man, easy-going and sociable. I love him like a brother. He and Elisa got married in their early twenties and had their daughter, Maria, right away. I met them through a friend who told me they were looking for a part-time nanny. I was a twenty-three-year-old struggling artist, so I applied and got the job. We've been like family ever since. They're both forty now and I'm thirty-seven, so it's been a while.

"Hey, Jack," Elisa said. "Cleo's been spending some time with Mirabel Townes' kids and she says a huge chunk of Mirabel's estate is going to the Scientologists. Have you heard anything about that from Derrick?"

Jack brought his plate and a wine glass over to our table, sat down and took a few bites. "Tastes as good as it smells," he said with a smile. "Sorry to be so late. Had some very indecisive clients. Anyway, about Derrick. I haven't seen him in a while. But from what I hear, it's no secret that his business has had some big losses. His financial picture isn't pretty. If he doesn't inherit most of Mirabel's estate, he could be in quicksand." He went back to his food and Elisa jumped in.

"I agree. Derrick must be fit to be tied if he's not inheriting the majority of Mirabel's money," she said. "From what I've heard, he's always needed it, which is probably why he never divorced her even though he's been involved with Judith for years."

"But why didn't she divorce him?" I asked. "Didn't she know about Judith?"

"I don't know. She never said anything and I never asked her. We mostly knew each other from political work and because Kari and my Maria were such close friends. She didn't talk about Derrick. The message I got was that her marriage was off limits and I respected that. But I figure she did know. It's not exactly a secret around town."

"I wonder why she stayed with him."

"She was a very loyal person. Steadfast. Never gave up on a cause. They'd been married over twenty years. She probably figured he'd come around eventually. And she was an idealist. Her passion in recent years was for her community work, political campaigns and environmental movements. I got the impression her marriage was on a back burner."

We talked a little more about the Townes family but none of us had anything new to add and I was eager to change the subject to escape more of Elisa's warnings. So we kicked back, shared some gossip, a few laughs, and more wine. After which, I slept soundly in their guest room, without any dreams of the Townes family.

Chapter 18

The next morning, after a quick breakfast at Elisa and Jack's and a brief stop at my house to change clothes, I drove over to Shady Terrace to visit Gramma. A week had gone by since the announcement of the closing, and the nursing home was bustling with family members—unusual for a Saturday morning. In the parking lot I saw a couple loaded down with bulky bags and boxes that they were stacking in their SUV. Looked like the moving-out process had already started. So much for my desperate hope that somehow the closing edict would be reversed.

As I entered Gramma's unit, I noticed Tanya the charge nurse coming out of Gramma's room. The multicolor-flower-patterned scrubs most of the nurses and aides wear here don't flatter her short wide figure, but her thick curly hair and huge brown eyes transform her into a beauty.

She hailed me as I walked down the hall. "Oh, Cleo, I'm glad you're here," she said. "Martha is agitated this morning. Keeps asking for your grandfather, James. This week, even the confused residents know something's up. Flora Gypsum refused to get dressed this morning—you know how she usually likes to get dolled up with jewelry, high heels and a hat. Right now she's still in her nightgown. And Peter Luth got so upset at breakfast, he threw his coffee cup on the floor. When it smashed, coffee splashed on Harriett Benesh and she threw a roll at him. It's affecting them all. They may not be able to talk about it, but they're tuned into the feeling of crisis."

I felt tears well up at the thought of my sweet Gramma being upset by cruel circumstances that she couldn't even understand, much less control. "It's so unfair," I said, holding back the tears. "Moving will upset them even more. And who knows where most of them will end up. It's not easy to find good places."

Tanya shook her head in agreement. "Don't I know it. All of us on the staff need to find new jobs and it's slim pickins out there."

Of course. The staff would be looking for new places too. Maybe I could get some leads from Tanya. "Have you found any places where you think you'd want to work?" I asked. "Gramma likes you and it would be nice for her to be where you go."

"The only offer I've gotten so far is from Easy Living Care Center," she said. "I'd rather scrub floors than work there." She headed off to answer a call light.

I continued down the hall to Gramma's room, remembering my own bad impression when I visited Easy Living and saw aides chatting with each other in the dining room when they should have been helping residents. Nothing about this move was going to be easy.

I took some deep breaths to calm myself. Gramma's sensitive to my moods and if she was already agitated, I didn't want to add to that. I found her in her bathroom trying to brush her teeth with a cake of soap. "It's too big for me," she complained, waving the soap in my face. "I need a different one."

I gently put my arms around her shoulders. "I'll get rid of that one for you," I said, reaching around and removing the soap from her hand. I gave her a kiss and a hug, helped her brush her teeth with her actual toothbrush, and eased her out of the bathroom into her bedroom. I pointed her toward the comfortable overstuffed chair she usually favors, but she was too jittery to sit. "Where's James?" she asked, pacing restlessly around her room. "He should be here by now." She looked worried.

I've long since given up telling her that Grampa is dead. She doesn't believe me and it's not something I want to argue with her about. So I make up reasons why he isn't there. Usually she accepts my excuses and quits asking for him. "He had a lot of meetings today," I said. "So I came to see you instead. Would you like to walk down the hall and see the fish?"

Watching the colorful tropical fish swim around in the extra-large aquarium worked its usual calming magic on Gramma, but didn't do much for me. I couldn't stop worrying about finding a good place for her. I wondered if there'd be a fish tank wherever she ended up.

All of which reminded me that I should check out more of the nursing homes in the booklet Tim had given us at the meeting. Not that I had forgotten—more like I'd put it in the back of my mind next to other unpleasant tasks I postpone like making dentist appointments and getting the tires rotated on my car. But I knew I had to move on this, so I told myself to suck it up and go visit more places. I gave Gramma a hug and said, "I need to go now. Do you want to stay here with the fish or go back down the hall?"

"Stay," she said.

I gave her a kiss, said goodbye, and moved toward the front door, wishing I could stay with her rather than face the task ahead.

As I stepped out into the parking lot, I heard, "Hey, Cleo, hold up a minute," from a man behind me. I turned around to see Derrick Townes dressed like he'd come straight from the tennis court.

I didn't feel like talking to him, especially given how unpleasant our last interaction had been. But he bounded over and stood in front of me looking as friendly and eager as a puppy dog. "Good to see you, Cleo," he said. A warm fuzzy smile spread over his face.

This guy has as many moods as a summer afternoon in the mountains, I thought to myself. And he goes from sunny to stormy and back with as little warning. I was wary and ready to shake him off.

But he was at least as persistent as his daughter, Lacey. He stood blocking the door to my car, talking to me like I was an old friend. "Bet you're not any happier with what's going on here than I am. This closing down thing is a huge mess." He shook his head and frowned slightly, then went on. "I had an early match in the tennis tournament this morning and then I came over to see Dad. I don't know what to do. He refuses to even talk about moving."

I decided a few minutes of polite conversation might be worth my time. Maybe he'd decide I wasn't as evil as Judith made me out to be. "So your father likes living here?" I asked.

"He didn't at first—after his stroke. Said he'd rather die than live in a nursing home. But he couldn't manage on his own and we couldn't take care of him. It takes two people to get him in and out of his wheelchair. The hospital social workers talked him into giving Shady Terrace a try and now that he's used to it, he likes it here pretty well. He doesn't want to think about any other places—says he'll just stay and let them tear the building down around him."

"What are you going to do?"

"Not sure. Have you found any good places for your grand-mother?"

"No. I'm just off to check out some more of the places on Tim's list," I said, hoping that now that I'd talked politely with him about his father, he'd back off and let me leave.

"Could I buy you a quick cup of coffee first?" he asked with an-other engaging grin. "I'd like to apologize for Judith's contrariness the other day. I was embarrassed. She gets carried away sometimes, doesn't realize how it comes across. Anyway I'd love to compare notes on this nursing home mess. Two heads are better than one and all that."

The idea of talking to someone who was in the same boat as I was with the nursing home search was appealing and I was curious about what he'd say about Judith, so I decided to join him. "Okay. How about Caffé Soleil over at Table Mesa? It's on my way and there's easy parking."

He agreed enthusiastically, so we drove off and met a few minutes later at the coffee place. Once we had our lattes and were settled at a table on the sunny outdoor patio, I pulled out the booklet Tim had given us at the meeting. "I've only seen a couple of the places on this list," I said. "Have you visited any of them?"

Derrick looked troubled. "Like I said, Dad doesn't want to move. I've been hoping we could derail this sale. Hugh Symes is rich, but he doesn't have a lot of friends in this town. You probably heard about the prairie-dog flap he got into with Mirabel. I think she had him by the short hairs on that one, but since she died her group has dropped the ball on it. I thought I could get his attention by threatening to revive that case and to rat him out on some other underhanded deals I know about, but he's not budging."

"So you actually threatened Symes, hoping you could get him to keep Shady Terrace open?"

"Damn right I threatened him. My father is on Medicaid and Symes is basically turning him out into the street. Dad has no money. He has to go wherever we can find an open Medicaid bed."

Given what Elisa and Jack had said about Derrick's finances, I figured he couldn't help his father pay for a nursing home. I could see why he was upset about the closing, but I thought his idea of derailing the sale was a lost cause. "From what Tim said, it sounds like the sale is a done deal," I said. "And we need to find new places before they all get filled up."

"Tim Grosso!" Derrick exclaimed angrily, nearly upsetting his cup. "I wouldn't trust anything that guy says. For all we know, Hugh may be paying him off."

I was getting used to Derrick's mood swings, but I was taken aback at the intensity of his attack on Tim. "Why would you say that?" I asked, then sipped my coffee and waited for his reply. When he didn't respond, I prodded him. "Tim's the chair of the Psych Department at the university and he does this nursing home thing as a volunteer."

Derrick looked around to see who was sitting within listening distance, then said quietly, "Tim and Mirabel were close until they had some kind of falling out last year. They worked on causes, went hiking, hung out smoking pot. I'm pretty sure he was encouraging her to leave me. The more time she spent with him, the more she talked about a divorce."

Whoa. Tim and Mirabel smoked pot together? Apparently Pablo was right about him. I also remembered what Elisa and Jack had said about Derrick staying with Mirabel because he needed her money. If Tim had been pushing Mirabel in the direction of divorce, I could see why Derrick would dislike him.

"It sounds like you didn't want a divorce," I said, wondering why he'd been having an affair with Judith if he wanted to preserve his marriage.

He leaned closer to me, a move I assumed was designed to keep the conversation private between us. For a moment I was distracted by the animal magnetism of this attractive man, his deep blue eyes meeting mine in an intimate gaze, but I shook off the feeling as he continued his story. "We hadn't had an intimate relationship for years," he said quietly. "But Mirabel was the mother of my children and we'd been together a long time. I wanted her to be different, but I didn't want to leave her. She didn't want us to split up either. We'd reached an agreement. She would stay with me and get out of the Church of Scientology, if I would give up Judith."

Yikes. Was this guy one of those good-looking athletic types who follows his impulses until he gets in trouble and then says whatever he needs to say to charm his way out? Had he really been planning to break up with Judith or had he just been playing along to get Scientology out of the picture? Did he and Judith think Mirabel had believed him and made the new will leaving all her money to him and his children? Did they bump Mirabel off like Angelica suspects so he could inherit the money and then be together after all?

I was carefully keeping my inscrutable therapist expression as this stuff was racing through my mind, but I needed to change my focus before I lost control and showed my alarm. I drew back away from him and said the first thing that popped into my mind. "You and Judith were breaking up?"

"I was about to tell Judith it was over the week that Mirabel died. Now there's no reason why Judith needs to know I had promised Mirabel I would leave her."

Why would he share such a cold self-serving thought with me? The only reason I could think of was that my original idea was true—that he and Judith had plotted together for him to deceive Mirabel—that he had never intended to break up with Judith, but he wanted Mirabel to believe he had. Now for some reason he wanted me to believe the lies he'd told Mirabel.

"Here's the thing," he said slowly, putting down his cup and turning his full gaze on me again. "Mirabel told me she'd kept her promise and made a new will that left out the Scientologists. But I can't find it. Her father, Vernon, handled all her legal stuff and he says he never drew up a new will for her. I think she did change the will, but I can't prove it. So I need you to contact her spirit or whatever Lacey says you can do and ask her where the will is. If you really want to help Lacey and Angelica, help me find that will so the Scientologists don't get money that belongs in our family."

Good grief. He thinks my Contact Project is like sending email questions to the dead. I didn't feel like explaining the whole process to him there and then, especially since it was Lacey who was my client, not him. So I gave the simplest answer. "I can't do that for you. I don't contact spirits for families. I help them do it."

"It would be much better for you to do it," he said. "I'll pay double what you usually charge if you can find out where the will is."

Now that it was obvious why he'd brought me there, I'd had enough. I stood up, collected my stuff, and said, "You have no idea what the Contact Project is. Now I need to go visit nursing homes."

Then before he had time to say another word, I turned and walked to my car.

Chapter 19

I visited another two disappointing nursing homes that Saturday afternoon. Afterwards to get my mind off the bad odors and dreary buildings, I went to my office to put some finishing touches on a presentation I was scheduled to give at a psychology conference in Denver the next week. I was excited about having gotten my paper accepted to this prestigious conference, and I wanted my presentation to be excellent. After I'd spent an hour tinkering with my Power Point slides, I took a break to check my email.

I noticed one with 'last minute conference changes" in the subject line, so I opened it first to see if I'd need to make any changes in my presentation. The words hit me like a ton of snow rumbling down a mountainside to smother an unsuspecting skier. I gasped for breath as I re-read the miserable message. "We regret that last-minute scheduling changes require us to cancel your presentation. Blah… blah…blah. Please consider submitting it for consideration at next year's conference. Blah…blah…blah."

Could they do this? Cancel me at the last minute? Did they have any idea how much time I'd spent preparing my presentation? Did they care? I grabbed my cell phone and called the number for the conference organizer. Of course I got voice mail. I left a message asking someone to call me about the email. Then I called Elisa's cell.

"Ouch! That's a kick in the gut," she said after I read her the email and asked my questions. "I'm SO sorry. I know how much this meant to you. But they can do it, Cleo. It's their conference. I haven't heard of it happening with that conference before, though. I wonder what happened."

"I guess they got a last-minute paper from someone they think is more impressive than I am," I said sadly.

"Maybe they didn't get enough conference registrations to hold all the sessions," Elisa said slowly. "Or maybe Judith Demar had a hand in this. She has a lot of connections in the academic community. Remember I told you she's a dangerous enemy."

"Seriously? You think she'd go that far? And what good would it do her if I don't know she did it? If she's trying to intimidate me, I need to know she got my paper removed so I know what she's capable of."

"Perhaps she'll find a way to let you know. Let's talk more about it later. I need to go now. I'm driving on Broadway and I have to get around a couple of busses."

I hung up, closed down my computer, locked up my office and went home to shower and change for the evening. Pablo was getting back from his Atlanta crisis-intervention training course in the late afternoon and we had plans to go to a party that evening at the home of some artist friends from the old days.

As I showered, I thought about how much I was looking forward to seeing Pablo, spending some time together, sharing all that had happened while he was away. His training schedule had been so intense that we'd only been able to connect for a couple of brief phone calls during the week. I had a lot to tell him. He didn't know about my meetings with Lacey, Angelica and Shane, not to mention Derrick and Judith, or Vernon and Glenna. But there was no way we'd have time to talk about all that before the party. I knew it would take a while to explain how I'd gotten so quickly involved in a situation he'd warned me away from.

I put on my favorite pair of sexy Joe's jeans—the ones that fit me like a second skin. After trying a few tops, I settled on a black lacey tank with a coral silk shirt over it. I wanted to look good, especially since I had to give Pablo news he didn't want to hear. I was just finishing styling my hair when Pablo showed up looking so scrumptious that I instantly threw myself at him for a huge hug. His powerful arms enfolded me and I smooshed myself into his solid muscular shoulders.

So much tension oozed out of me that I felt ten pounds lighter.

"I'm glad to see you too," Pablo said tenderly, tipping up my head for a soft sweet kiss. I almost suggested we skip the party altogether. But before I could, Pablo read my thoughts, met my eyes and said, "You look great, but let's go to the party first. It will be fun to see Mel and Jerri and everyone. We can leave early and come back here."

Mel and Jerri were a couple when we were all in college studying art. They got married not long after and had a couple of kids who must be about eight and ten now. Jerri has done well as an illustrator and Mel started a greeting-card company that ended up being bought out for millions. They are the big success story of our class. I don't see them much anymore except at occasional gatherings of old friends, and it's always fun to catch up.

I love their house. It's an old Victorian near downtown. They spent a whole lot of time and money remodeling it, carefully keeping its historic character, while adding modern finishes like a state-of-the-art gourmet kitchen and luxurious bathrooms. The restored original woodwork, hardwood floors, and crown molding give it an old-world charm that makes me feel like I've been transported back to a more gracious genteel time.

The living room was bursting at the seams by the time Pablo and I found parking and got to the house. We waded into the throng, grabbed a couple of glasses of wine, shared hugs and laughs with old friends, and soaked up the festive ambiance as we drifted here and there. After an hour or so had gone by, he was across the room and I was deep in conversation with Celine—a friend I hadn't seen for years because she had gotten married and moved to Seattle. She and her husband had only recently moved back to Boulder where she was managing a Vitamin Cottage store. "Maybe I should come in and get something to help me with all the stress I've been under lately," I said. "But I never know which supplements to choose."

"We have the perfect solution for you, Cleo," she said enthusiastically. "Pamphlets with questionnaires you fill out about how you're feeling and then after you add up your answers you can see what vitamins and supplements you need to take to feel better."

Suddenly a man behind me put his hand on my shoulder and interrupted us. "I couldn't help but overhear," he said. "And I have to tell you, Cleo, that vitamins and supplements aren't what you need to relieve stress."

I whipped my head around to see who was calling me by name and giving me advice, and was surprised to see my ex-boyfriend Brian. Amazing! He'd been here a year and I'd never seen him at all. Now twice in one week, I run into him. What are the odds?

I felt flustered and a bit taken aback. "Brian! What a surprise running into you again," I said. "This is my friend Celine. She's a manager at Vitamin Cottage. So what do you have against vitamins?"

"Pills aren't the answer to people's problems," he said emphatically. "They're not going to help you and they may make you worse. And relying on medication keeps you from finding permanent solutions to your issues."

"I don't think it's fair to call vitamins and supplements medication," Celine said. "Our products are all natural and our approach is holistic…"

"That's not the point," Brian interrupted. "Stress and pain are caused by a reactive mind. You need to get free from your reactivity and learn to understand yourself and your life if you want to be happy."

Celine didn't reply to him. Just made a quick getaway, saying she had to catch up with her husband across the room.

Brian stayed put, his hand still firmly on my shoulder. "Cleo, your survival is important to me. I've found the way to flourish and prosper and I want to share what I've learned with you. I owe you that to make up for the way I behaved when we were together. You'll be so much happier after you learn the truth about how we can solve our own problems."

I'd heard enough. First he butted into my private conversation and now he was telling me what I needed to do to be happy? I pulled away from his grasp and looked him straight in the face. "Wait a minute, Brian. Since I saw you last I've gotten my doctorate in psychology and I'm a licensed therapist, so I don't think I need a Scientologist giving me advice about my mental health."

He moved closer. His familiar smell washed over me, bringing back sexual memories of our time together. I was feeling a little lightheaded. "What do you know about Scientology?" he asked. Have you read *Dianetics*? Anyone who has not read *Dianetics* remains ignorant of the most important breakthroughs on the subject of the human mind."

I stepped back, regrouped and took a minute to decide how I wanted to answer. I considered just making an excuse to get away from him, but I wanted to find out more about his involvement with Mirabel Townes. So I bypassed his questions and said, "I didn't know you were a Scientologist until we ran into you at the gallery the other day. After you left, Faye said something about you being a Scientology friend of the former gallery co-owner Mirabel Townes."

"Poor Mirabel," he said quietly. "Drowning like that in her own backyard. So sad. She was a person of good will who worked hard to take care of the planet."

"I know she was a Scientologist, too. Did you know her well?" I asked, hoping he'd spill some secret info about Mirabel's position in the Scientology community. I was looking for a clue as to whether she had become disenchanted with them and possibly written them out of her will like Derrick said she did.

But instead of taking the bait, he pushed back. "How did you know Mirabel?"

I took a few sips of my wine while I pondered my reply. How to say enough to keep him talking about Mirabel without telling him too much about my involvement with the Townes family?

"I didn't know her," I said. "But I know her daughter, Lacey. She happened to mention that her Mom had left a lot of money to Scientology, so I'm guessing Mirabel was a pretty active member."

Brian scowled. "I can only imagine the evil Lacey is spreading about us," he said, bitterly. She tried her best to undermine the progress Mirabel was making with us, told her we were brainwashing her. Insisted Scientology is a cult, accused her mom of being gullible,"

"Was Mirabel having second thoughts about Scientology because of what Lacey was telling her?"

"No," Brian said, still frowning. "She mostly tried to help Lacey see the truth. Encouraged her to look at how her criticisms of Scientology were coming from her own mistakes and insecurities. But Lacey refused. Her mind is closed."

He stopped and seemed to go inward for a minute. I could see his body relax as a smile returned to his face. "But let's talk about you," he said, putting his arm around my shoulders. "You said you've been under a lot of stress lately. I'd love to have you come in and take our free stress test. I can tell you some fantastic stories about what other people have achieved with Scientology methods."

As I was debating the best way to wriggle out of the conversation and Brian's arm, Pablo suddenly appeared at my side. "There you are, Cleo," he said softly, completely ignoring Brian. "Are you about ready to leave?" Then he turned to Brian as if he'd just noticed him. "Oh, hi Brad," he said, nonchalantly.

"It's Brian actually," Brian said, tightening his grip on my shoulders. "Cleo, before you go let's set a time for you to come by the office so we can talk more about getting rid of your stress."

I wrenched free of Brian's arm and took Pablo's hand. "Pablo and I need to leave now, Brian. And as I said before, I'm quite capable of solving my own problems."

"I'm talking about way more than solving your problems," Brain said fervently. "I'm offering you a way to a higher state of awareness where you can gain lasting happiness."

"Hey, give it a rest, Brad," Pablo said. "This is a party, not a revival. Get yourself a drink and have some fun. We have to go."

As we wended our way through the crowded room to the front door, I thought about how Brian seemed to be a strange new person, sort of a high-pressure salesman for his newfound religion. If—as Shane had said—Mirabel had been drawing back from Scientology, what sort of pressure would Brian and his fellow believers have put on her?

Chapter 20

Surprisingly, once we'd left the party the Brian episode didn't intrude on our evening. Back at my house, we tumbled into bed and made love, eagerly giving in to our pent-up desire. Afterward, I nestled into his chest. "I missed you," I said. "It's been a hard week."

"Problems with your Gramma?" Pablo asked drowsily, hugging me close. "I know that's tough for you."

"True, but there's more," I said. "You probably don't want to hear it all now, so how about I tell you in the morning?"

No answer. He was sound asleep. So I turned over, relieved to put off until another day catching him up on my involvement in the Townes' family drama.

It all hit the fan the next morning at my kitchen table over fruit and bagels when I told him about my various meetings with Lacey, Angelica, Shane, Derrick, Judith, Vernon and Glenna and my agreement to help Lacey and Angelica. Pablo heard me out without reacting—his cop training—then started questioning me. "Why, Cleo? Why do you want to get involved?"

I spread some strawberry cream cheese on my bagel and tried to stay relaxed. "It's not that I want to exactly," I said. I flashed on a vision of Angelica, so verbally stoic, yet betrayed by the tears on her cheeks. I wanted to hug her, hold her hand and wipe away her tears, but that wasn't what she asked of me. She wanted me to help her solve the mystery that tormented her. "It's that Angelica is so sure that Mirabel didn't drown accidentally, and she has no one to help her find out what really happened." I took a bite of my bagel and waited for the next question, hoping this wasn't going to go the way I was afraid it was.

Unfortunately he moved right into confrontational mode. "How are you going to be able to help her when she's a minor child whose parents have forbidden you to work with her?" he asked in a steely voice.

Ouch. He's so quick to find the weak spots and zing right in. I tried to sound patient and reasonable as I replied. "I can't help her directly. You're right about that. All I can do is help Lacey contact her mom. It will be up to Lacey to help Angelica."

Now Pablo was in full interrogation mode—not even bothering to eat. Just gulping coffee and spitting out questions like, "Do you really think you can contact a dead woman and find out more than the police can?"

"The police have already refused to investigate any further. They won't do anything unless someone can prove the drowning wasn't an accident."

We went on like that for a while. Question. Answer. Question. Answer. Our food sat untouched. Our voices escalated. Our tempers flared. Finally Pablo stood up, carried his dishes to the sink, and said, "Enough, Cleo. I don't want to talk about this anymore. Boulder has a police department. Let them handle it. You're in way over your head here, and you're likely to get hurt. Investigating murder—if there even is a murder here—is no job for a therapist."

I stood up too. "Never mind, Pablo. It's my decision to make and I've decided to help Lacey and Angelica. I was hoping you'd understand, maybe even help me think it all through. But forget it."

"I wish I could forget it," he said as he headed into the bedroom to collect his stuff. "Nothing's ever simple with you, is it? If you really wanted my help, you'd pay more attention to what I say. I'm the cop here, not you." He grabbed his backpack and walked out, leaving me wondering why I'd even bothered telling him about my week.

I decided to refocus and de-stress by taking a walk down to the Pearl Street Pedestrian Mall—the six-block area that is the heart and soul of Boulder, with people-watching, street performers, food, shopping and more. It was a sunny fall Sunday and as I walked toward the mall I saw the usual throngs of Boulderites out bicycling and walking. I knew the hiking trails would be full as well. If the sun is shining in Boulder—which it usually is—people feel almost obligated to be outside doing something active.

The bicyclists reminded me of how Brian and I used to bike up to Ward, a tiny mountain town known as a bastion of aging hippies. Hard to imagine the Brian of today hanging out in Ward. He had turned into a completely different person than he was when we were together a dozen years ago. The guy he used to be would have run as fast as he could away from someone promoting Scientology like he did last night. He would have laughed out loud at the idea that joining a cult is the way to get rid of stress and find lasting happiness. I wondered what had changed him so much. If it was Scientology, they must be a powerful group.

Suddenly I noticed that I was passing Faye's gallery and it was open. I decided to stop in to talk to Faye about the value of Gramma's paintings and get her ideas as to whether we could sell more of them quickly if Gramma needed to move to a more expensive place. A couple of people were wandering through the gallery, shadowed by a young sales associate. I peeked behind the curtain at the rear of the gallery and found Faye at her computer in the back room. "Hey, Cleo," she said giving me a wide smile. "I was just going to take a break. Would you like some tea?"

"No thanks," I said. "I just had breakfast. But you go ahead. And maybe I can ask you a couple of questions while you drink it."

She put a tea bag in a sky-blue pottery mug, filled it with hot water from an electric kettle, and took it over to a table next to a small couch and a side chair. We sat. I admired the exquisite necklace she was wearing—Native American handcrafted sterling silver with turquoise. She sipped her tea. I filled her in on Gramma's situation. "What a shame, Cleo," she said, setting down her cup and putting her hand on my arm. "I hate to think of Martha having to live in some of the places I've heard about. I hope you can find a good one."

"I'm trying," I said, working to hold back tears. "But I haven't found anything yet. I may have to hire people to care for her at home. That would be a lot more expensive than Shady Terrace, so I was wondering what you can tell me about the market for Gramma's paintings right now. I may need to sell some of the ones I have to pay for her care."

Faye had drawn back her hand and was looking off in the distance with a pained look. She sighed and turned toward me. "I'm afraid it's not a good market at all right now," she said. "I wouldn't advise putting more of Martha's paintings up for sale. It's likely to bring down the prices for the ones already on the market."

My heart sank. If Gramma needed more money, where would we get it? "Could you show me the figures on the paintings that have sold in the last year?" I asked. "The money goes into her trust and I haven't paid as much attention as I should have."

"Sure. But could we do it next week? I'll need to gather up all the information."

Shouldn't she have that on her computer where she could access it with a simple search? I thought about pushing her on that, but before I figured out a polite way to phrase it, she said, "I'm sorry, Cleo. I haven't gotten the books completely straightened out since Mirabel died."

"Oh, right. She was a co-owner. So I guess Derrick owns half the gallery now."

"No. I own the whole thing. Mirabel had a clause in her will leaving me the gallery. The Church of Scientology is inheriting the building, but the gallery gets to stay in it rent-free. I'm lucky because from what I've heard, the Scientologists are raising the rent on the other tenants. Your Scientology friend was in here the other day telling me about the new rents. He seemed a little surprised when I pointed out that Mirabel's will said that I don't have to pay rent for the gallery."

I ignored her comments about Brian and the Scientologists. While I was a little curious about how much the Scientologists were raising the rent, I didn't want to give the impression that Brian or his actions were important to me. So I responded to what she'd said about inheriting the gallery. "Wow! You own the gallery. And the free rent should help with the gallery expenses," I said.

"It will help," she said. "But it's not easy to make ends meet in the gallery world these days. Sometimes I think…"

Before she could finish her thought, we were interrupted by Tim Grosso standing in the doorway of the back room. "Hey, Faye," he said. "I came by to drop off that book I promised you last night. I had to stop by my office this morning, so I grabbed the book while I was there." He held out a slim hardbound volume with a gold title on the spine. I was curious of course, but I was at the wrong angle to read the title.

Faye jumped up, took the book, and gave Tim a kiss and a big hug. "Thanks a bunch, Tim," she said sticking it over on her cluttered desk. "Would you like some tea?"

"If I'm not interrupting you and Cleo, tea would be great," he said with a smile.

I figured they might like some privacy and I needed to get going anyway, so I said, "Actually I was just about to leave. As you know, Tim, I have nursing homes to visit."

As I stepped out of the back room, I felt drawn to look again at Angelica Townes' paintings. Possibly her art would help me understand her better. I noticed the placard next to her work. Somehow I'd missed reading it when I looked at her painting before—probably because the gallery had been so crowded. It read, "Angelica Townes, an unusually gifted ten-year-old artist, has been painting since she was two. Her paintings are inspired by her visions and dreams, and have deep spiritual meanings. Her use of luminous color surrounding the faces represents emotional states reflected in auras that she sees encircling the faces of many people she meets."

So Angelica paints the auras she sees. I'd heard that each color of the aura surrounding a person's head has a precise meaning, indicating a specific emotional state. I wondered what color aura she saw around me and what information she took from that. But wait—if she had this ability, couldn't she just look for which one of Mirabel's family, friends or acquaintances had a bad aura and figure out who drowned her mother? If, that is, someone actually did drown Mirabel.

And if Angelica can actually see auras. And if auras actually exist and mean something.

As my focus turned away from Angelica's paintings, I noticed I could hear Faye and Tim talking and I heard my name. I moved a little closer, as if examining another painting, and stood quietly listening.

"I was just telling Cleo how hard it is to keep the gallery going," Faye said. "I can't imagine what I'd do if I had to pay the big rents the Scientologists are charging the other tenants in the building."

"I'm kind of surprised that they own the building now," Tim said. "Mirabel once told me she was rethinking her decision to leave it to the Scientologists."

"How long ago was that?" Faye asked.

I knew I shouldn't stay and continue to eavesdrop, but I couldn't force myself away.

"About a year ago," Tim said. "As you know, she and I weren't on such good terms anymore, so we hadn't talked lately. I figured Derrick and Shane talked her out of leaving the building to the Scientologists. They both have expensive tastes and neither one of them likes to work hard enough to support their lifestyles."

"That's true," Faye said. "But at least Derrick has an actual job. Shane spends all his time on the computer. I know Mirabel was worried about him, especially after she found out that he was making money by creating fake documents like over-twenty-one IDs that he sells to college students."

So Shane's income wasn't all from Gyaki-Birquit. Not too surprising that he knew how to use his computer skills to create fake IDs, but I was surprised to find out he was doing it. Even though I had no idea how I would explain myself if Faye and Tim caught me listening, I had to hear more. I slipped behind the door and held my breath.

"Not only that," Faye went on, "Mirabel suspected he was also running an ID theft and forgery scam, buying electronics and gift cards with stolen credit card numbers and selling them on eBay."

"No kidding," Tim said. "The little weasel stole one of my credit cards—probably when Mirabel and I were in the hot tub—and used it to buy some things online before I realized it was stolen. The credit card company took responsibility and they didn't seem to care about finding out who took it, but I kept after it until I tracked it down to Shane."

Yikes! This was getting juicier and juicier. I knew I should leave before one of them came out and found me loitering behind the door. But my curiosity kept me rooted to the spot.

"Really? Shane stole your card?" Faye sounded shocked. "How come you never told me about that?"

"Old history," Tim said apathetically. "It all happened before you and I got together."

Then Faye asked exactly the question I would have asked. "So did you tell Mirabel?"

Tim sounded a bit reluctant to be having this conversation, but he answered her question. "Oh yes. I went to her and said I'd give her a chance to get Shane to straighten things out and make amends and if Shane did that, I wouldn't press charges."

Once again, Faye asked the question that was on my mind. "So what did Mirabel say?"

"At first she didn't believe me. I guess that was before she suspected what Shane was up to. But I convinced her to talk to Shane. She finally got him to admit it. You know how forceful Mirabel could be. He gave back the card, but refused to take responsibility for the charges. Mirabel came back to me and offered to pay the credit company back herself, but I turned down her offer. I wanted Shane to take responsibility."

Hmm…So Tim decided to push Mirabel even knowing how tough she was. Wonder where that got him. Faye wondered too. "So what happened?" she asked.

Tim sighed. "Mirabel and I had a big fight. She said she felt responsible for Shane's problems because she hadn't been a good enough mother to him. She was unwilling to put any more pressure on him. I said I was going to the police."

"So did you?"

"No. Mirabel threatened me back that she'd talk to the police about those slightly illicit plants I grow. The whole thing ended in a standoff and we hardly spoke again after that. Sad. We'd been such good friends for so long."

At that point, I somehow came to my senses and realized I'd never be able to explain why I was still in the gallery after I'd said I had to leave ten or fifteen minutes ago. I tiptoed off toward the front door, trying to take in and make sense of all I'd just heard. No wonder Shane doesn't want to try to contact Mirabel. They had some huge issues. And who else knows about Shane's illegal activities?

I wandered out of the gallery in such a haze of confusion that I ran smack into a man on the sidewalk outside. I would have landed on my butt if he hadn't grabbed me. "Oh. I'm so sorry. My head was somewhere else," I said breathlessly. Then my head cleared and I noticed that for the third time in a week I was face to face with Brian.

Chapter 21

We have to stop meeting like this," Brian said with the deep laugh I'd always loved. I found myself laughing along with him, despite my irritation with him the night before. This amiable Brian was the guy who used to be so good at cheering me up. Now that we've literally run into each other again," he said, "let me buy you a cup of coffee."

I was shaken by the conversation I'd just overheard, but not so rattled that I'd fall for a ploy to subject myself to more Scientology proselytizing. "Thanks, but I'm in kind of a rush," I said. "I have a lot of things to get done today." I turned to leave, but he still had hold of my arm.

He let go, but stood blocking my path. "Come on, Cleo. It's only 11:30 and it's Sunday. Surely you can take a few minutes for coffee. It's such a nice day. Here we are right in front of Spruce Confections. We can sit out on the patio, drink some excellent coffee and catch up on the past ten years. You can tell me more about your therapy practice."

Coffee on the patio did sound tempting and after my fight with Pablo, being with Brian had its charms. It was a gorgeous day, and I wasn't looking forward to my next task of checking out more nursing homes. Tim had suggested that I go on the weekend to see what conditions were like when staffing was lighter, and I did intend to go that day. I wanted desperately to find a good place for Gramma, but I find visiting those places depressing. Fortifying myself with coffee first would give me energy.

I was also very curious to find out how and why Brian had changed so much. But I definitely didn't want any lectures about how to handle my problems. So I laid out my terms. "Okay. A quick coffee. But only on the condition that you don't try to convert me to Scientology. If you start that again, I'm leaving."

"Fair enough," he said. "Let's go grab a table." We headed for the spacious flagstone patio to the east of the small bakery where we laid claim to an empty gray metal table littered with sections of the Sunday paper. While Brian went inside to the counter to get coffee, I sat and read an article about a prairie-dog linguist who had spoken at a recent meeting of the Boulder Prairie Dog Action Group. According to this guy, prairie dogs have the most sophisticated communication system that anyone has shown in animals. For example, he said they have different words for tall human in a yellow shirt, short human in a green shirt, coyote, deer, red-tailed hawk and many other creatures. Wow—who knew prairie dogs were so smart? No wonder Mirabel and other local activists had gotten laws passed in Boulder years ago to make it illegal to harm them or to destroy their burrows. I could only imagine the foul language those rodents must have used to describe Hugh Symes after he plowed their burrows under.

My ruminations were interrupted when Brian showed up with the food. "I remembered that you like blueberry muffins," he said, setting one in front of me next to a fragrant cup of coffee. I realized that I was ready for another breakfast, since my first one had been spoiled by my argument with Pablo. The coffee smelled delicious and the muffin looked equally yummy.

I quickly forgot about the prairie dogs as I focused on enjoying the rich sweetness of the muffin set off by the spicy full-bodied coffee blend. Then I remembered my manners. "Thanks, Brian," I said. "This is great."

"At least some things haven't changed," he said. "You always were a coffee freak. But it sounds like you have made a lot of changes. Fill me in."

"Wait a minute," I said. "I've made a lot of changes? You've made a complete U-turn. Tell me about your life."

He gazed off to the left for a minute, as if looking for inner wisdom. Then he sighed and said, "You—more than most people—remember how I was, Cleo. I had a great time but nothing really mattered to me. The way I let you go is a good demonstration of that. After I'd been in California a while, I realized I was aimlessly wandering through life, going nowhere. I found myself struggling to find some meaning and purpose. A friend introduced me to Scientology and I knew right away I'd found what I was looking for. Now I can't imagine my life without it."

I recoiled at his singing the praises of Scientology again. What was I thinking when I asked him to tell me about his life? I sort of wanted to pursue the philosophical aspects of his conversion. But I didn't want to encourage him to spread the gospel. So I asked about another aspect of Scientology that I had a hard time imagining him having accepted. "I've heard they charge their members a fortune for everything."

He smiled. "It does cost a lot," he said. "But I'm exchanging my money for getting clear of my problems and moving to a higher state of spiritual awareness. It's important to balance inflow with outflow. Actually I get more than I give. Believe me, if it wasn't worth the money I wouldn't be paying for it. But it's not only worth the money I pay, it's worth way more. If it cost ten times the amount I pay, I'd find the money to do it. If it was a hundred times more, I'd pay that."

He took a drink of his coffee, then said, "Now it's your turn. How did you go from artist to therapist?"

I tried to condense ten years into fifteen minutes, telling him about my realization that art was never going to support me, about getting my doctorate in clinical psychology and becoming a grief therapist, and about how Gramma got Alzheimer's and Grampa died a few years after that. I left out any mention of the Contact Project or contacting spirits.

He drank his coffee, munched on his muffin, and listened intently without interrupting. When I finished, he said, "So is that why you're involved with Mirabel's family? Because you're a grief therapist?"

I thought back to what I'd said to him about the Townes family. Last night I'd told him I knew Lacey and that Lacey had told me her mom had left money to Scientology. But that was it. Other than that, I hadn't said anything about the Townes family. "What do you mean 'involved'?" I asked.

"I mean the way you've had meetings with them this week—not just Lacey, but Shane and Derrick and even Mirabel's dad, Vernon. Are they all having grief therapy?"

What? Did Scientologists have a big spy network all over Boulder? I took another long drink of my coffee to keep my anger from boiling over and thought about what I wanted to say. My first instinct was to demand he tell me where he was getting his information. How did he know I'd had those meetings? Had he been following me since I ran into him a week ago at Faye's gallery? Or had he been following members of the Townes family? I didn't want to show my anger or fear about being spied on. And I didn't want to give him any more information than he already had. So I kept my cool and sidestepped into therapist mode.

"Brian, you must know that I can't talk to you about confidential issues like who is or isn't my client," I said. "When you said you wanted to hear about my therapy practice, I didn't know you meant you wanted private details about clients."

I noticed a quick flicker of anger pass over Brian's face, but he pushed it under right away. It was almost like a shade coming down over a window. In the old days he would have exploded like fireworks on the fourth of July. I figured he'd learned this control from his years of scientology training. He leaned forward and gave me what probably passed for a sincere look among his current friends—but I recognized the old Brian phony I'd-never-lie-to-you look. "I'm sorry, Cleo," he said softly. "I didn't mean to pry. It's just that the Townes family has been through so much and I wondered how they're doing. I hope those kids are okay."

I believed that he was wondering about them in some way, but doubted that he was concerned about their welfare. I said nothing—a well-known therapist tactic to keep the other person talking.

After about thirty seconds went by, he said, "Okay, I get that you can't talk to me about the Townes family. But I can still talk to you about them. You don't have to answer. Here's the thing. I knew Mirabel pretty well and I know she didn't trust Derrick. And for good reason. He's not a nice person. Maybe you know that now that Mirabel is gone, we own the building the Scientology offices are in. Mirabel left us the building in her will, but Derrick has been saying she made a new will that left us out altogether. I don't think she did that. She never told me she was making a new will and as far as I know, no one has seen a new will. Our lawyers are investigating."

Mirabel's will again? Brian was the third person who'd mentioned it to me. First Shane—who said that Mirabel had left bunches to Scientology. Then Derrick—who said she had changed the will to leave out the Scientologists. But Derrick also said he couldn't find the new will. So why are the Scientology lawyers involved?

"Mirabel talked to you about her will?" I asked. "She was only in her forties. Why was she talking about a will? Was she expecting to die young?"

"Scientologists are encouraged to make wills," he said. "I'm sure you know Mirabel was a wealthy woman. She was also a socially responsible woman who wanted to be sure her money would go where it would do the most good."

"So are you afraid Derrick's right and she did change her will?"

Brian leaned close and put his hand lightly on my arm. "I don't think she did," he said, dropping his voice to a familiar intimate tone. "But Derrick's been spreading that story all over town. Cleo, I know you're a person who cares about truth and justice. I'm asking for your help here to expose some destructive lies. Do you know whether or not Derrick actually has found a new will? Do Mirabel's kids know?"

Amazing! He really thinks I'm so naïve that he can pump me for information and I'll just dump it in his lap? His manipulative charm may have worked on me when I was in my twenties, but I am more mature and way beyond that now. I displayed my hard-won maturity by keeping my temper as I responded to him calmly but firmly as I pulled my arm away from his grasp. "I really need to go. Thanks for the food."

Brian looked shocked. I guess his tactics for winning people over usually worked better for him. "Hang on, Cleo," he said, reaching for my arm again.

But I yanked my arm away as if from a hot radiator. "Enough, Brian," I said quietly as I stood up and pushed in my chair. "Let it go. You'll have to find another source to answer your questions." I turned and walked off toward my house. Brian didn't follow me.

Chapter 22

By the time I got home, I had put Brian and his questions out of my mind, replaced by my concerns about finding a place for Gramma to move. I had my list of nursing homes to check out that afternoon and I set out on my tour as soon as I got home. Visiting nursing homes isn't on anyone's list of favorite ways to spend a Sunday afternoon. Stepping into that setting is a quick and uncomfortable way to face your own mortality.

I went to see three places on my list that afternoon, each more depressing than the last. There's no mistaking that these places are the last stop in this life. You can almost smell death in the air. You see it in the frail twisted bodies of residents slumped in wheelchairs, staring vacantly into the distance or perhaps looking inward at their past lives where they were young and happy. They seem to have nothing to live for, yet they continue to cling to life, some reaching out to touch any visitor who comes close enough, others calling out, "Can you help me?" to anyone who walks by.

To be fair, I reminded myself that Shady Terrace had its share of residents like this as well. The difference was that I knew them, knew details about their lives and families, knew who they were before they ended up in their current state. I saw them as individuals who I could empathize with, and that made all the difference.

So I tried to tour the nursing homes as an objective observer of the conditions, care and comfort level of each place. I tried to envision Gramma in each place, but I couldn't do it. When she entered Shady Terrace, I was in graduate school, totally swamped with work.

It was Grampa who visited places and made the choice. He loved her so much, yet he knew he couldn't take care of her at home anymore. Looking back, I realized in a new way how hard it must have been for him. But he made it easy for me after she moved to Shady Terrace, going with me to visit her, pointing out the positives for her being there, until I got familiar with the place and her living there. This time I was on my own and way out of my depth.

By the end of the afternoon, I needed to reconnect with Gramma, hoping I could somehow absorb from her some feeling as to what would be the right choice for her. So I headed for Shady Terrace. It was nearly five when I got there, so the residents were already lining up outside the dining room. I found Gramma sitting on a couch in the hall next to a man named Clyde who had taken a fancy to her lately. Clyde listed drastically to one side when he walked and generally seemed to be in danger of taking a major fall. But sitting, he looked almost normal. He could sound fairly normal too until you realized he said the same things over and over.

They were holding hands when I walked over to their couch. "Hi, Gramma. Hey, Clyde." I said, reaching down to give Gramma a hug. "You two look comfy."

"I'm ninety-seven-years-old, you know," Clyde said, starting in on one of his recurring themes. "Wait till you're my age. Then you'll know about aches and pains."

"If I look as good as you do when I'm ninety-seven, I'll be happy," I said, playing along with his game the way I always do.

"That's too old. You're not ninety-seven," Gramma said. Hard to know if she was addressing Clyde or me. My mind wandered a bit as I began wondering where Clyde was going to move to and whether she'd miss him if they ended up in different places. Good thing I'd come over to see her. Now I realized I'd completely overlooked finding a way to keep her with the friends she's made at Shady Terrace. Yet another factor to consider in my search.

Aides were ushering the residents into the dining room, so I helped Gramma and Clyde to their feet and walked with them slowly. I kissed Gramma goodbye at her table and headed off down the hall toward the door.

As I passed through the main entryway, I saw Tim Grosso at a table over in a corner talking to a couple. I decided to sit down and wait a few minutes to see if I could get a chance to talk to him about the nursing homes I'd visited.

Sure enough, the couple stood up and gathered their things to leave. I walked over and stood nearby so I could get Tim's attention as soon as they left.

"Do you have a few more minutes?" I asked. "I've visited several places and I'm kind of discouraged about what's out there."

"Of course, Cleo." Tim said, pulling out a chair at the table. "Have a seat and fill me in on what you've seen and what you're thinking."

Naturally, the conversation I'd overheard that morning between him and Faye jumped into my mind. But I couldn't bring that up, so I put it to the back of my mind and told him about my reactions to the nursing homes I'd visited ending with my qualms about moving Gramma to any of them. "I just can't bring myself to put her in any of those places. I'm starting to think about bringing her home and hiring someone to take care of her when I'm not there. She has money, especially if we can find a way to sell more of her paintings. Faye says it might be harder than I thought to sell the paintings, so I need to have a better idea of what home-care might cost. Do you know?"

Tim had been sitting quietly listening with an air of concern, which I noticed was looking more and more like a look of deep worry. "It is expensive—usually $18 to $25 an hour—so you have to figure on at least $7500 a month, and that's just for twelve hours a day, which means you have to do the night care. And from what you've said about her wandering at night, you probably would need someone at night as well."

"That would be pricey, but it's possible that she might be able to afford it," I said. "If I did decide to go that way, would you recommend using an agency or hiring someone privately?"

"It depends," he said. "It's not easy to find good reliable people and you can have problems either way."

"Oh, right," I said. "I remember you telling me the other night at the gallery that your father was ripped off by his housekeeper. Do you mind telling me what happened?"

Tim looked embarrassed, almost furtive. "My father never trusted me with his finances," he said. "Never let me know how much he had or how much he spent. Then unfortunately he met a sexy, charismatic young woman who completely beguiled him. She was a massage therapist who moved here from Texas, apparently unaware of the oversupply of massage therapists in Boulder. When she had trouble making a living giving massages, she went to work for an older couple my dad knew. Later they moved into assisted living, and my dad inherited the housekeeper. As soon as I met her, I was wary. She didn't fit my idea of a housekeeper. I tried to warn Dad about her but he said he was entitled to the pleasure of a gorgeous housekeeper if he could afford it. Then he accused me of putting my future inheritance ahead of his comfort."

I didn't know what to believe. Had Tim been looking out for his father's best interests or was his father right about Tim's priorities? I waited for him to go on.

"Here's where it gets sticky," he said. "I assumed Dad was paying her well, but I had no idea how much. After he died I found out he had transferred the title of his condo and his car over to her. It was all done legally, so there was nothing I could do. I tried to find out how much more of his money she might have gotten away with. But it was hard because he had added her name onto his bank account. Again perfectly legal. And talk about being blind to reality, Dad's lawyer was an old friend of his, nearly as old as Dad. He arranged all that and apparently didn't think anything of it. But here's the punch line. After Dad died, his lawyer grabbed Glenna—the housekeeper—for himself and now she's living with him. Probably ripping him off just like she did Dad."

Omigod! Wait a minute—Glenna? Could this be the same Glenna who is living with Vernon Evers? Images of him signing over assets after several bourbon-on-the-rocks came to mind. "Was your father's attorney Vernon Evers by any chance," I asked.

"Yes, Mirabel Townes' father," Tim said. "You know him?"

"He's been my grandparents' attorney forever," I said. "And I had the dubious pleasure of meeting Glenna last Friday when I went over to talk to Vernon about Gramma's trust to find out more about her financial situation and how it affects this move. Glenna seems to be kind of volatile. Did you warn Mirabel about Glenna?"

"I tried, but she was mad at me about something else—it's a long story—and she refused to listen."

Oh, right. That long story about Shane and the credit card. But I couldn't say I knew about that. So I turned the conversation back to Gramma's situation. "Of course Gramma's situation would be different because she'd be living with me, so I'd know more about what any caregiver is up to. And, anyway, Gramma doesn't have control of any of her money. It's all in trust. So she can't give anything away."

"That's a point. I guess your concerns would be more about cost and finding reliable caregivers—and deciding whether you want to have her living with you."

I thanked Tim for his help and drove home running Gramma's options through my head over and over, hoping to stumble on a solution I hadn't thought of yet. But no new ideas popped up. I was leaning more toward bringing her home—after all it is her house—if she had enough money to pay for caregivers. Not caregivers like Glenna though, that's for sure.

I pondered the sticky ethical issues involved in whether Glenna had duped Tim's dad and how she might be duping Vernon Evers. On the one hand, these older men had earned their money and if they wanted to give it to Glenna in exchange for care and whatever else, shouldn't that be their choice to make? On the other hand, Glenna was a strange one. Who knew what she was up to?

Had Mirabel actually listened to Tim's warning about Glenna? I wished I knew. I remembered Shane saying that Mirabel thought Glenna was after Vernon's money, and was trying to get him to dump her. I got a sudden impulse to add Glenna's name to the list of people who wanted to get rid of Mirabel.

Chapter 23

I got up early the next morning. I love starting my week with a Monday before-work yoga class. Determined to put the Townes family issues out of my mind, I welcomed the focus on breathing and body alignment. I left the session with a relaxed body and a clear mind, ready for a busy day with grieving clients.

At my office, I was much too busy to think about anything else until about 4:00, when I looked up from some complicated patient insurance forms to find Angelica standing silently in front of my desk watching me. "Angelica!" I shrieked in a very untherapist-like voice. "What are you doing here? And how did you get in without me knowing it?"

"I tried the door and it was unlocked, so I came in. I was quiet so as not to disturb you. I have to talk to my mother about my dad and Judith, and I need you to help me reach her."

She stood very still with her usual glassy calm air as if nothing out of the ordinary was going on. Good grief. She was a strange child. But, as usual, I felt drawn to this ten-year-old girl set adrift by the death of her mother. She seems both perfectly peaceful and vulnerable at the same time in a way that speed-dialed my helpfulness gene. I still didn't know if she was special with unique abilities, but I did know she needed help. I wanted to solve her problems, but what could I do? For sure I couldn't talk to her here.

"Angelica, you know I can't do that," I said reluctantly. I didn't want to put her out on the street, so I said, "You need to go home. I have my car out back. I'll drive you."

"Cleo, it's important that I talk to my mother. I know things and I have a bad feeling about what's going to happen. You're the only one who can help me, and I can tell that you want to help."

I tried to couch my severe message in as soft and kindly voice as possible. "Angelica, I can't help you because your father won't allow it, and if I don't get you out of this office I'll lose my license to practice and I won't be able to help anyone. So please let me take you home."

Her face fell. "You don't understand. You're stuck at a level of conflict because you can't see the energy beyond that. But I'll go with you."

Stuck because I can't see the energy? That sounded like something Tyler would say. Probably something Tyler had said. Maybe Angelica truly is tuned in to a higher plane.

Balancing my anxiety over having Angelica in my office with my desire not to make her feel rushed out, I locked up the office and led her out to my car in the parking area behind. "Where do you live?" I asked, as we buckled ourselves into our seatbelts. She gave me directions to a house in northwest Boulder so I headed north on Broadway. "Angelica, you've told me you're an Indigo child and you're the first Indigo I've ever met," I said as we drove along. "I'd love to hear more about what it's like for you if you're willing to tell me."

She remained silent and still, looking out the window on her side of the car. I wondered whether I had crossed a line by asking. Should I apologize? But after a few minutes, she turned toward me. "I don't mind telling you, but it's hard in some ways because I don't know what it's like not growing up Indigo."

"I understand," I said. "You can only tell me about your own experiences."

She looked off to the side again as she began to speak "As long as I can remember, I've known things that other people don't seem to know. Sometimes I know what's going to happen before it does—like when the phone's going to ring and who is calling and why. And I can see auras. Yours is mostly turquoise, so I know you're a good listener and a caring person. When I was little, I thought everyone could see the colors around people, but then I realized that most of them don't.

I know I'm different than most kids my age. Some of them think I'm weird. But that's okay. There's no way they can understand."

"What is it like to feel so different from other kids," I said.

She looked pained, like an ordinary ten-year-old who felt marginalized would look. "Sometimes it's hard," she said. Then her expression changed back to her wise Indigo smile. "But mostly I don't want to be like them," she said quietly. "They're just trying to all be the same. I don't need them. I'm my own best friend."

Whew. That attitude could make for problems at school for sure. "Is it hard to go to school when you feel that way?" I asked.

"The thing I hate about school is that you have to be there every day," she said, "and I'm not the same person every day."

She was silent for a minute, smiling to herself. Then she said, "Turn left at the next street."

She guided me along a couple of curvy streets lined with upscale houses set on large landscaped lots, and into the driveway of a huge two-story white house on an extra-large wooded lot. Just as I pulled in, a black SUV zoomed around the corner and into the driveway right behind me. Oh great, here I was with Angelica, stuck in their driveway. And unfortunately for me the driver of the SUV turned out to be Judith Demar. As Angelica opened the car door and got out, Judith jumped out of her car, ran up and grabbed her by the arm. "Where have you been?" she asked angrily. "You were supposed to wait for me after school. I don't have time to spend all afternoon looking for you."

Angelica ignored her and turned to me. "Bye, Cleo," she said. "Thanks for the ride." That would have been the time for me to say, "You're welcome," and drive off into the sunset. But Judith's SUV was still blocking my way out of the driveway.

As soon as she heard Angelica say, "Bye Cleo," Judith noticed me sitting in my car. "What are you doing with Angelica?" she shrieked. "I know Derrick and I made it clear last week that you do not have our permission to treat her."

Angelica started toward the house, but Judith grabbed her arm again and pulled her back. "Not so fast," she said. "I want to know what you and Cleo have been doing."

I took a deep breath to calm myself, then spoke quietly and evenly. "I gave her a ride home, Judith. No treatment." Which was essentially the truth. No point getting Angelica in hot water by reporting that she'd showed up at my office. I continued in my calmest voice, "Now, if you'll move your car for a minute so I can get out, I'll be out of your way."

Judith ignored me and faced Angelica in a confrontational stance. "I need some answers here. Why are you getting a ride home from Dr. Sims when you knew I was coming to pick you up at school?"

Uncharacteristically, Angelica looked angry. She stuck her face right back in Judith's and said with a typical pre-teen sneer, "You're not my mother and it's no business of yours what I do or who I see. You think you know everything about my dad but you don't. Two weeks before my mom died, I heard Dad promise her that he wouldn't see you anymore."

With that, Angelica turned and stalked off toward the front door without waiting to hear what Judith might say in return. Judith looked like she'd been slapped. Then to my surprise she sank down onto a wrought iron bench under a big tree and burst into tears.

So she isn't a totally tough nut after all, I thought. I wondered whether she was upset at the news that Angelica had hurled at her, or whether she was mostly frustrated at her inability to get along with Angelica. Either way, I wasn't feeling especially sympathetic, but I did need her to move her SUV so I could get out of the driveway and be on my way. I couldn't bring myself to yell a reminder about moving her SUV while she was sobbing, so I took a deep breath, got out of my car, walked over and stood next to the bench.

"I know this afternoon hasn't gone the way you hoped it would," I said, "but I want you to know that all Angelica and I did together was drive here."

Judith stopped crying and sat silently looking at the ground beneath her feet. Then she looked up at me and said, "Despite what she thinks, I don't hate Angelica and I don't want to hurt her. I can see she's a troubled child and I'm trying to help her. But she's arrogant and willful and Derrick encourages that behavior by letting her have her own way most of the time. He thinks he can't say no to her because her mother died. I'm having a hell of a time getting him to see how she manipulates him with this Indigo nonsense."

I wondered again why Derrick was relinquishing his parental role to Judith. And why was she telling me all this? After insisting that there was no way I could treat Angelica, was she trying to draw me in to the family drama in a way that would support her point of view? No way was I going to respond to anything she'd said. "I can see you're frustrated, Judith," I said quietly. "Maybe you and Derrick should find a couples counselor to discuss this with. But I need to get back to my office now, so could you please move your car and let me out?"

She nodded silently, got up and backed her car out. I quickly got in my car and drove off. I noticed my cell phone beeping from inside my purse to let me know I had a message, so I grabbed it out and checked the caller ID as I drove. It was Lacey. I punched in my code and listened to her message.

As usual, she sounded frantic. "Cleo, I thought Grandad could help me get Dad to let Angelica work with you and then Angelica could be the one to contact Mom. But Glenna doesn't approve of your work and Grandad won't go against her. I tried one more time to get Dad to give in about letting Angelica work with you, but it was no go. So I'm giving up on that. I can see that I need to be the one who does your contact session, so we need to schedule one ASAP. Call me back. Please, please call!" she begged with her usual dramatic urgency. "We can't waste any more time."

The more I thought about the mess the Townes family seemed to be in, the more I myself wanted someone to reach Mirabel. Maybe she'd been murdered and maybe she hadn't, but either way it seemed that it would be good for them to find out what they could. So, when I got back to my office, I called Lacey and set up a contact-session appointment for Wednesday.

Chapter 24

Before one of my clients starts a contact session, I like us to spend some time together in a place where the deceased loved one lived or worked—ideally a room that contains things that person used often. Being in the room sets the scene, and telling me about the deceased person's daily life helps the living person remember and move into the space of the deceased.

I agreed to meet Lacey at their family home where she and Angelica lived with Derrick. Judith was also living there most of the time and I didn't want to risk running into her, so we set up our meeting for 1:30 Wednesday afternoon when she would be teaching a seminar at the university.

Lacey was waiting for me on the front porch when I drove up. She ran over to greet me as I got out of the car. "I'm so excited," she said, "I woke up this morning with a strong feeling that Mom is waiting to hear from me. I can't wait to get started."

Of course the process is more complicated than she thought, but I didn't want to dampen her enthusiasm, so I just said, "Great. Let's go right in to your mom's office."

She led me through the front door into an airy two-story entry hall, with a large living room off to the left, a long hall heading off to double French doors at the rear of the house, and a staircase at the right leading to the second floor. The house had a cheerful feeling, enhanced by the hardwood floors and buttery yellow walls that magnified the sunlight streaming in from a skylight high above. "What a lovely house," I said.

"Mom and Dad designed it," she said. "It was their dream house. Too bad they weren't happier living in it."

"Maybe they were in the beginning," I said. "How long ago did they build the house?"

"About ten years ago," she said. "It was right about the time Angelica was born. Kari was five then, Shane was thirteen and I was twelve. And you're right—they were happy then. At least they seemed happy. But what does a kid know about how happy her parents are? Well, Angelica knows lots of stuff about adults, but I never had her special abilities."

I would have liked to explore her childhood memories further, but time was short and we needed to move on with what we needed to do before Lacey's attempt to contact her mom, so I said, "We need to be around some of your mother's things so we can focus on her and begin to feel her essence. Are her clothes and jewelry still here? People's favorite things take on their essence."

Lacey frowned. "Mom's essence isn't in her clothes or jewelry," she said. "We should go to her office. That's what she cared about. None of us has felt up to sorting through all that stuff. I think Dad's searched through it looking for a new will, but otherwise it's pretty much the way she left it." She led the way down the hall toward the back of the house, then up four steps to a large kitchen and family room. Mirabel's office was a small room off the family room. Other than a big window that looked out on the flower garden and wooded grounds behind the house, there was nothing much to look at. The room was jammed with papers everywhere—covering a wide desk that faced the window and stacked in boxes on the floor. "Mom was always going to get this stuff organized," Lacey said sadly, "but she never got around to doing it."

"I know the feeling," I said. "Papers seem to multiply in an office." Then to move us along with the process, I said, "Can you feel or imagine your mother in this room like she used to be?"

Lacey laughed. "No problem. In my mind's eye I can see her sitting right there at that desk, talking on the phone, sifting through a stack of papers. That's how she spent most of her time when she wasn't off at meetings. I'd say this is for sure the best place in the house to feel a connection."

There was no place to sit in the office other than Mirabel's desk chair, which also held a box of papers. "Let's just sit on the floor," I said. After we made ourselves as comfortable as we could on the floor, she began to tell me about Mirabel's work in the community. But we were quickly interrupted by a glaring Derrick standing in the doorway.

"What's going on, Lacey? Why is Cleo here and what are you doing in Mom's office? Surely you could find a more comfortable place in the house than this to sit and talk."

I wasn't any more pleased to see him than he looked to see me. I hoped Lacey could give him a quick answer that would satisfy him enough that he'd leave us alone.

"We're in here because it's the place that most helps me feel close to Mom," Lacey said. "Cleo's going to help me try to contact Mom today and I need to start out by being around stuff that was important to Mom so I can get a strong feeling of her."

Derrick's frown turned into a smile. "You sure picked the right room for that, even if you do have to sit on the floor," he said in a much pleasanter tone. "Mirabel wasn't home much, but when she was, this was where you'd find her."

Lacey didn't smile in return. She just looked up at him and said, "Dad, we need to get on with what we're doing here, so could you please close the door and give us some privacy."

He made no move to step out of the doorway. No longer smiling, he said, "I'm glad to hear you're going to contact Mirabel. When you do, you need to find out something for me. Your mother told me she'd kept her promise and made a new will that left out the Scientologists. But I can't find it. Vernon handled all her legal stuff and he says he didn't help her make a new will. I think she did, but I can't prove it. So you need to ask her where it is."

Oh, no. The will questions again. I thought I'd already made it clear to Derrick that we weren't going to give Mirabel his messages.

Lacey jumped to her feet. "Dad I don't want to talk about this. Now you need to go." She reached for the door—I assumed to close it in his face. But he was blocking her way.

"You haven't answered me, Lacey," he said. "I made a simple request and I'd like you to be courteous enough to give me an answer."

I was still sitting on the floor looking up at them as they both stood facing off in the doorway. I considered getting to my feet and joining them, but I couldn't see anything to be gained by involving myself in their argument—especially since it was a discussion Derrick and I had already had. So I waited quietly.

Lacey planted her feet right in front of Derrick and leaned in, close to his face. "Okay, here's your answer," she said in a steely voice. "No, no and no! I'm not going to ask Mom about her will. That's not what this is about. This is for me to connect with Mom and talk to her about what I want to say. I'm not your messenger. If you have questions about her will, you should take them up with Grandad or try to contact Mom yourself." She snickered. "Of course Mom wouldn't be likely to want to do you any favors if she knows about how Judith has moved in here and what the two of you are doing to Angelica. And I figure she does know because dead people can see everything. So good luck with finding out anything about her will."

Lacey's voice had risen to a shrill, almost hysterical point by then. Her agitation was not at all the right preparation for her upcoming contact session. I finally decided we needed to get out of there and get her calmed down. So I stood up, put my hand on her arm and spoke slowly and firmly to Derrick. "Look. I told you that the Contact Project is not a messenger service. You need to back off now and let Lacey do this the way she wants to do it." Before he could reply, I turned to Lacey and said, "Come on. We need to go now."

Derrick held his ground in the doorway, blocking our way. "Listen, Lacey," he said angrily. "If more than a third of your mom's money goes to Scientology, we'll all be in trouble. Maybe you don't care for yourself, but if you care about Angelica as much as you say you do, you'll want to find that new will. So for once in your life stop being selfish and think about what's best for the whole family."

Could Derrick really be in such a dire financial situation? He sounded desperate. I began to wonder whether he might be deeply in debt.

Lacey put her hand on his chest and pushed him. "Move," she said. "We need to go." He looked angry enough to push back or maybe even slap her, but he got control of himself and stepped back out of the doorway. We hustled through and headed down the hall to the front door.

"I'm very disappointed in you, Lacey," Derrick yelled after us. "I thought you cared about this family."

"I care more about this family than you do, Dad," she yelled back. And before we closed the front door behind us, she leaned in and took her parting shot. "I'm beyond disappointed in you, Dad," she screeched. "You don't care about anyone but yourself." She slammed the door shut.

In the driveway, I turned to her and said, "I'll meet you at my office. Do your best to calm down while you're driving there. Don't think about your dad and how you're mad at him. Think about your mom and how much you miss her."

Lacey nodded. "Sorry," she said, "he just ..."

"No more about him," I reminded her. "Let's go now."

We each got in our cars and drove off toward my office. Whew! What a state she was in. The time we spent in Mirabel's office was pretty much a disaster as far as setting her up for the contact process. If she was going to have any chance of reaching Mirabel, I needed to help Lacey smooth out and quiet her mind.

Chapter 25

Back at my office, I took Lacey for a walk over to Boulder Creek. Autumn is a great time of year at the creek. The water level is lower than in summer, but the sun dancing off the reds and yellows of the leaves reflects in the water below creating a soft leisurely space. I love to sit on a bench overlooking the creek, soaking up that tranquility.

I found my favorite bench and suggested to Lacey that we sit quietly and relax for a few minutes. Then I said, "It would be helpful for you to think about your mom for a bit before we go to my office and use the apparition chamber. Try focusing on a time when you and she were in synch, enjoying each other. It doesn't have to be recent. Does a time like that come to mind?"

Lacey sat quietly for a few minutes. Her face softened. She said, "I remember my sixteenth birthday. Mom wanted to have a special day with me—which was a huge surprise, since she was mostly too busy to take off a whole day to be with me or any of us kids. My birthday is in March. She let me skip school—another huge surprise—and we went skiing at Winter Park. It was one of those spring skiing days that comes right after a heavy snow. Sunny, not very cold, bright blue sky, no crowds. We had some terrific runs and we ate lunch outside on the deck of that food place at the top of the mountain. It always amazes me that you can ski and the sun is warm enough to be able to eat outside. We sat there eating pizza slices, relaxing in the sun, laughing at a couple of snowboarders talking about the spills they'd taken in the morning. It was one of the most fun days we ever had together."

"A wonderful memory," I said. "Can you think back and picture your mom on that day? Remember how she looked, what she was wearing, and like that."

"Definitely," she said. "Mom had a fabulous down ski jacket that I always loved. It was a black and white Spyder that she used for hiking and snowshoeing as well as skiing. Mom was always physically active and in great shape until the last few years when she got such bad arthritis. So, yes, I can still see her in that jacket and her black ski pants schussing down the hill with her hair blowing in the wind and a huge grin on her face." Tears welled up in Lacey's eyes and she sat silently for a few minutes. Then she said, "We didn't have nearly enough good times like that, and now it's too late."

We sat by the creek for a while longer before we walked slowly back to my office. There I took Lacey into the apparition chamber. I have it set up in a small windowless room, just big enough for the four-foot square mirror on the wall about three feet above the floor, and the easy-chair inclined backward that sits in front of it. The mirror and the chair are surrounded by a black velvet curtain that creates a small booth so the sitter can gaze into the mirror and see only a pool of darkness. The only illumination comes from a fifteen-watt bulb in a small stained-glass lamp behind the chair. The theory behind this is that throughout history people have reported seeing visions in reflective surfaces such as clear pools of water, polished brass cauldrons, crystals, and mirrors lit in the midst of blackness. The apparitions appear as the viewer gazes into the clear dark pool.

I asked Lacey to remove her watch so she wouldn't be focused on the time, then got her situated in the chair. "Take some deep breaths and relax," I said. "Try to clear your mind of everything except thoughts of your mother, and then gaze deeply into the mirror. Don't try to rush it or make something happen," I cautioned her. "Just be here. You can stay as long as you want. I'll be right across the hall in my office if you have any problems. When you're done, just come out and we'll talk."

I work hard not to expect or even hope for any particular outcome when a client is in the apparition chamber. Once they are in there, it's their process. Whatever happens, happens. I use the time to work on patient charts, insurance forms, or whatever projects will keep my mind occupied.

So once Lacey was settled, I went across to my office and started working on my notes for the class I would be teaching on Friday. I was deeply involved in reading an account of double-blind experiments designed to investigate whether mediums can contact the dead, when I heard the apparition chamber door open. I got up and went out to the hall. Lacey ran up and squashed me in a big hug. "She came! Mom came! I saw her. I talked to her. It was amazing!" Lacey's words tumbled over themselves in her excitement.

I hugged her back and waited quietly until the cascade of disjointed words stopped and she released me. Then I said, "That's wonderful, Lacey. Let's go sit in the counseling room. I'll get you some water and you can tell me what happened." She followed me into the room and sat on the sofa, looking a bit dazed, but happy and more relaxed than I'd ever seen her. I brought her a glass of water and sat across from her in my usual wing chair. "Tell me about it," I said.

Lacey sighed then began speaking softly. "I sat there for a long time, just thinking about her like you said I should. But I couldn't see anything in the mirror and I was getting discouraged. Then all of a sudden I heard her voice. She said, 'Take your time, Lacey, and think about what you want.' That's something she often used to say to me, so I thought maybe I was imagining her voice. But I looked up and there she was in the mirror, just sitting there looking out at me. I was so happy to see her that I started crying. She said, 'Don't be sad for me. Don't cry. I know it's hard to imagine, but I'm fine.' I tried to tell her how sorry I am that we didn't get along better before she died, but she started fading away when I was saying that."

Lacey stopped and took a big gulp of water, then set the glass down on the table in front of the couch. She grabbed a tissue from the box on the table and blew her nose. I waited to see what else she had to say.

She sat for a few minutes looking off to her left as if trying to recollect something. "Could you get me some paper and a pen?" she said. "I want to make some notes before I forget any of what Mom said to me.

"Of course," I said. I got up, walked down the hall to my office and brought her a pen and a pad of paper. She began scribbling furiously and kept at it for about ten minutes. Then she looked up. "Okay," she said. "Now I can finish telling you. When Mom started fading away, I yelled at her not to go yet, that I needed to find out what had happened to her in the hot tub. She came back and somehow stepped right out of the mirror and hugged me. I could really feel her. Does that usually happen?"

"Sometimes," I said. "But it's different for everyone. Did your Mom talk about what happened to her?"

"No," Lacey said sadly. "I told her Angelica thought someone pushed her under the water and we wanted to find out about it, but she didn't really answer me. She just said, 'It's all about money. Some of them will do whatever they have to do to get it. And the others don't see what's happening. It's hard to see through that fog.' I asked her to tell me what that meant and who she was talking about, but she didn't answer." Lacey stopped and stared off into space, looking a bit forlorn.

"What do you think she meant about the money?" I asked. "Do you think she was talking about your dad and the will he's looking for?"

"I don't know," Lacey said. "But Angelica told me that Dad and Judith have been arguing a lot about money lately. It sounds like his business isn't doing well and he doesn't have as much money as Judith thought he did."

"Was that all your mom said?" I asked gently. "Did she disappear after she talked about the money, or did she say more?"

Lacey shook her head and looked back at me. "No she didn't disappear right then. She started kind of humming that Beatles song, 'Let It Be.' And then she said, 'I love you, Lacey, and I love Shane, and I love Angelica, and I know you'll look out for her. Keep Angelica safe. She needs you.' She hugged me again and it felt warm and wonderful. Then she let go, stepped back, and looked me in the eye with a serious expression. She said, 'My dad needs some help, too.' After that she faded away."

"I wonder what she meant about Vernon," I said. "Do you think your grandfather is in some kind of trouble?" I remembered Tim Grosso's warning that Glenna was probably ripping off Vernon just like she had ripped off Tim's father. But I wasn't sure I should mention that to Lacey.

"We all know Grandad drinks too much, and he's a little forgetful," she said. "But aside from that I thought he was doing okay." She looked down at her notes for a minute, then looked up at me. "Actually, I'm really confused about most of what Mom said. Maybe Shane could help figure it out. Can you come with me to Shane's apartment?"

At first I was inclined to just send her off on her own. But it was after 5:00 by then and I had no more clients scheduled for the day and I was very curious about what Shane would have to say. So I said, "I guess I could do that. But how do you know he'll be home?"

"Shane's always home plugged into that computer world where he lives. Let's go in my car and I'll drop you back here after."

Chapter 26

Shane's apartment was one of many in a large complex in northeast Boulder. We parked in a visitor spot and walked down a long sidewalk past a pool and a clubhouse. Judging from the people I saw soaking up the late afternoon sun on their balconies, beer bottles in hand, the complex attracted mainly young college-student types. Lacey stopped at a staircase in a well of one of the three-story buildings. "These building all look alike to me," Lacey said. "It took me a while to be able to find my way around. Shane's on the third floor of this walkup. I don't know why he lives here. He's not a student, but he says it suits him, so I don't argue with him about it."

At the top of the stairs a small landing led to two apartments. Lacey knocked on the door of the one on the left. No one answered, so she knocked again, more loudly this time. "He's probably on the computer with earphones as usual," she said exasperatedly. "Let's try the door." She turned the knob and pushed open the door to what was one of the trashiest apartments I'd seen in a long time. Pizza take-out boxes, beer bottles, and what looked like hundreds of super-sized soft drink cups competed for floor space with various bags and boxes filled with who knows what. The light was dim, perhaps to obscure the mess or maybe so there would be no glare on the screen of the oversized laptop that sat on a low table next to an extra flat-screen monitor.

Shane sat on a pillow on the floor in front of the computer, totally engrossed, and as Lacey had predicted, he wore earphones as he typed away. He didn't notice us until Lacey walked over behind him and tapped him on the shoulder. I expected him to jump in surprise or maybe show some irritation that we had let ourselves in, but instead he kept on typing for a minute and then turned around to look at us. "Oh, hey, Lacey, Cleo," he said languidly. "What's up?" I wondered if his immersion in the game kept him mellow or if he was stoned or on some kind of tranquilizer.

The graphics on his computer screens showed a futuristic city populated by thin shimmery characters darting around and flying over buildings. In the middle, in an area that resembled a town square, some of the characters looked to be involved in a meeting or perhaps a contest. I was immediately captivated and wanted to see more, but Lacey had different ideas. "Shut that game off, Shane," she said. "We have important news to discuss."

Shane turned back to his screen. "Sorry, Lacey," he said indifferently. "It's not a good time. I'm busy. You could have saved yourself some trouble by calling before you came all the way over here."

Lacey was in no mood to be blown off. She yanked off Shane's earphones and grabbed his shoulders with both hands and twisted him around until she could stick her face in his face. Then she shrieked at him so loudly that I feared for his eardrums. "Shane, listen to me! I talked to Mom. She had things to say to us." Shane stood up facing her and moved her toward a futon couch littered with papers.

"You don't need to shout, Lacey. I can hear you." He pushed most of the papers off the couch. "Chill. And sit. You too, Cleo. Have a seat and you can both tell me what happened." I joined Lacey on the futon and Shane moved his pillow to sit on the floor facing us.

Lacey pulled the notes she had made at my office out of her purse and stuck them in Shane's face. "Look. I wrote it all down so I wouldn't forget."

Shane pulled the notes out of Lacey's hand. "It's all about money," he read aloud. He looked puzzled. "What does that mean? What's all about money?"

"That's just it," Lacey said, her voice rising again. "I don't know."

Shane looked down at the notes again, read for a minute, then closed his eyes and sat silently. We watched and waited. Finally he opened his eyes and spoke, wearily. "Let's get this straight, Lacey.

You got Cleo to help you contact Mom, and it actually worked, and all she told you was that people will do stuff to get money? Oh yeah, and that you should take care of Angelica and that Grandad needs your help. None of this is actually news. Sounds more like a daydream than a contact with a spirit to me."

For some reason people seem to think they can ask questions of a spirit and get targeted answers like they would in a Google search. It's hardly ever like that. More often, people get a strong feeling of connecting with the dead person and then hear some message—often one they find confusing. I didn't want to start into a lecture about it, so I decided to see what Lacey would say.

"No, Shane, it wasn't a dream. I saw her and I felt her. She was there. And what I wrote down is what she said. Now I need you to help me make sense of it."

"So she sent you a message that it's all about money and you want me to explain that to you?" Shane asked flippantly.

"This is not a joke, Shane," Lacey said sternly. "I need your help. Who do you think she was talking about when she said it was all about money? And when she said some people will do whatever they have to do to get money, and the others don't see what's happening because it's hard to see through the fog? We have to figure out what she meant by that."

"Okay, let's say you did really see her and that's what she said," Shane said cautiously. "Why do you think it's so important?"

"She said it right after I told her Angelica thought someone pushed her under the water and we wanted to find out about it," Lacey said. "So I think she was saying that whoever killed her was motivated by money. But that could be a lot of people—the Scientologists inherited money, Dad inherited money, which could indirectly be money for Judith. Faye got the gallery. Even you and I and Angelica inherited money."

"Sometimes these messages aren't as direct as they seem," I said. "Just because she was talking about money, doesn't mean she was pointing at the ones who will inherit."

Shane perked up and looked more interested. Maybe thinking of the message as more complex was engaging his gaming experience. "Right," he said. "It may not be that simple. She could have been saying that someone wanted her gone for reasons connected to money, but not necessarily so they could inherit her money."

"Like who?" Lacey asked.

"Like Glenna. Before she died Mom told me she was worried that Glenna was after Grandad's money. Mom had even talked to the DA about Glenna and she was trying to get Granddad to dump her. Maybe Glenna knew. And that developer Hugh Symes that she got into that prairie dog fight with. She was bringing a suit against him that could have cost him a bundle if she successfully stopped his project. And what about her drug-dealing former friend, Tim? They had a fight and weren't speaking. Maybe he was afraid she'd turn him in to the police."

Lacey threw up her hands. "Enough, Shane. Stop. You're adding to the confusion, not helping. Mom didn't say anything in the contact session about any of the people you mentioned."

"But Shane has a point," I said. "We have to consider everyone who might have a motive. Like I said before, we can't assume your mom's message would be clear and easy to follow. Spirits don't usually talk that way."

Lacey jumped up and began pacing around the room, dodging piles of clutter. "Good grief, Shane, this place is a mess. How can you live like this?" she asked as she dislodged a pizza box from her foot. "Oh, never mind. Let's get back to Mom. With so many suspects, if she can't or won't give us a clear message, what can we do?"

Shane had been gazing off into space, not looking like he was paying much attention to Lacey. Then he turned his head in her direction. "Sit, Lacey," he said. "How can I think when you're roaming the room like that?"

Lacey returned to the couch next to me, where she perched on the edge nervously clasping and unclasping her hands.

"When a situation presents too many options, a player needs to narrow them down and focus on the most promising ones," Shane said slowly. His steadiness was a marked contrast to Lacey's agitation.

Probably years of experience had taught him to ignore her drama.

But Lacey continued her rant. "This is not a game," she shrieked. "We're talking about our mother here."

"Games aren't that different from life, Lacey," Shane said patiently. "If you want to get anywhere, you have to think smarter than the other characters and you have to make a plan to challenge your opponents."

An intelligent, mature, perceptive observation. In fact it sounded like something Pablo might say. I decided I'd been underestimating Shane. I wondered whether he applied this philosophy to his entire life, and, if so, how it played out. Did it influence his long-term plans? But that was a tangent I didn't need to explore. I pulled my mind back to the immediate situation. "What sort of plan do you have in mind, Shane?" I asked.

"I'm thinking we could shake up the possible suspects by leaking out something about Mom having told Lacey someone murdered her. We add extra bait by saying Mom said that she did make a new will and that it made some big changes. Then watch everyone very carefully to see what they do."

An alarm bell rang in my head. What if Mirabel was actually murdered and the killer believed Lacey had gotten new information from Mirabel's spirit? Would Shane's plan put Lacey in danger? I decided to hear the whole plan before I brought that up. "Do you have a list in your head of all the suspects we'll be watching?" I asked.

"There's Dad and Judith," Lacey said. "They wanted Mom gone so they could get married and have her money. And Dad thought he had convinced Mom to make a new will leaving out the Scientologists. So he and Judith figured they'd get most of the money."

"And the Scientologists," Shane said. "They knew she wasn't as committed as she used to be, so they probably wanted her gone before she disinherited them." Shane held up his hand and began ticking off more suspects on his fingers. "There's Glenna. Mom was trying to convince Grandad she was ripping off his money. There's Tim Grosso. Mom knew about his marijuana growing business and she was mad at him, and I think she threatened to turn him in. There's Faye, inheriting the gallery. There's that developer Hugh Symes.

Mom was costing him a fortune with her prairie dog crusade. Is that enough people to watch?"

"Do you think these people would believe your mom actually talked to Lacey after she died?" I asked. "Most people don't believe in spirit contacts."

"Maybe they will and maybe not," Shane said. "But if someone killed Mom, he or she might get pretty worried about what Lacey knows about how Mom died, or about a possible new will turning up."

"Wouldn't that put Lacey in danger?" I asked. "If there is a murderer out there who thinks Lacey knows something, that person might come after her."

"I'm not worried," Lacey said. "I've been studying aikido for self-defense for ten years now. At my level, I can handle whatever they're likely to come up with."

Spoken with the typical overconfidence of a twenty-four-year-old.

"Unless they have a gun," I said.

"Come on, Cleo. This is Boulder. We're not talking about gang members. I seriously doubt any of them will come after me with a gun."

"I don't think any of the people we're looking at would take the chance of bumping Lacey off in a way that was obviously murder," Shane said. "That would be a serious tactical error that would attract the police and probably get the killer caught. If they tried anything, it would be something they could make look like an accident—like what happened to Mom. So don't be standing on the edges of any cliffs, Lacey, or driving on steep mountain roads where someone could easily run you off."

This was getting creepy. I began to wonder whether Shane could distinguish between online- game battles and real-life confrontations with real-life consequences. I could hear Pablo in the back of my mind warning me what a terrible idea this plan was. "Maybe we should think about this for a few days," I said. "I don't want to do anything that will put Lacey–or anyone else–in danger."

"No, Cleo. Timing is everything," Shane said. "Today is the day Lacey talked to Mom, and Dad knew she was doing it today, so that probably means Judith knows too. Today is when we need to get the information out. Once we lose the freshness, we lose our impact."

"I agree," Lacey said. "And how is waiting a few days going to make any difference anyway? Let's go ahead. I'll leak the news to Dad and I'm sure he'll tell Judith. And I'll call Grandad. He'll probably tell Glenna."

"What about Faye and Tim?" Shane asked.

"I can tell Faye when I take Angelica to the gallery tomorrow," Lacey said.

"Faye will probably tell Tim," I said. "They have a thing going on."

"So that leaves the Scientologists and Hugh Symes," Shane said. "I know a couple of people who could spread this around in a way that is likely to reach Hugh."

Should I offer my help in reaching the Scientologists? I was reluctant to do it, didn't want to get involved at that level. But I remembered Tyler telling me not to just float around when Angelica was out there alone in the mean waves. I felt obliged to participate in the plan along with Shane and Lacey.

"I found out recently that I know one of the Scientologists who was close to your Mom," I said. "He's someone I knew a long time ago and when he found out I was involved with your family, he started pumping me for information. I refused to tell him anything, but I'm sure he'll be interested if I offer to share something with him."

"Sweet!" Shane said. "We're a team on a quest. Let's move on to the next level of play. We have our assignments, let's get to it. And keep in touch as news comes in." He stood up, took his pillow, and went back to his computer.

I was still trying to decide whether this plan was a huge mistake as Lacey and I got up and headed toward the door. On my way out, I glanced at Shane's computer screen and there among the shimmery characters flying around, I briefly glimpsed a surfer in black shorts. Tyler? Was this a sign he approved of our plan and my part in it? Strangely, I felt reassured.

Chapter 27

It was nearly 7:00 p.m. by the time Lacey dropped me off at my office. I was starving but I wanted to straighten the place up before I left so it would be ready for my morning clients. Just as I was about to leave, my phone rang. My caller ID said "Elisa calling." I was tempted not to answer, because I knew she wasn't going to like the idea that I'd signed on to Shane's plan to smoke out Mirabel's murderer. But I had promised Elisa I'd keep her in the loop, so—reluctantly—I picked up.

"Hey, girl. Have you eaten yet? I'm just leaving a meeting. It's lasagna night at Pasta Jay's. Want to join me?"

As soon as she said lasagna, I could taste it—the homemade noodles, gooey cheese and seasoned ground beef baked in Jay's famous Marinara sauce. "That does sound yummy," I said. "I can be there in fifteen minutes. Does that work for you?"

"See you there," Elisa said.

As I walked the few blocks from my office to the homey corner restaurant, the enticing smell of garlic welcomed me. A few people were waiting outside to be called for tables, so I put my name in with the hostess. Elisa showed up about five minutes later and we were lucky enough to get a table next to one of the floor-to-ceiling windows with a view of the foothills.

Some Boulderites insist Pasta Jay's is just for tourists, but the restaurant actually has lots of devoted local fans. I'm one of those. I love Pasta Jay's delicious garlicky marinara sauce and its cozy atmosphere of brick walls, red checkered tablecloths, posters, flowers and candles. The delicious fresh Italian food is more comfort than gourmet—but

I've never had a dish there that I didn't enjoy.

Elisa and I ordered a bottle of Chianti, a house salad to share and the lasagna special. We chitchatted about nothing much until we were set with our wine, garlic bread and salad. Then Elisa asked, "Have you found anything for your grandmother yet?"

I sipped my wine, then said, "No. I visited a couple more places on Sunday, but I couldn't imagine Gramma in any of them. Like I told you the other day, I've been thinking about bringing her home and hiring a round-the-clock caregiver." I stopped to spear and eat some greens with gorgonzola, then continued. "I talked to Tim again about it and he reminded me that if I hire privately I might end up getting someone dishonest or worse. Of course I know that but I plan to be careful who I pick. He said his own father got ripped off by a caregiver and it's not so easy to find someone honest."

Elisa fished around in the salad to get some beets and garbanzo beans with her lettuce. "Maybe it's better to go through an agency," she said, as she steered her full fork toward her mouth. She ate the bite, then finished her thought. "Agencies have to do background checks on their employees."

"Agencies are a lot more expensive," I said. "I'm trying to find out what Gramma can afford. I talked to Faye about selling more of her paintings, but she said the current ones aren't selling well, so we shouldn't put more on the market."

"That seems strange, "Elisa said. "Martha's work was always in such demand."

"Times change, I guess," I said. "I haven't been following the art world much lately."

"Do you know how many of Martha's painting sold in the last year?"

"Not really. I figured Faye was on top of it so I didn't have to be. And I got busy and stopped keeping up."

"Thinking of what you've been busy with, how are things going with the Townes family?"

The waitress brought our lasagna, so I waited until she left, then took a deep breath and began to fill Elisa in on all that had happened in the few days since I'd called her Saturday afternoon to vent about the rejection of my conference paper. Stopping now and then to eat, I hit all the highlights—Derricks's agitated search for Mirabel's new will; Brian's creepy questions about my meetings with various Townes' family members; the startling conversation I overheard between Faye and Tim about Shane's fake ID business; the grim information Tim gave me about Glenna ripping off his father; my unsettling encounter with Judith after driving Angelica home; Lacey's satisfying contact with Mirabel in her session today; and finally the disturbing agreement Lacey, Shane and I had just reached at his apartment.

"Whew—all that since Saturday and it's still only Wednesday!" Elisa said, pouring more wine into both our glasses. "You're up to your neck in this Townes' family mess, Cleo. I thought you agreed to be extra careful with what you promise people who come to your Contact Project. I distinctly remember that after that mess you got us into last summer, you swore you'd never go after another murderer, no matter how much someone begged you."

I took a swig of Chianti. She had a point. Both of us had been in terrible danger last summer as a result of my helping a young widow discover who pushed her husband off a cliff. But it was Elisa who was taken hostage and almost got killed. "Look," I said, "I understand why you're upset and I want you to know I'm not expecting or asking for any help from you. I'm only telling you all this because you made me promise to keep you in the loop."

"It's not myself I'm worried about," she said. "It's you. Because of your lack of good judgment last summer you lost clients, you almost had your psychotherapist's license revoked, and you nearly got killed. Wasn't that enough excitement to at least last out the year?"

We both returned to our food, which gave us a break from conversation to let the tension dissipate. We're the kind of good friends who push each other's limits, but also know when to back off.

I smiled at her. "Come on, Elisa. You know I'm not in this for excitement. I feel that I have to help Angelica and Lacey. They need me."

"You're a therapist," she said carefully. "I don't have to tell you that feeling needed can be a trap. How is Pablo taking you getting back into the detective business?"

I sighed. "Not well, of course. We had a big fight Sunday morning after I updated him on the details. He says I'm in way over my head and that I should let the police handle it. He went home mad and I haven't heard from him since."

Elisa smirked. "Could be a good thing, given all that's happened since Sunday. I don't even want to think about what he'd say about the plan you hatched with Lacey and Shane to try to trap someone by spreading false information."

I didn't back off or look away as I replied. "I agree that may not be the best idea, but Shane was very persuasive and I didn't have a better suggestion."

She moved her face a little closer to me, keeping her eyes locked on mine. "How is it going to work, exactly?" she asked. "Once you spread the lie around, what will you do?"

She had me there. I looked down. "I'm not sure. We haven't thought it all the way through. I guess we'll see what happens, and go from there."

"Let's hope what happens isn't someone getting killed," Elisa said, pushing her advantage.

I made one final attempt to win her over—admittedly a feeble one. "You're overreacting."

Before Elisa could reply, the waitress stopped at our table to ask if we wanted take-out boxes for what was left of our dinners. We were both stuffed so we asked for the boxes and the check.

We let the conversation go at that point, each of us convinced that the other was missing the main point—but neither of us in the mood to push it any further.

I got home to find trash strewn all around my driveway, back yard and patio. An unpleasant surprise. Both my trashcan and my recycling bin were overturned. I cursed myself for neglecting to tie down the bins, leaving them vulnerable to the wind, which had picked up during the evening.

But then it occurred to me that a person might have done this. Someone going through my trash looking for something, or someone who wanted to send me a message. No, that was crazy. I'd probably been listening too much to Elisa and Pablo's warnings.

In any case, I had a mess to clean up, and the sooner the better because in my neighborhood trash can attract bears, especially in the fall. I turned on the back patio light and started in. While I gathered up orange-juice cartons, junk mail, and miscellaneous trash, I thought about my promise to Lacey and Shane to share our fake Mirabel message with Brian. The more I thought about it, the less I wanted to do it. I certainly didn't want to tell Brian that Lacey had talked to Mirabel in a contact session at my office. In fact, I didn't want to talk to Brian at all. On the other hand I had promised.

By the time I had all the trash back where it belonged, I still hadn't decided what to do. I drifted over to a chair on my back patio, sat down, and gazed off at the foothills behind my house, hoping for inspiration.

"Yo, Cleo. Quit worrying about nosedives. Make your stance fit the wave."

Not exactly the inspiration I was looking for, but there hovering over the middle of my back yard was Tyler on his surfboard.

"Tyler! Where have you been? There's lots going on and I haven't seen you for a week—except maybe in Shane's computer game. Were you there?"

As usual, he stayed on message, ignoring my question

"Cleo, you can't sit in the channel and watch. Get into the lineup. Get wet. Even wipeouts are fun."

"Fun? What are you talking about? This is dangerous stuff!"

"I told you, you need to believe in yourself. Don't back down. You'll blow it if you miss the good wave."

Then, gracefully riding the crest of some virtual whitecap, he sailed off into the night sky.

Chapter 28

Ihad trouble sleeping that night and woke up in a funk the next morning. To settle my mind, I decided to go for a short hike in the foothills behind my house. The wind had died down overnight and the morning was sunny and warm enough to hike in a light sweatshirt. As I climbed the steep trail, I leaned into the rhythm of my breathing, keeping my thoughts quiet. I relaxed, enjoying the scent of pine needles, the feel of the breeze on my skin, the stretch of my muscles and the autumn colors of the bushes and trees around me. As I often do, I marveled at the way nature blends the many shades of red, gold, yellow, brown and green in a way that I've never captured to my satisfaction in a painting.

On my way back down, I let myself reflect on last night's conversation with Tyler. I couldn't pretend I didn't know what he was telling me to do. I needed to help Angelica and keep my commitment to Lacey and Shane. I decided I would call Brian and invite him to drop by my office later. I could have met him for coffee at a safe neutral place like the Trident Café, but I wasn't afraid of him. I figured that meeting him in my own space—the space where I operate as a professional—would give me confidence and more control over our interaction.

Of course if I really wanted control, I could have told him our planned story over the phone. Maybe I should have. But I told myself that it would be less awkward in person and also I'd be able to see his reaction. Truthfully, though, there was a little something else drawing me toward seeing him again. He might be a Scientology nut but he still had those smoky eyes, and that sexy smile when he wanted to use it. Given the way my relationship with Pablo was going, I guess I felt like kicking up my heels a bit.

He sounded surprised to get my call. "Hey, Cleo. Good to hear from you. I didn't mean to upset you the other day. Can we write that off, start over, and be friends again?"

"Friends? Is that what we were? I'll have to think about that. But, yeah, I'd like to make a fresh start, and I have some information for you. Can you drop by my office for a cup of tea this afternoon? Anytime between 3:00 and 5:00 works for me. I'll be here preparing for my class tomorrow."

"Sure. But don't keep me guessing. What kind of information?"

"I can't go into it now, Brian. My next client is due any minute. Come by later. I'm at 736 Pearl." As soon as I said that, I remembered that he knew everything I'd been doing for days, so he probably knew quite well where my office was. And now I'm inviting him in. Elisa may be right about my need for excitement.

He showed up at 3:15, so I guessed he must be eager to hear what I had to say, eager to see me, or both.

He was all smiles and charm with an autumn bouquet of sunflowers and chrysanthemums in hand. "Again, I apologize for Sunday—and, come to think of it, for Saturday night too. I know I was pushy. I promise not to do it again."

"Fair enough," I said. "Thanks for the flowers." I took the bouquet and led him back into the counseling room where I had turned on my electric teakettle and set out mugs and an assortment of tea bags.

"Nice office, and in the high-rent district, too," Brian said. "Your practice must be doing well to afford this."

"I'm doing pretty well," I said as I got a vase out of a cabinet, filled it with water and stuck the flowers in. I didn't want to get into explaining about how the endowment for my Contact Project pays the rent, or even mentioning the Contact Project. So I let that topic drop. "Help yourself," I said, gesturing toward the kettle. "I think the water's hot enough."

We each made ourselves a mug of tea and moved over to the seating area, where I sat in my usual wing chair and Brian sat on the couch opposite me. Earlier I had put a plate of cookies and some napkins on the coffee table.

"Hey, oatmeal cookies with raisins. My favorite. You remembered," Brian said picking up a cookie and a napkin.

Hmmm—had I remembered that? I had taken a quick trip over to the tiny Lolita's grocery a few blocks up on Pearl to get some cookies. But I wasn't aware of specifically trying to get Brian's favorite. "Enjoy," I said.

Brian took a big bite of his cookie, chewed slowly, then picked up his mug and sat back, looking quizzically at me. "So what's the information you mentioned?"

I took a drink of my tea to fortify myself before I plunged in. Then I said, "I thought about your question about whether Mirabel's kids know if she made a new will. There's no reason not to answer that."

Brian looked up sharply. "Really? They told you something? What do they know?" He sounded like an impatient prosecuting attorney who would not be denied an answer.

His sudden intensity put me on edge. But I kept that feeling under wraps. After years of experience with volatile people I know how to keep my voice calm. I replied carefully, "They have some information that she did make a new will and that it had some big changes."

Brian slammed his mug down on the table, slopping tea over the sides. "What kind of changes?" he demanded, wiping at the spilled tea with his napkin.

Whoa. I wasn't prepared for him to react so strongly. I felt like telling him I'd made a big mistake inviting him and that he should leave. But I was also curious about his vehement responses. Why was he this upset about a possible new will? Did he have reason to believe that Mirabel would have disinherited the Church of Scientology? So I said, "They don't know what might have changed. What changes do you think she might have made?"

He got up and took his mug and the soggy napkin over to the

counter where I had put the kettle. I figured he was trying to regain his composure, so I waited quietly. He walked back over to the couch and sat down again, looking less agitated. "I have no idea what changes she might have made, Cleo," he said. "But any changes could have a big financial impact on the Church of Scientology. That's why I'm asking you. Does Derrick Townes have the new will?"

"They don't know that either."

I could see him trying to control his anger, but it welled up in his face like mercury rising in a temperature gauge until he lost the struggle and boiled over again. "Christ! Why don't they just ask him?" he asked furiously.

I was beginning to worry about what Brian might do next. Shane's plan had been to tell people not only about the new will, but also that Mirabel might have been murdered. If Brian got this upset about a new will, how would he react to the rest of my story? But I had signed on to the plan, so I continued. "Derrick's children aren't close to him. You probably know he's been having an affair for a long time. And they're worried that there's something suspicious about how Mirabel died."

Brian glared at me. "What do you mean, suspicious?" he challenged. "I thought the police said it was an accident."

I felt myself shrinking in response to his aggressiveness, but I took a deep breath and forged on, speaking slowly and deliberately. "They did rule it an accident. But that doesn't mean it was. The police have been wrong before."

Brian finally got a grip on his emotions. His face relaxed and his voice softened. "Will the case be re-opened?" he asked.

"I don't know."

"How are they going to find the will?"

"That's all I can tell you, Brian." I rose to signal him that it was time to leave.

Brian didn't get up or say anything, just sat there looking at me for a minute. As a therapist, I'm used to letting silences build rather than filling the space, so I waited quietly. Finally he stood up and said, "I do appreciate your telling me about the will, Cleo. I don't mean to be pushy again, but I sure would like to know where that new will is, if there is one."

"Now you know what I know, Brian. What are you going to do with this information?"

"You have no idea how important this is, Cleo," he said, looking defeated.

I walked out into the hall moving toward the front door. He followed. "Thanks for coming by," I heard myself say as he went out the door. I wasn't really glad he'd come. In fact, I regretted inviting him. But the automatic social response slipped out anyway. I hate it when I do that.

After Brian left, I spent another couple of hours preparing for the next day's class, which was going to be about the Afterlife Encounters Survey, a five-year international study of friends and family members' reports of their encounters with deceased loved ones. The study, completed in 2002 by a former hospice worker and director of the Elizabeth Kubler-Ross Center, found that ninety-eight percent of the 596 respondents who had experienced at least one afterlife encounter reported that their encounters brought them comfort that did not diminish over time. This finding is one of the reasons I believe so strongly in the benefits of my Contact Project.

I got so involved in the material that I was able to put Brian and the Townes family drama out of my mind until I was on my way home. But then my regrets about my interaction with Brian resurfaced. What was I thinking? There was no way I wanted Brian back in my life in any ongoing way. We had problems when we were together years ago and that was before he became a Scientologist. Plus now he seemed kind of threatening.

I realized I was missing Pablo. Usually when we have a fight we each need a few days to cool off, but it was Thursday and our fight had been Sunday morning. We should be over it by now. As it turned out, Pablo was thinking along the same lines. About ten minutes after I got home, he showed up at my front door with a pizza and a six-pack of Fat Tire—my favorite local microbrew beer.

"Hey, babe. We got off track, but let's not rehash it. We know by now that we don't have to agree about everything to have fun together. What do you say?"

"I say I've been missing you too," I said, as I took the beer from his hand and headed for the kitchen to put it in the refrigerator. He followed me, put the pizza box on the kitchen counter, and turned toward me with open arms. I flew into those arms and squashed myself against his solid body. It felt like home. We hugged, kissed and headed for the bedroom, leaving the pizza cooling on the counter.

Later in the kitchen as we quenched our thirst with frosty brews while we reheated the pizza, Pablo said quietly, "Cleo, do you understand why I don't want you getting involved in investigating a possible murder?"

"Because of what happened last summer?"

"That and the fact that you're not a trained crime investigator and you have no backup if things escalate. I know you're following your heart when you try to help people, but I don't want to lose you because you got in over your head."

His tenderness disarmed me. I put my beer down on the table and gave him a hug. "Pablo, I know you're coming from a caring place when you try to protect me. But it feels too protective, like you're limiting me, smothering me a little." I pulled him over to the table and we both sat sipping our beers for a few minutes.

Then I reached for his hand and continued making my case. "Remember, I'm not the twenty-one-year-old art student you were in love with sixteen years ago. After you left me for your grand adventure, I grew up and learned to enjoy my independence. Helping people is my career and I'm good at it. I'm a professional and I find it upsetting when you try to tell me how I should work with my clients. Advice is one thing, but I have to make my own decisions. Surely you can see that."

He gave my hand a squeeze. "I hear what you're saying, but it's hard for me to watch you driving off a cliff without trying to do anything about it. As a cop, I see a lot of ugliness and I don't want you to be caught in that."

I let go of his hand and went back to my beer. "Pablo, you have to trust that I'm being careful. I learned some hard lessons last summer and I won't put myself in that kind of danger again. Can't we just drop this and enjoy our pizza? Like you said, we don't have to agree on everything."

"Okay, Cleo," he said reluctantly. "But can you at least promise that you'll call me right away if you find yourself in danger—that you'll let me help before it escalates?"

"I will," I said. "Let's get another beer and take our pizza in the living room. I have this week's episode of *Boston Legal* recorded. Watching that should take our minds off this discussion."

We ate and drank as we laughed at Alan Shore and Denny Crane resorting to outrageous tricks to win questionable cases. I mused to myself about how easy it is to see how television characters overreach and how hard it is to recognize that tendency in myself.

Pablo left about 10:00 p.m. to go back to his Longmont apartment because he had an early morning meeting. I reviewed my notes for the next morning, took a long shower and went to bed.

But I tossed and turned, unable to sleep as worries crept in like a bunch of slimy squiggly garden worms creating tunnels in my mind. I was too stubborn to admit it to Pablo or Elisa, but deep down I was beginning to agree with them that I might be in over my head. The more I thought about it, the less I liked it. I had agreed to help because Angelica touched me in a way I couldn't explain. And because Tyler had repeatedly insisted that I must help her. But now I was involved in a duplicitous plot with Lacey, whose emotional stability was erratic at best, and Shane, a slacker and petty criminal. None of this felt good to me.

I slept fitfully for a bit, then woke up in a sweat. What if Elisa's warning about my safety was right? What if the trap Lacey, Shane and I had set did lead to another murder? I'm the adult professional here. Should I pull them back? Otherwise, wouldn't a bad outcome be my fault? I needed to step back and rethink my involvement. I resolved to call Lacey and Shane the next morning to call off the plan. We should go back to everyone we had lied to about what Mirabel had said and tell them the truth.

Unfortunately, my second thoughts came too late.

Chapter 29

A frenzied pounding on my front door woke me up at 6:00 a.m. My first sleepy inclination was to pull the covers over my head and hope whoever was making the racket would go away. But the knocking continued. As I grew more alert, I panicked. What if something had happened to Pablo and the police were here to tell me about it?

Swallowing my fear, I jumped out of bed, ran to the living room and looked out a side window. No police. Instead I saw Lacey, disheveled and weeping, banging frantically on my door. "Cleo, wake up. Open up," she howled.

I was so relieved not to see cops that I wasn't even irritated at Lacey for waking me with one of her dramatic tantrums. I just opened the door and stood there waiting to find out what she wanted. She nearly fell into my living room. "Something horrible has happened," she shrieked. "Grandad is dead." She fell against me, sobbing on my shoulder.

Okay, just because someone is a drama queen doesn't mean she never has a reason to lose it. I had misjudged her. This time her hysterics were merited.

I hugged her and rubbed her back until her sobbing subsided. Then I led her to the kitchen, sat her at the table, and put the kettle on for tea. Once she calmed down, I asked her to tell me what had happened.

"Grandad fell down the stairs last night and died." She began crying again.

"What a horrible accident, Lacey. I'm so sorry," I said, handing her some tissues.

She dabbed at the tears, but kept crying. "It's worse than that," she moaned. "I have a terrible feeling it wasn't an accident."

I almost lost my cool and bombarded her with questions. I wanted to know all about his fall and why she thought it might not be an accident. But I didn't want to set her off again. "Who was there when he fell?" I asked.

She blew her nose and grimaced. "No one knows. Maybe he was alone, maybe not. Maybe he tripped. Maybe someone pushed him." Her voice was shrill and her words tumbled over each other.

I put my arm around her shoulders and spoke quietly. "Slow down. Why would you think someone pushed him? Tell me what you know."

Lacey wiped her eyes and took a deep breath. "Glenna called the whole family from the hospital last night. Grandad was already dead when I got there. Glenna said she'd been out at a church meeting and got home around 11:00 p.m. She said that when she got there, she found him unconscious at the bottom of the stairs and she called 911. An ambulance came and took him to the emergency room, but he never regained consciousness. He died right after he got there." Lacey put her head in her hands and sobbed.

Her recounting the details wasn't only to satisfy my curiosity. It's what people do after a traumatic event. Reviewing the particulars aloud has a grounding effect that helps the sufferer cope with shock. Lacey needed to talk. I got her some more tissues and comforted her.

After a bit, she stopped crying, sat up and faced me again. "Dad and Glenna got into a huge fight at the hospital," she said. "She yelled at Dad that it was all his fault. She said Dad came over in the afternoon to see Grandad and that they argued and after Dad left, Grandad was upset and drank a lot. She said that's why he fell down the stairs. Dad yelled back at her, saying if Grandad wasn't safe to be alone why didn't she stay with him."

My kettle was boiling, so I got up to turn it off and get a couple of mugs and a selection of tea bags. "What did Glenna say about that?" I asked as I put the mugs and tea bags on the table.

Ignoring the tea stuff, Lacey plowed on with her story. "Glenna said she offered to stay, but Grandad said he was fine and she should go ahead and go to her meeting. Shane thinks Glenna may be lying and that she actually pushed him down the stairs. He says a few days before Mom died she told him that Glenna had gotten Grandad to give her money and had probably convinced him to put her in his will. Shane says Glenna could have easily come home earlier than she said she did and pushed Grandad down the stairs and then pretended he had fallen before she got there."

Lacey finally stopped, took a deep breath and turned her attention to the tea bags. After we had each put a tea bag in our mug, and I had filled them with boiling water, I returned to my chair and the conversation. "What do you think happened on the stairs?" I asked.

She looked down into her tea. "I don't know. Maybe someone killed him."

I wondered whether our misinformation plan had anything to do with Vernon's death. "Did you talk to your dad and your grandad like we planned?" I asked. "Did you tell them that you contacted your mom and that she told you she had made a new will and that someone had murdered her?"

She nodded. "I told Dad, but I didn't get a chance to tell Grandad. Dad was all excited thinking he'd get more money in a new will. I guess that's why he went to see Grandad."

"Do you think your dad came back after Glenna left for church and got into another argument with your grandad and pushed him?"

She began to cry again. "I'm afraid that could be it. I feel terrible. We never should have made that plan. But now you have to help me find out what happened. I came here because I have to contact Grandad right away to ask him how he fell."

I handed her a box of tissues and waited while she blew her nose. When she looked up, I spoke gently to her. "We can't try to reach him now, Lacey. In the first place, you're much too upset. And, besides that, I have a class to teach this morning. It sounds like you've been up all night. Is that true?"

She straightened, pulled back her shoulders and sat tall. "Yes, but I can handle lack of sleep."

I smiled, but stayed firm. "It's not good for the contact process, though," I said. "You'll do much better if you're rested and relaxed. Here's what I think we should do. I'll go teach my class, and you go home and get some sleep. Then come to my office this afternoon at 4:00. If you feel relaxed and ready, we'll give the apparition chamber a try."

Lacey looked like she wanted to argue more, but then seemed to think better of it. "Okay," she said. "It will be hard to sleep, but I'll try."

I showed her out and ran for the shower so I could get ready for class. In the shower I remembered my fear that something had happened to Pablo. I knew he was fine, but I wanted to hear his voice. Also, it occurred to me that if I could reach Pablo, he could probably find out what the coroner said about Vernon's death. Maybe Vernon had a stroke or some other physical problem that made him fall. When I got out of the shower, I turned on my phone to give Pablo a call. He didn't pick up, so I left him a message. Then I noticed a message had come in for me the night before. It was Tim Grosso asking me to stop by his office after class.

All through class I was preoccupied with thoughts of Vernon, as well as concern about why Tim wanted to see me. It was hard to concentrate on my lecture and I think it showed. I let my PowerPoint presentation lead me listlessly along. The students looked bored and didn't engage in discussion. Ordinarily I would have felt bad about putting so little energy into my teaching, but that morning I just wanted to get out of the classroom and move on with my day.

As soon as class was over, I stuffed my laptop and papers into my backpack, hustled out of the room, and made my way through the throngs of students to the stairway at the end of the hall. As I climbed the two flights to Tim Grosso's office on the third floor, I almost lost my balance when a young guy sprinted past me on my left. I couldn't help but think about Vernon falling to his death on his stairs the night before. Creepy. Did Glenna really find him at the foot of the stairs or did she push him down there? Or did someone else push him down while she was out?

Another faculty member was leaving Tim's office just as I got there. Tim beckoned me into his cluttered office to a chair near a large window that overlooked a grassy quad. "Thanks for stopping by, Cleo," he said as he sat down behind his desk. "I thought it was time to talk about how your class is going. I'm sure you remember my saying when we originally talked about this class that the department sees it as an experiment. So I think it's important that we check in periodically about progress and concerns."

Uh-oh, this sounded ominous. I thought the class had been going well—leaving aside today, which there was no way he could have gotten complaints about already—but I worried that his words were setting the stage for a rebuke. And his demeanor confused me. Over the past two weeks, we'd been sharing personal information about problems with my grandmother and his father, but now he was Mr. Department Chair acting like he didn't know me at all outside the university. Since he was playing it that way, I decided to respond in kind. "I'm happy with the class," I said. "Most of the students participate in class discussions and some of them have done extra reading on topics that interest them and brought the information back to the other students."

Tim nodded. "I'm glad to hear the students are involved in the material," he said. "But I hope you're being careful to keep your interactions with them focused on the class. One problem with a topic like paranormal psychology is that it can get more personal than is appropriate for a university class."

I had no idea what he was getting at, so I simply nodded and tried not to look as clueless as I felt.

He waited a few seconds and then apparently realized that I wasn't going to say anything. "What I'm getting at here, Cleo, is that it's come to my attention that you're professionally involved with one of our students, Lacey Townes, and possibly with her younger sister—a minor child—against the parents' wishes. This is the kind of thing that can escalate to a publicity nightmare for the university and this department. I'm sure you remember that when we talked initially about this class, I expressed my concern that it might become controversial, possibly sensationalized in a way that would reflect badly on the university.”

Had Judith Demar complained about me? My gut churned and jolts of energy coursed though me. I had to force myself to stay in the chair and pretend to be calm. “Lacey Townes dropped my class before we began working together,” I said in my best professional voice. “I insisted on that so there would be no conflict of interest. And I’m not working with her younger sister. Lacey wanted me to, but I’ve made it clear that I can’t work with a minor child without permission.”

Tim nodded. “That’s good as far as it goes,” he said. “But your involvement with a student—even though she has withdrawn from your class—doesn’t look good. And when that student is from a prominent local family, it opens up more possibilities of bad publicity.”

I wondered whether he’d considered the possibilities of bad publicity that went along with a department chair growing marijuana. Good grief, what a hypocrite! But I couldn’t bring that up. So I said nothing and waited to see where he would go next.

“Bottom line, I would be much more comfortable if you ended any professional relationship you have with Lacey Townes or anyone in her family,” he said.

I stiffened. He had roused my rebellious streak, strengthened by a lifetime of arguments with my father who finds something to criticize about almost anything I do. I knew I’d better get out of his office before I said things I’d regret. So I said, “I hear your concern and I’ll think about what you said, but I need to get back to my office now.” I stood up, picked up my backpack and walked out.

“Let me know what you decide,” he said to my retreating back. I didn’t turn around.

I walked down the stairs and out the side door onto campus. The sun was shining, but I was in a fog. Questions and angry feelings vied for my attention. Could Tim require me to drop Lacey as a client? I couldn’t see how. She’s not my student. She’s over twenty-one. And she’s not even a psychology major. My professional work with her has nothing to do with her classes at the university. My whole interaction with him felt like a power play on his part. But why does he care this much? Does Judith Demar have that much clout? How would she, when she's in a different department? Who else might be whispering in his ear?

I decided I wasn't going to let myself be intimidated. What was the worst thing that could happen if I refused to drop Lacey as a client? Tim could decide not to hire me to teach another class. I am an adjunct instructor after all, with no guarantees beyond the current semester. And while I care about teaching and I like the credibility of being associated with the university, I'm not going to buckle under to an unfair demand.

My commitment to Lacey felt firm and strong to me and I was resolute in my decision to help Angelica. Despite my past doubts, I was clear that I was making the right choice.

Suddenly I felt better, lighter. I relaxed into the festive atmosphere of a good-weather fall Friday on campus and walked on toward the parking lot.

Chapter 30

I was almost to my car when I realized that I'd forgotten to turn my cell phone back on after class. When I did, there was a voice mail from Pablo answering the message I'd left him earlier. "Hey, Cleo. Unless something comes up I'm here in the office most of the afternoon. Call me."

I dumped my stuff in the car, sat on the edge of the front seat and hit his number. He answered on the first ring. "Hey, babe. What's up?"

The sound of his voice gave me a warm melty feeling. "I missed you," I said. "Last night was fun. I wanted to hear your voice this morning."

"That's sweet," he said. "Last night was great. But you knew I had an early morning meeting. Did you really call me at 7:30 this morning just to hear my voice?" He sounded skeptical.

"You're right," I said. "I did have another reason for calling, too. I promised to keep you in the loop with what's happening with the Townes family and there's been another death—maybe a suspicious one. Did you hear about Vernon Evers?"

"Hear what?" Pablo asked in his matter-of-fact cop's voice. Maybe he hadn't heard, or maybe he wanted to see what I knew before he said more. He never tips his hand, even to me.

I decided to assume he didn't know and filled him in on what Lacey had told me, including her suspicions.

He listened quietly, then paused briefly before he spoke. "You want to be careful here, Cleo," he said, calmly but firmly. "Lacey Townes has a tendency to leap to conclusions with no evidence. She looks at an accident, imagines it's murder, and makes empty accusations. If you want to help her, you need to get her to back up and look at the facts."

Wait a minute. Isn't he leaping to conclusions about Lacey? I almost jumped in with that, but reminded myself of his caring concern the night before, took a deep breath, and answered him in my calm therapist voice. "We really don't have many facts. Actually I was hoping you could help with that. Is there any way you could find out what the coroner's report said about Vernon's death?"

"It's too soon. The coroner won't have written his report yet. Why don't you ask Derrick Townes what the hospital physicians told him?"

"Derrick's a suspect," I said. "I can't ask him."

"You have to have a murder before you can have suspects, Cleo."

My emotions got the better of me and I spoke out of frustration. "Oh, here we go again," I said exasperatedly. "The police are going to say Vernon fell down the steps by accident, and then they won't investigate. The whole thing will be swept under the rug."

"Cleo, you know that's not the way the police work." Pablo sounded irritated. "If a death looks suspicious, there will be an investigation. The Boulder police might already be looking into the death. But they're not going to tell me about it because I'm in the Longmont PD, not the Boulder PD. And they're certainly not going to tell you about it because you're not even a cop."

I could see this was going nowhere. Plus it was almost 2:30 and I needed to eat something before I met with a client at 3:00. So I backpedaled. "You're probably right, Pablo. We don't have enough information to know whether Vernon fell by accident or not."

Of course I didn't mention that Lacey was going to try to get that information by contacting Vernon's spirit that afternoon. Just thanked Pablo sweetly for his concern and told him I had to go grab some lunch.

I hustled back to my office, ate some yogurt and an apple from my frig, and met with my 3:00 client. By then it was nearly time for Lacey's appointment. She showed up on the dot of 4:00, bounding into my office. Her eyes were puffy and her face was drawn, but she looked much more rested than she had earlier. "I'm so ready to talk to Grandad and find out what happened," she said. "Can we start right now?"

"Hold on, Lacey," I said. "I know you want to get right to it, but reaching a spirit isn't like making a phone call. I need to help you relax and focus before you go in there. Let's go sit in the counseling room and you can tell me some of your best memories of your grandfather."

I had her lie on the couch and close her eyes. Then I led her through some deep breathing exercises. When she was relaxed, I said, "Now keep your eyes closed and remember some good times you spent with your grandfather. Try to see him and hear him as he was then. Can you tell me about a time you remember?"

She lay quietly for a few minutes. Smiles flickered across her face. Then she said, "When I was little and Grandad had his office on the Pearl Street Mall, I used to love to go there with him. My favorite place in the office was the floor-to-ceiling windows that looked over the mall. I'd sit on the floor and watch the people going by. Grandad would be working at his desk, but he'd come over and sit with me some of the time and make up stories about the people we could see—like this one lives in a haunted house with twenty-seven dogs all named Buster, or that one is under a magic spell that makes him wear plaid shirts that are too small for him every day. He'd have me rolling on the floor laughing," she said with a broad grin.

"What a great wonderful memory, Lacey. How about when you were older? Can you recall happy times with him?"

She took a minute, then began slowly. "He was so great when I was a teenager." Her face turned sad. "I don't think I ever thanked him enough for all he did for me back then."

I wanted her to stay focused on positive memories and not descend into grief, so I redirected her back to her experiences. "Can you tell me about something fun you and he did together when you were a teenager?"

"Sure. But there's so much it's hard to pick only one."

"You don't have to choose the best example. Just go with whatever comes up."

"Okay, I'm thinking of a time he took me with him on a trip to

New York City. He had some meeting to go to and I'd never been to New York. My parents were always too busy to take us on trips. It was fabulous. We stayed at The Carlyle on Madison Avenue with amazing views of Central Park. He arranged for someone to take me to museums and shopping while he was at his meetings and at night he took me to shows. We saw *Chicago* and *The Phantom of the Opera*. I felt like a princess." Again the huge grin.

I let her bask in the memory glow a few minutes before I began to bring her gently back to the room, open her eyes and sit up. We moved into the apparition chamber, where I got her comfortably situated and reminded her of the procedure of staying relaxed and thinking of her grandfather while gazing intently into the mirror. Then I left her there and went across the hall to my office, keeping my door and my ears open.

An hour later, I was working through a stack of insurance paperwork when Lacey opened the door from the apparition chamber to the hall. I got up and went to her. She wasn't jumping up and down with excitement like the last time—just standing quietly looking a bit bewildered. I put my arm around her shoulders, led her to the couch in the counseling room, and got her a glass of water. I also got her a pen and some paper so she could make notes like she had done the other time. She sat quietly sipping the water and staring off into the distance.

I sat across from her and waited until her gaze turned to me. Then I said quietly, "Would you like to tell me about what happened?"

"It took a lot of waiting," she began slowly, "but he came. He was in the mirror, but he didn't come out of it and touch me like Mom did. He smiled at me and said, 'I love you Lacey. Don't be sad.' I asked him what happened on the stairs and he said, 'It was my time to go, Lacey. Don't be sad.' I kept trying to tell him that I wanted to know whether he fell or someone pushed him, but he never answered that question."

At that point Lacey stopped talking and began writing slowly. After she'd covered about half a page on the pad I'd given her, she looked up. "Grandad said some stuff about Mom. I wanted to write down his words before I forgot." She looked down at the notepad. "He said, 'Mirabel didn't trust people. She thought money turned people bad. Maybe she was right.' I asked him who she didn't trust but he didn't answer that either. Somehow I couldn't seem to ask him the right questions." Lacey was looking increasingly troubled.

"No, Lacey," I said. "It's not your fault if you didn't get the answers you were looking for. I don't think there are any right questions. Talking to spirits isn't that easy. They're on a different wavelength. Mostly you have to take what they give you and try to make sense of it. Did he say anything about her will?"

Lacey began clasping and unclasping her hands nervously. "Not much," she said. "He just said something about how it's easy to change a will. Then he faded away." She sighed and leaned back into the couch looking exhausted.

I worried that she was blaming herself for not getting more information from Vernon. "It sounds like you found contacting you grandfather more frustrating than helpful," I said. "Sometimes that happens."

Lacey stared down at the floor for a moment and then shook her head. "No, I'm glad I saw him," she said. "It was good to hear him tell me that he loves me and not to be sad. But I didn't find out what happened to him on the stairs. Even though I got a strong sense from him that it doesn't matter, I want to know what happened."

"It sounds like you're saying that it was good to see him, but you want more answers."

She frowned and continued. "Right. I really didn't find out anything. We still don't know who killed Mom or how Grandad died or whether there's a new will. Maybe I should try to contact Mom again?"

I needed some time to process all that had happened in the last few days and I thought she did also. Plus I was hoping the police would come up with some information about Vernon's death that would lead us to some answers. "This has been an intense time," I said. "Let's give it a few days. Maybe you and Shane and I can talk early next week about where to go from here."

I was tired, she was tired and I missed the signs of an impending explosion. With no warning she jumped up off the couch and began pacing the room, screaming, "No! No! No!"

I stood and walked slowly toward her. "What, Lacey?" I said softly. "What is upsetting you?"

She turned toward me, waving her arms and crying. "Waiting doesn't work," she shrieked. "Give it a few days—that's what Mom and Dad kept saying about Kari before she died. I would tell them that she wasn't eating anything, that her ribs and hip bones stuck out like a skeleton, that she was exercising for hours every day. I'd push them to do something and they'd say, 'Let's give it a few days.' And then it was too late. In a few days she was dead."

She stood in front of me sobbing, "Bad things are happening," she cried. "I'm scared for Angelica. She's the one who says she knows Mom was murdered. I'm afraid whoever did it will go after her next. We need to stop them before Angelica has some horrible accident that isn't really an accident."

I put my arms around her and let her cry until I could feel that she had released much of her tension. Then I led her back to the couch and sat with her. "I know you want to take action right away," I said, "but we don't even know if there's a killer out there. As you said, your contact sessions with your mother and grandfather didn't give us any new information about how they died, which makes me think that their spirits aren't going to tell us about that."

"Are you saying I shouldn't try to contact them again?" Lacey asked.

"I'm saying that I don't think you should contact them again to ask whether or not someone killed them. Neither of them gave you an answer when you asked that before. You may have another reason to try to contact one of them later to resolve unfinished issues you have with them or to say goodbye in a way that feels more complete to you. But I don't think the next few days is the time to do that."

"But what about Angelica? How can we protect her?"

"Here's a suggestion. It's Friday afternoon. I'm sure Angelica is upset about her grandfather right now and could use some time with her big sister. Can you be with her over the weekend, watch over her without being too obvious about it?"

Lacey thought for a minute. Then her eyes lit up. "Yes, I can do that. There's a gallery in Aspen that has a show of paintings by a young girl about Angelica's age. Faye suggested she go see it, and I said I'd take her sometime in the next month. We'll do it—go up tomorrow and come back Sunday. And she won't be going to school Monday either because of Grandad's funeral. So I can be with her then too."

My relief at the idea of getting both Lacey and Angelica out of the vicinity, even if it was only for a couple of days was tinged with concern about where we would go from there. I tried to tell myself that by Monday the whole situation might look so different that our fears for Angelica's safety would disappear. But I didn't really believe that.

Chapter 31

Early Saturday morning I sat at my kitchen table drinking coffee and reading a front-page newspaper article about the closing of Shady Terrace. Entitled, "Seniors forced out in the cold," the article quoted a communications director from the national office of the corporation that owned Shady Terrace. He said that although the corporation is selling the building, which means the residents will have to relocate, Boulder has other options available.

He made it sound so simple. Just sign up for one of the other options. I wondered whether he'd ever had to look for "options" for someone he loved. I pitched the newspaper into the recycling bin and gathered up the materials I had collected about Gramma's options. I had the housing guide that Tim had given me, my notes from the family meeting he'd held two weeks ago, and materials from the nursing homes I'd visited. But nothing spoke to me. I knew I hadn't found anything that was even close to being right for my beloved Gramma.

Just then my phone rang and the Shady Terrace phone number popped up on my caller ID. Yikes! Could they possibly have yet more bad news for me?

But it wasn't bad news. It was Betsy, one of the Shady Terrace social workers, with an intriguing possibility. "Some of us on the staff have been working on finding a way to open a small assisted living house," she said. "We couldn't take Medicaid—at least not in the beginning, because it takes so long to get approval. At first we could only take the private-pay residents, so we're trying to talk to as many of them and their families as we can to see who might be interested.

Would you like to hear more about it?"

Would I? Someone up there must have been listening to my prayers. Maybe Grampa found a way to influence events down here.

"I'd love to hear about it, Betsy," I said eagerly. "What's the plan?"

"It's too complicated to go into on the phone," she said. "So we're trying to tell families about it in some small meetings. We're having three today—one this morning at 10:30 and two this afternoon, one at 1:30 and one at 4:00. Could you possibly make one of those times? The meetings will only take about an hour."

I could hardly wait to hear their plan. "Absolutely, Betsy," I said. "I'll be there at 10:30."

I got over to Shady Terrace at 10:00 so I'd have time to visit with Gramma before the meeting. The place was taking on a deserted air. Empty rooms and empty beds. Reminded me of one of those aging shopping malls with too many vacant storefronts and too few customers.

As I walked down the hall to Gramma's room, I noticed one of the residents, Flora Gypsum, sitting on her usual hall couch. Flora typically dressed like an aging glamour girl, with fancy clothes and caked-on makeup, which she was still able to apply herself despite her confusion. She also had her hair done every week by the beautician who visited Shady Terrace. Today Flora wore a fancy green and yellow print dress and a black hat with an orange feather. But instead of her usual high-heeled shoes, she wore fuzzy pink slippers—a very unusual flaw for her.

As I stopped next to her, I noticed that she didn't have her newspapers, which she typically carried with her everywhere. Of course she can't actually read them anymore, but she seems to enjoy holding them and looking at them. Probably reading the paper was once an important part of her daily routine.

"Hi, Flora," I said, "How are you today?"

"Bad," she said. She looked troubled. "Some people here are lost and no one can find them. There are only a few of us left."

Where to begin? Who knows what she thought had happened to the missing residents? It must be frightening for her. But it wasn't my place to have a discussion with her about the closing of Shady Terrace. I had no idea what she'd been told or what she understood. Anything I said might very well upset her more.

"My gramma is still here," I said. "You know Martha. I'm on my way to see her now. Would you like to come with me to her room?"

"No," she said. "I need to wait here in case my friends come by."

Ouch. This was sad. But I knew Flora well enough to know that arguing with her would only agitate her. "Okay," I said. "Maybe you'll see her at lunch."

I continued on down the hall to Gramma's room, where I found her sitting dispiritedly in her armchair staring into space. I walked slowly over and knelt down next to her chair. She startles easily, so I always give her time to adjust to my moving into her space. "Hi, Gramma," I said, putting my hand gently on her arm. "How are you feeling?"

She gave me a bewildered look. "Who are you? Did you come to buy a painting?" she asked.

Oh dear. It was one of those days when she doesn't recognize me. Even though I'm used to it, my heart always drops when it happens.

"Gramma, it's me, Cleo, your granddaughter." I said.

"Have you seen my husband James?" she asked.

"No," I said. "He must be away. Would you like to walk down the hall and see Flora? I just saw her sitting on the couch." I don't try to correct Gramma's confusion. It's better to gloss it over and redirect her attention somewhere else.

"No," she said.

"How about some music?" I asked, putting on a CD of one of her favorite piano concertos. She closed her eyes and seemed to relax into the music. I sat on the edge of her chair with my arm around her and we listened together for about fifteen minutes. Then I kissed her good-bye and went off to the conference room to hear about Betsy's plan.

Several people were already sitting at the long table. Besides Betsy from Social Services, I recognized Mary Ellen, the Director of

Nursing, and Joanna, the Activity Director. A short blonde woman introduced herself as Allie, the daughter of a resident, and we were shortly joined by a gray-haired woman who I recognized as the wife of a resident, accompanied by a middle-aged man she introduced as their son Henry.

After Mary Ellen welcomed us and we'd gone around the table greeting each other or in some cases introducing ourselves, she began to tell us about a new and different kind of nursing home model. "A geriatric physician named William Thomas came up with a plan—called the Eden Alternative—to de-institutionalize existing nursing homes by changing their culture to be more of a community," she said. "We've used some of his ideas here like having our garden where residents help grow vegetables we eat and giving residents choices of times for their meals. I wanted to do more but Shady Terrace is a big place and change is hard." She stopped briefly for a drink of water. We all sat in rapt attention waiting to see what would come next.

She continued. "Now with the closing, Betsy and Joanna and I got to talking about Dr. Thomas's newest development called a Green House. It's a small homelike group home with lots of plants and visits from animals and children," she said enthusiastically. "We have a dream to start our own group home like a Green House. We could keep some of our residents together and offer jobs to some of our staff."

Wow! This sounded amazing. It also sounded like a huge under-taking to pull off in the time available.

The gray-haired woman asked one of the first questions that had come to my mind. "Wouldn't it take a long time to build or even modify a place to meet all the Health Department regulations?"

Betsy jumped in. "We've found the perfect place, actually. It was a small assisted living home that closed last year and the building is for sale. It has room for nine residents and it already meets all the regulations."

"And it has a big yard with a deck and lots of room for a garden," Joanna said with a big smile. "Our residents would love it there."

I so wanted this to be possible. But my practical side had doubts. These women were young, probably in their thirties. How could they afford this? Nursing home staff aren't highly paid and the project sounded like the sort of thing it would be hard to get financing for. I tried to phrase my question tactfully. "How about the financing to buy the building?" I asked. "Would that be a problem?"

"It could be," Mary Ellen replied. "But we have one investor who is willing to put up about half of what we need and we're hoping you and other families will be our partners in this venture. If we can find nine families who would like to have their family member move to our group home, and if those families are willing to invest enough to cover the rest of what we need for startup costs, we can do it."

Before I could open my mouth, Allie, who was there representing her mother, asked the exact question I was about to ask. "How much of an investment would you need from each family?" My mother has been able to pay privately here, but she doesn't have a lot of extra money."

Exactly Gramma's current situation. Her small monthly trust income combined with her Social Security and Grampa's retirement annuity provided enough money each month to cover her private room at Shady Terrace and her personal and medical expenses. But her ongoing expenses were high enough that she didn't have a large reserve of extra money. The last statement I remembered seeing showed about $20,000 in her savings account.

"With the cost of the house, plus furnishings and other setup costs, we figure we'd need $50,000 from each family," Mary Ellen said. Yikes! $50,000! Where would Gramma get that much money? And even if she had it, could she afford to sink it into this undertaking?

As if she'd read my thoughts, Mary Ellen continued. "This would be an investment, which means the families would be partners in the venture. And the families would be co-owners of the building, which would be security for much of your investment. The three of us—Betsy, Joanna and myself—don't have much money to put in, but we would donate our time in the beginning to get this started."

"You'd have to pay other staff, wouldn't you?" I asked. "What are you thinking our monthly charges would be?"

"If we can get $450,000 from the families to add to the $450,000 we have from our original investor, we'll have the $900,000 we need for setup. Then we can provide the room and board and care for the same monthly charge you're paying now at Shady Terrace," Mary Ellen said. "And we believe you and your family member will be getting significantly more value for your money."

Joanna stood up and handed each of the three of us potential investors a stack of papers. "We realize this is complicated and you'll want a lot more details," she said. "So we've prepared written plans, financial statements, and contracts for you to review. We're inviting all the families of private-pay residents to come to one of these meetings in the next few days. We need to act quickly, so we're asking you all to let us know by the end of next week if you're interested. Then we'll have another meeting next weekend for all the interested families, and move on from there."

Our hour was almost up by then. We asked a few more questions, then gathered up our papers and went our separate ways to think over the proposition.

For me, the main thinking I needed to do was about where to come up with the money. I loved the idea of a small group home set up to be a community rather than an institution. And from all I'd seen in recent years, Mary Ellen, Betsy and Joanna were genuinely motivated by their concern for the best interests of the residents. Of course I knew this was a risky venture, but after all my searching I hadn't found anything else even close to being this promising. So the risk was probably worth it for Gramma.

As I drove home, I ran through possibilities for raising the money. One big problem was that I knew virtually nothing about Gramma's trust. Grampa hadn't wanted to leave me with the job of managing Gramma's money. To spare me that task—which he said shouldn't be my responsibility—he had set up her finances to be handled by a bank and by her attorney, Vernon Evers. To be honest, math and money management aren't my strong suit, so I was relieved to have that aspect of her care in more capable hands. I got copies of quarterly statements from the bank—which is how I knew the amount in her savings account—but all I knew about her trust account was the monthly income. I had been planning to get the details from Vernon

Evers, but now I had no idea who would be handling it or whether I could get $30,000 out of it in a lump sum.

I couldn't see how I could raise the money personally. I had almost no savings and I didn't think any bank would loan me $30,000. Maybe I could sell Gramma and Grampa's house. But that would take months or longer to get a good price. Plus the house was in Gramma's name, not mine, so selling it would probably be complicated. Also, I had promised Grampa that I would do everything I could to keep the house in the family.

Selling some of Gramma's best paintings looked like a better idea. I had several at home and in my office that had never been on the market before. These were paintings she had done at the height of her career when she was winning awards and selling her work to private collectors.

But I had no experience selling Gramma's paintings. That had all been handled by Faye or previous gallery owners. Gramma hasn't produced any new paintings for the past dozen years or so due to the progression of her Alzheimer's, so her recent sales have all been from older never-sold work and that has all been through Faye's gallery. Other galleries around the country may have some of Gramma's work for sale but those are previously owned pieces being sold by the original purchaser. Gramma gets nothing from those sales, so I hadn't tried to follow them.

Unfortunately I hadn't kept up very well with Faye's sales of Gramma's paintings. I probably should have, but I wasn't in charge of her money and until now she'd easily had enough to meet her needs. Since Grandpa died, I'd been focused more on visiting her often and making sure she got good care than on checking on sales of her artwork. I had trusted Faye to market the paintings that she had on hand. But she still hadn't shown me the figures for recent sales, and she'd admitted that the gallery was struggling financially. I wondered whether I could trust her to put out the energy and resources to sell any of my collection of Gramma's paintings.

I decided to go to the gallery and insist on an accounting of recent sales and prices. If I didn't like what I heard, I might consider selling the paintings from my collection through some other means. I liked Faye, especially since she'd been so supportive of Pablo's work, but I needed to get this money for Gramma and I needed it quickly.

Chapter 32

I stopped at home for a quick lunch, then went downtown to Faye's gallery. I braced myself for an uncomfortable conversation. I wasn't looking for friction, but I was determined to push Faye enough to get specific information about Gramma's recent sales.

Faye was alone, working at her desk when I arrived. I pasted a smile on my face as I walked over and stood in front of her.

"Hey, Faye," I said in the most genial voice I could manage.. "I got some good news about Gramma this morning."

She looked up, smiling. "Wonderful," she said. "What's up?"

"Some of the Shady Terrace staff plan to start a small group home, very homelike, not institutional. I think it would be perfect for her."

"That does sound like great news."

"There's only one catch. They need an upfront investment from the families of the people who move there. We'd be partners in the venture with the building as security, so it looks reasonable to me. But I don't know if Gramma has the cash available. I might have to sell some of her paintings that I have at home."

Faye bristled and tapped her pen sharply on her desk. "That's not a good idea. I told you it's not a good market right now," she said in an exasperated tone. "If we release more of her paintings, I'm afraid they won't hold their value.." She continued making the annoying clicking sound with her pen.

I didn't want to argue with her, but I was determined to get some answers. "You might be right, but before I make any decisions, I need some information. Like how many of her paintings have sold this year?

How many do you have in storage, and how many of those are you actively marketing now? What prices are they selling for?" I waited.

She closed her eyes. Then opened them and looked me in the eye. "I've been putting off telling you this, Cleo, because it's not good news. Only a few paintings have sold this year and those for lower prices than I'd hoped. It seems that Martha just doesn't have the fan base she used to have."

My heart sank. How could this be happening? "How many exactly and for what prices? Show me the figures," I demanded.

"All right, Cleo, take a look." She called up a database on her computer and typed in "Martha Donnelly." A page came up, showing that only three paintings had sold this year, each for around $1,500. These were large framed oils—48" x 60". I was stunned. Gramma's large paintings have usually sold for $5,000 or more. I stood there staring at the page in disbelief.

"How did this happen?" I asked. "And why didn't you tell me earlier?"

"The art market is down overall," she said. "And a lot of Martha's fans were older than she is, so they're not around anymore. Her work isn't as popular with younger collectors. I decided to go ahead and sell at lower prices and take the loss to get her name out there again. I didn't tell you because I kept hoping sales would pick up."

I wasn't ready to accept this dire forecast without doing some research of my own into the art market. But I couldn't see much point in discussing it further with Faye.

I struggled to contain my anger. I wanted to get out of there before I lost my temper and said something I'd regret. "Okay, thanks for the information," I said as I turned to leave. "I guess I need to think about whether I can find some other way to come up with the money." As I headed off toward the front door and let myself out, a wave of sadness washed over my anger. I realized that I was grieving for all that Gramma had lost to her horrible disease, and missing Grandpa more than ever. He would have handled this tough situation she was in so much better than I could.

Pablo had invited me to a family dinner at his parents' house that evening. I enjoy hanging out with his family so I looked forward to the evening as a welcome break from my worries about Gramma. I drove out to his house in Longmont so we could go together in his car to his parents' house nearby. It was so good to see him and get that big hug I'd needed all day, that I found myself in tears.

"Hey, what's going on," he asked as I pulled away and fished in my pocket for a tissue. "Is this about Vernon Evers?"

"No," I said wiping my eyes. "It's about Gramma. But I don't want to be late for your parents. I'll tell you on the way over."

As he drove, I filled him in on the new place the Shady Terrace staff was setting up, Gramma's need for money to move there, and what I had learned from Faye that afternoon. "I'm so frustrated," I said. "I don't know what to do next."

"Hey, we can work this out," Pablo said. "After dinner let's go over to my house and do some searches on the internet to see what we can find out about prices for paintings. We can look up some artists we know or know about and see how their prices stack up against what we expect. And we can see if we can find any of Martha's paintings for re-sale and check the asking prices."

"Thanks. That's a great idea," I said as he parked the car in front of his parents' Victorian house in the historic district of Longmont. As I always do, I admired the wide tree-lined street and the meticulously cared-for houses, especially Pablo's family home. Pablo's father remodeled the house himself, restoring the woodwork and hardwood floors, and added a large deck in the shady back yard.

His parents Fernando and Juanita welcomed me to their comfy home with open arms and loving words. In many ways I feel more comfortable with them than I do with my own parents. I'm pretty sure they would like to see Pablo and me married, but they never bring that up—at least not with me.

It was too cool for the deck on that October evening, so we sat in their spacious living room where Juanita had laid out a platter of tiny corn tortillas topped with refried beans, chopped tomatillos, onions and cheese. Pablo grabbed us each a cold beer from the kitchen and we munched on the snacks while his parents bombarded me with questions about what I'd been doing.

I was partway through telling the story of Gramma's predicament, when Pablo's sister Sofia arrived with her husband Eduardo and their two young kids, three-year-old Miguel and five-year-old Lucia. The kids were excited to see us, especially Pablo, and to show off their new shoes—black Spiderman athletic shoes for Miguel and shiny pink patent Mary Janes for Lucia. After we oohed and ahhed over the shoes, Lucia turned to Pablo and said, "Where's Mia? I want to show her my shoes."

Pablo looked surprised. Apparently he hadn't realized that five-year-old girls tend to be both talkative and indiscreet. If he'd been bringing Mia to family gatherings and hoping to keep that a secret from me, his cover was blown.

"Hush, Lucia," said her mother before Pablo could answer. "You have plenty of people here to see your shoes."

"But I want to show them to Mia," she whined.

Juanita jumped up and took Lucia's hand, "Come, Lucia," she said, pulling her in the direction of the kitchen, "I need you to help me get some juice for you and Miguel."

Pablo also sprang to his feet. "Hey Miguel," he said, "Let's go out back and see how fast you can run in those new shoes." Miguel grinned and followed Pablo.

I wasn't happy to find out that Mia was still hanging around and that Pablo had brought her to events with his family, but I didn't want to deal with those feelings that night. I had way too much going on to add another problem to my already overloaded brain. And in all fairness Pablo and I don't have an exclusive relationship and that's as much my choice as it is his. Plus, I didn't want to talk about Mia with Pablo's family any more than they did with me.

I quickly engaged Pablo's sister Sofia in a conversation about her impressions of local nursing homes. Sofia's a hospital nurse, so I figured she could tell me something about the condition of patients who came to the hospital from various facilities. She had a lot to say, unfortunately none of it very encouraging. By the time Juanita called us to the dinner table, I was more convinced than ever that I needed to find the money for Gramma to move to the new place.

Dinner was a delicious dish of lean pork marinated in a Mexican spice and citrus mixture and sautéed with onions, peppers, garlic, jalapeño chili pepper, tomato, and cilantro. We piled the succulent mixture into soft flour tortillas, which we rolled into cone shapes and topped with fresh avocado salsa. Heaven!

I relaxed and let the Mia episode go, so I could enjoy the evening. Not to say I wouldn't bring it up with Pablo later, but I couldn't see any point of obsessing over it during dinner. And Pablo was being especially attentive and engaging. We ate, drank, talked, laughed at the kids' cute comments, and lingered at the table over dessert the way families do when they take time from their busy everyday lives to enjoy each other's company.

After we'd all pitched in to clean up and do the dishes, Sofia and Eduardo took their kids home for bed. Pablo and I left also, respecting his parents' habitual early bedtime.

We headed over to Pablo's house. He rents, but needs a house rather than an apartment so he can use the garage and basement for his sculptures. It's a quiet two-bedroom brick ranch—standard issue with white walls, beige carpet, beige mini-blinds. Pablo's furniture is basic as well—beige futon couch, black wooden entertainment center and matching coffee table. But the place comes alive with Pablo's own style because of his abstract metal sculptures scattered in various nooks and corners. The cats, dogs, chickens and other animals that he builds from rusty steel tools, blades, gears and other recycled stuff, create a quirky welcoming committee of silent pets.

I hadn't mentioned Mia on the way over and neither had he. I considered asking him about her before we started our internet search on art prices, but decided against it. My upset over Mia was less important than my concern for Gramma. I wanted to get to the internet search; I wanted to continue enjoying Pablo's company; and I didn't want a repeat of an argument going nowhere.

We started with Google searches on some artists whose work we knew. But we found that rather than listing prices for their art, most of the artists suggested customers purchase their work through galleries or contact them directly for price information.

"They're probably not putting prices up because it will upset the gallery owners if the artist undercuts them by selling their own work on a website for less than the gallery prices," Pablo said. "Which we can do when we're not paying the gallery commission."

"Right," I said. "So let's look at some gallery websites for prices."

We started with galleries in the west and southwest—Denver, Santa Fe, Taos, L.A., San Francisco and Seattle. Some galleries showed prices, others didn't. Prices varied by artists and we hadn't heard of many of the painters, so it was hard to judge whether or not prices were lower than usual.

"Let's look on eBay," Pablo suggested. "Lots of art is on there, so it might be easier to find work by artists we know. Or maybe even some of Martha's work up for re-sale."

On eBay, we clicked on art, then clicked on paintings. The site showed over 38,000 paintings for sale by dealers or resellers, nearly 3,000 for sale by artists, and another 8,000 or so unspecified. We began to browse through the listings, which included original oil paintings, watercolors, and acrylics of all sizes; as well as giclee prints and other reproductions. But the prices were much lower than Gramma's work. Many were priced at under one hundred dollars and most were under a thousand.

"I don't think we're going to find much work comparable to Gramma's here," I said scrolling rapidly through the pages. But just as I was about to close the site, a familiar image popped up. "Wait—I see one of Gramma's paintings," I said, clicking to enlarge the image. It was a luminous abstract of Colorado's state flower—the white and lavender columbine—nodding gracefully on a sunny mountain slope. Gramma had named it "Flower Power."

"No, Cleo," Pablo said. "That's not Martha's work. Look there, it says it's original art signed and dated by the artist, Monique Hixon."

"But I remember that painting," I insisted. "This Monique Hixon must have copied Gramma's work. And look at the price. Good grief!

She's selling it for $250. Gramma's probably sold for $5,000. How can she get away with this?"

"We don't know yet if she's getting away with anything," Pablo said. "Let's not jump to conclusions. We can try searching for Monique Hixon to see what else she has on eBay."

"Okay," I said, typing the name into eBay's search box. I clicked art as a category, then started the search. Several hundred listings for this Monique person popped up. I scrolled through and found five others that I was sure were Gramma's. All were listed for sale by eBay seller TheBestArt4U in a private auction. No information was given about either the artist or the seller, except the seller ratings which showed good performance on shipping time and providing the item as described in the listing.

I was steaming mad. "This is fraud," I screeched, jumping up and pacing the room. "No wonder Faye thinks we can't get good prices for Gramma's paintings. If people can get these cheap reproductions, why would they buy her originals?"

Pablo stayed in his chair and didn't react to my angst. "Has Martha already sold these paintings that you think this woman copied?" he asked evenly.

"Yes those have all been sold," I said impatiently, continuing to pace. "Oh, and I just remembered, they were all photographed for a book of her paintings, which is probably how Monique or whoever she is was able to copy them."

"Okay they've been sold. So these copies, or whatever they are, aren't competing with Martha for sales. At most they'd be a problem for someone re-selling the works."

"Sold or not, they're Gramma's copyrighted images," I groaned. "If collectors who've bought her work see those copy-cat paintings selling for a fraction of the price they paid, they'll feel cheated and won't want to buy any more of her work. I can imagine all her artworks becoming worthless. It's a disaster for her." I circled back to stand in front of him. "How can you be so calm about this scam? How would you feel if someone was copying your work?" I shrieked. "We need to report this woman to the police."

Pablo laughed. "Cleo, I am the police," he reminded me. "And I know we have to get the facts before we can do anything."

Bottom line, I knew he was right about getting the facts. So I sat with him at the computer for another two hours doing internet searches. EBay doesn't make it easy. We couldn't find out anything about the seller or the so-called artist. And when we looked at procedures for reporting problems, it was all about issues of not getting what you ordered. We finally discovered eBay's Verified Rights Owner (VeRO) program where people can report violations of their intellectual property rights, but the instructions said that only the intellectual property rights owner can report potentially infringing items or listings. Obviously Gramma was in no position to make a report and anyway I wouldn't want to upset her by telling her about this scam.

Our Google search on eBay art fraud came up with over a million hits. The sites we looked at weren't encouraging. Apparently getting action from eBay is difficult and winning a lawsuit against them is unlikely. And as far as suing the seller, victims say that even if you can identify the seller, the documentation you have to collect for a lawsuit is complex and problems are multiplied if the seller is in a different state—which is usually the case.

We were both so tired and discouraged by then that we went to bed and went right to sleep. Not the romantic Saturday night we'd envisioned earlier, but then again, at least we weren't arguing about Mia.

Chapter 33

In the middle of that night, I woke both of us up screaming. Pablo shook me until I struggled out of a nightmare where I had been stuck in a thick damp fog closing in on me and filling my lungs so I couldn't breathe. In my dream I was terrified as I tried to escape the killer fog before it choked me. Finally it lifted, briefly disclosing a grassy meadow in the distance, where I saw Grampa beckoning me forward. He called me to join him, and I tried, but no matter how fast I ran, I couldn't get there. Then the viselike mist returned worse than ever. I was completely disoriented and the fog was strangling me. I couldn't find the meadow or Grampa again no matter which way I turned. I screamed and woke up.

"I was suffocating and I couldn't get out," I sobbed. "Whichever way I ran was worse than where I'd been before. The fog was swallowing me up. It was horrible!"

Pablo held me close. "It was just a dream, Cleo. Put it out of your mind," he said in a sleepy voice, hugging me tighter. "You're safe here. Think about something else and go back to sleep."

As I snuggled into Pablo's arms, my heart rate slowed, my breath came more easily and I eventually got back to sleep. But I was still feeling weird when we got up late Sunday morning. My vision of Grampa had been so vivid that I wanted to call him to ask why he was summoning me to the meadow. I feared he was trying to warn me that time was running out to find the cash Gramma needed to move. I had promised him that I would take care of Gramma and now everything in her life was falling apart.

I wiped away some tears as I walked to the bathroom to grab a quick shower while Pablo made some coffee. While he showered I got a little breakfast together. He doesn't keep much food around, but I found some bagels and cream cheese and a couple of apples. Briefly, I wondered whether Mia had laid in the bagels and cream cheese for an anticipated morning after. But I quickly banished that train of thought to my think-about-it-later drawer. I couldn't allow myself to focus on Pablo's relationship with Mia when I had so much else going on.

When Pablo joined me at the kitchen table, we ate and discussed what to do next about the eBay art fraud. "I think I should tell Faye what we found," I said. "Maybe she's run into this sort of thing before and knows something about stopping it."

Pablo knit his brow. "Wait, let's think about this," he said slowly. "I like Faye, but we have to consider that she could be involved in the fraud in some way. Let's hold off on talking to her about it."

"Really?" I asked. "You think she's involved?"

"No, I don't think she is," he said. "But I've been surprised before. We can't rule it out, so let's not tell her just yet that we've uncovered it."

I thought he was being way overly suspicious, but that's how cops are trained. And I really had no reason to talk to Faye about the fraud right away, so I went along. "Fine," I said. "I won't say anything to her. I think I'll look through Gramma's old files in the studio and see if I can find names of collectors who have bought her work. Maybe if I call some of them, I can sell some of the paintings I have without going through a gallery."

"Sure," Pablo said. "That could work. And when I go in to work later, I'll see what I can find out about eBay fraud and identifying eBay sellers."

I didn't want to linger any longer in Longmont, so we kissed goodbye and went our separate ways—Pablo to the gym and me back to Boulder. As I drove, I obsessed over the inconclusive results of our eBay searches the night before. I couldn't believe someone could rip off my Gramma so easily and, even worse, that it could be so hard for me to do anything about it. Sometimes it seems like everything is set up in favor of people who prey on others. I've heard Pablo complain often enough that his hands are tied in bringing the guilty to justice. Now I get his frustration about that in a whole new way.

Desperation had me by the throat. I had to do something to stop this fraud right now. Legal channels are fine when you have the time, but time wasn't on my side here. I began to wonder if there wouldn't be some way to use under-the-table tactics to catch Gramma's scammer. Of course Pablo couldn't do that, but I felt justified in doing whatever I could, given the circumstances.

Suddenly I thought of Shane. I remembered that conversation I had overheard between Faye and Tim about Shane running an ID theft and forgery scam, buying electronics and gift cards with stolen credit card numbers and selling them on eBay. He sounded like someone who knew his way around eBay and wasn't bothered by ethical or legal issues. Of course I couldn't tell him I knew about that, but I could appeal to him as someone who knows the internet better than most of us. Maybe he could help me find a way to unmask the scammer.

It was nearly noon by then, which didn't seem too early to call him, so I did. He wasn't exactly excited to hear from me. "I don't even have time to get my own work done," Shane said after I'd asked him if he could help me with an urgent internet problem regarding my Gramma's art sales. "If it's about art, why don't you ask Faye to help?"

"Look Shane, I'm desperate and I really need your help," I said. "I know you're busy, but I need an internet expert, not an art expert. If I could stop by for a few minutes and show you what's going on, you'd be doing me a huge favor." I probably wouldn't have pushed him that way if it hadn't been for Gramma, but I didn't feel even a little bit guilty when he reluctantly agreed that I could come over.

I had to knock so long and hard before he answered his door that I was about to open it and let myself in. But suddenly there he was, barefoot, wearing baggy shorts and a wrinkled tee shirt, and blinking as if he'd emerged from a dark cave. He beckoned me in and I followed, gagging slightly at the rotten smell that came from inside. The place didn't look like he'd done any cleaning or thrown anything out since Lacey and I had been there on Wednesday. His blinds were closed and I struggled to avoid tripping over trash in the dim light, which came from his laptop and extra monitor glowing on the coffee table.

"Hey, Cleo," he said half-heartedly. He had a spacey look, like he might be hung-over or high. I began to doubt my judgment. Good grief, what was I thinking coming to a spoiled, slacker kid who lived in a virtual world, when I needed help with a serious real-life problem? But there I was and there was no denying he's way savvier about the internet than I'll ever be. After he brushed papers off his futon couch, we sat and I explained about Gramma's need for money and the eBay fraud. Then I directed him to the eBay pages Pablo and I had found the night before.

"I can see why you're upset," Shane said, "but from what I know about eBay the sellers can describe the items they're selling any way they want and there's essentially no oversight as to authenticity. EBay takes pretty much a hands-off approach to fakes or stolen property or whatever. The way they see it, they're a marketplace, not a retailer, so what's sold is the seller's responsibility."

Ouch. This didn't sound good. "How do I find out who the seller really is and how to get in touch with whoever it is so I can stop this fraud?"

Shane rolled his eyes. "EBay isn't going to tell you who the seller is. If you want to know, you'll have to be your own detective. You'll probably have to spend way longer than you have to find out who it is."

I drooped in despair. "What else can I do? Are you saying it's hopeless?"

"I'm saying that it doesn't sound like trying to stop the internet art fraud is the way to go right now. If I were you, I'd forget the eBay thing and work on selling your grandmother's real paintings for now."

I took a moment to think about his advice. "But Faye isn't getting good prices for Gramma's paintings."

"Or at least that's what she's telling you," he said, skeptically.

Did he know something compromising about Faye? And if he did, would he tell me? "What do you mean? Do you think she's lying to me?" I asked.

He shrugged. "I told you before that the gallery isn't doing well financially. Her situation is pretty desperate. You might want to be careful how much you trust her. Maybe she's selling the paintings for more than she's telling you and keeping the extra for herself. Or—how do you know that she still has all your grandmother's paintings that she says she hasn't sold?"

Whoa—panic time! I was definitely losing my cool. I would have gotten up and walked around the room to relieve some tension, but the floor was too cluttered. So I stayed put on the futon couch as I pushed on with more questions. "What are you thinking about Faye?"

"Have you seen the paintings lately? How do you know she hasn't sold them and not told you so she could keep all the money?" He lounged back with a sphinxlike look that reminded me of Angelica.

I squirmed. "You're making some serious allegations here, Shane. Why would Faye cheat my grandmother? Her gallery has been representing Gramma for years."

"Like I said, Faye's been under some serious financial pressure lately." His tone was downright cocky.

I decided to confront him. "How do you know so much about her finances? Did your mother tell you?"

"Not exactly."

"So how then? I can't believe you if I don't know the source."

He paused, staring off into the back of the dark room. Then he turned to me. "Okay. Here it is. But I don't want Lacey to know about this. If you tell her, I'll deny every word of it."

"Okay," I said inquiringly.

He straightened up and looked me in the eyes as he explained. "Last spring I was looking for something on my mom's desk and I ran across a list of her passwords. She was on my back about some stuff so I decided to check out her emails and see what she was saying about me. I read a lot of her emails for months—both the ones she sent and the ones she got."

"Wasn't it risky that she'd find out?"

"Not really. I only went on her account in the middle of the night when I knew she wouldn't be on it. And I was very careful to mark all her emails unopened after I read them."

"What does all this have to do with Faye's finances?"

He held up his hand to silence me. "Just listen," he said. "I'm getting to that. In about March I read an email from Mom to Faye about creative bookkeeping Mom had uncovered. Apparently the gallery had some big losses, which Faye had covered up, and she ran through the reserves by continuing to take a big salary even when the gallery wasn't bringing in enough to cover it. That got me interested so whenever I saw an email to or from Faye, I read it. Mom was asking Faye a bunch of questions about the gallery's bills, pressuring her to be more accountable, and threatening to come in and go over the books. For months Faye kept blowing her off, making excuses. By summer Mom was questioning Faye's ability to run the gallery. Mom gave her an ultimatum—get the gallery financially stable or Mom would dissolve the partnership and take it over. Then Mom died and Faye inherited the gallery, so I guess she gets to keep running it." He sat back and waited for my reaction.

"I agree, that sounds serious," I said. "Did you tell your dad about it after your mom died?"

"Of course not," he said exasperatedly. "Then I'd have to tell him I'd been reading Mom's email. I did give him some strong suggestions to check out whether Faye owed Mom money for gallery expenses, but he said that was a small deal and he had more important things to do."

"Why don't you want Lacey to know about this?"

He scowled. "Lacey already doesn't trust me. I don't want her to know I was reading Mom's emails."

"But maybe Faye is the one who murdered your mother," I objected. "Don't you think Lacey should know what you found out about the conflict between them?"

"Like I said, I can't tell Lacey about that without telling her I was reading Mom's email. But one of the reasons I came up with the plan to say Lacey found out that Mom made a new will was to try to smoke Faye out. I wanted to see how Faye would react because she would probably be afraid Mom wrote her out of this new will, which would cancel out the old one."

We sat silently for a minute—at which point I realized that it was time for me to go. I wasn't going to get any more help here. I thanked Shane and headed for the door.

He didn't bother to get up, but fired off one parting shot. "I did some online research about the art gallery business," he said. "Owning a gallery is the second-worst business to be in, after restaurants. They go bankrupt all the time. Faye has a big advantage not having to pay rent."

I sighed as I closed the door behind me. Of course I knew that galleries are financially risky. But I was hoping Shane was wrong about Faye's gallery. If it folded, what would happen to Gramma?

Chapter 34

Vernon Evers' funeral was set for late Monday morning. Should I go? He was my grandparents' lawyer, but it's not as though I knew him well. On the other hand, Lacey and Angelica might expect to see me there. Right. Probably I should be there to support them. Of course Glenna wouldn't want to see me there, but I knew the funeral would be huge, so she probably wouldn't even notice me. So, okay. I re-scheduled my clients, put on my black dress and headed off to the service.

It was a dreary day—cold and rainy—just like the weather for funerals in the movies. As I drove across town to the imposing Baptist church east of Boulder where the ceremony was to be held, I thought about Vernon and Glenna. Would she inherit in a big way from his estate? They weren't married, so she wasn't automatically entitled to anything by law. From what Tim had said about her, it was highly likely that she had manipulated him into putting her into his will for a big chunk. Did she push him down the stairs to hasten that inheritance along? A horrible thought, but Shane and Lacey seemed to think it was possible.

I was so angry at that point that I almost missed the turn to get to the church parking lot. I hate the idea of someone taking advantage of an elderly person and I hate even more the idea that she might get away with it. If Glenna had been ripping Vernon off, we needed to find a way to show her up for the manipulative fraud that she was.

The parking lot was already two-thirds full when I pulled in. I followed the crowd to the front of the building, where we filed in to the solemn strains of an organ playing "Shall We Gather at the River." The music calmed my mood and pulled me into the moment. I chose a seat in a back pew and looked around. The church was nearly full, lots of grey-haired men in suits and older women in dark dresses. At the front of the church, slightly to the left of the aisle, sat a substantial copper casket topped with a colorful flower spray of roses, carnations, delphinium, daisies and freesia. On the right of the aisle a lectern was flanked by two large standing baskets of white mums and lilies.

Funerals remind me that life is a short ride. As I sat there waiting for the service to begin, I thought about the way we move through life pretending to ourselves that we have all the time we need. And then it's over. There's so much I haven't done—never been married, never had children, never been to Europe, never took piano lessons, never hiked Colorado's highest peaks. The list could go on and on. I resolved to take some time soon to re-evaluate my priorities.

I looked down at the printed program an usher had handed me on my way in. The cover had a picture of Vernon and his dates of birth and death. By my quick subtraction, he was seventy-eight when he died. In his obituary inside, I read that he was a graduate of Harvard Law School and had been a practicing attorney in Boulder for fifty years, as well as a city commissioner, community activist and a major player in local citizen environmental groups.

He was predeceased by his wife Ruth and only child Mirabel. I remembered that Elisa had told me Ruth was from a very wealthy cattle-ranching family. That's where Mirabel's money came from. According to Boulder gossip—and Elisa—Mirabel's grandparents had set up trust funds in their wills for both their daughter Ruth and their granddaughter Mirabel. The grandparents died when Mirabel was young, so she started getting trust fund income when she was eighteen. When Mirabel's mother Ruth died suddenly of a heart attack two years ago, the principal remaining in her trust was divided equally between Vernon and Mirabel. I didn't know how much that was, but I knew Mirabel had millions and I assumed Vernon did as well.

And now maybe Glenna would be a millionaire. Thinking of Glenna, there she was wearing a smashing black suit with jeweled cuffs and leading the family processional down the aisle. She walked alone, weeping copiously and wiping her eyes with a lacey black handkerchief. Either she was truly grieving or she was an excellent actress.

Behind her were Derrick and Judith, followed by Shane, and then a middle-aged couple I'd never seen before. But Lacey and Angelica weren't part of the group. Alarm bells rang in my head as I scanned the crowd. Could something have happened to them on their trip to the mountains? I couldn't imagine Derrick walking calmly down the church aisle if Lacey and Angelica were in trouble. Maybe they didn't want to be in the public eye with their grief and were watching from some secluded spot in the church.

The minister came out from a side door and motioned to Glenna who started the service by reading the twenty-third psalm. She stopped crying before she stepped up to the lectern and her voice was clear and still as she began, "The Lord is my shepherd; I shall not want."

I listened and tried to keep thoughts of Lacey and Angelica out of my mind. Following the scripture reading a soloist sang "Softly and Tenderly Jesus is Calling." Next a local attorney who had served with Vernon on the city commission delivered the eulogy. He spoke of "Vern," his long-time friend and colleague as a good noble man who lived for bettering the community. He praised Vern's high moral and ethical standards and reminisced about his many passions and successes.

Derrick told an amusing family story about Vernon teaching the grandchildren to ski, and Shane told one about how he taught his grandfather to use the internet. They both thanked him for all he had done for their family. Friends and colleagues who had worked with Vernon over the years talked about how he had attended countless community meetings negotiating and debating long into the night, how he possessed unique skills to organize people with broad viewpoints, and how he often served as the cool head to heated opinions.

It was good to hear these fond remembrances of Vernon with no mention of his recent memory problems or heavy drinking. He truly had been a distinguished attorney, held in high esteem for his contributions to the community.

Glenna came back to the lectern to invite us all to stay for refreshments, and take time to mingle and share our remembrances of Vern. The pallbearers escorted the casket up the aisle; family members followed and then the rest of us began to exit, row by row. Since I was at the back, I was one of the last to move out into the lobby.

I followed the crowd down the hall into a large airy room where long tables held fruit and cheese trays, coffee, tea and juice. Shane was standing alone on the far side of the room, Blackberry in hand, typing madly with both thumbs. I made my way over and stood in front of him until he looked up. "I didn't see Lacey or Angelica," I said. "Are they here?"

"No," he said, looking back at his Blackberry to check an email message.

"I'm surprised they would miss the funeral," I said. "Has something happened to them?"

He continued typing. "No, they're fine."

"So where are they? I need to talk to Lacey."

"They're stuck in the mountains somewhere. You can call Lacey on her cell."

I was getting sick of his aloof attitude. Was he deliberately withholding information to annoy me? I had no patience for his passive-aggressive behavior, so I walked away—back across the room out to the hall, took a quick trip to the ladies room and then walked down the hall a ways to a small quiet Sunday School room. I took out my cell phone, which I had turned off during the service. As soon as I turned it on, I saw that I had a missed call from Lacey. She'd left a voice mail, but all it said was, "Call me. It's important."

I was just about to call her back when I heard raised voices coming from slightly further down the hall. I peeked out the door and saw Derrick, Shane and Glenna facing each other in what looked like a stormy exchange. They seemed too involved in their confrontation to notice me, so I stayed just inside the doorway and listened.

"That's not acceptable, Glenna," Derrick said angrily. "We have a right to look through Vernon's office to see whether he made a new will for Mirabel."

"No you don't," Glenna said. "Vernon left me his house and all its contents. If you want an inventory of what's in the house, you can call the attorney who is handling Vern's estate. Here's his card."

"You bitch," Shane said bitterly. "You may have fooled Grandad but we know what you are. You took advantage of an old man's weakness to get him to write you into his will and then you pushed him down the stairs so you could get the money faster."

Wow, that was getting right to the point. Apparently Shane didn't feel constrained to wait for evidence, a coroner's report or a police investigation.

"That's enough, Shane," Derrick said, putting his hand on Shane's shoulder. "Making accusations won't get you anywhere. Let's talk to the lawyer."

Glenna ignored Derrick's attempt to tamp down the fire. "I'm sick of your bullshit, Shane," she said vehemently. "You're way more desperate for money than I am. Vern always said you can be a very pushy kid when you want something. Maybe you pushed your mother under the water in her hot tub so you could inherit and maybe you got so angry you pushed Vern down the stairs when he didn't come up with her new will like you wanted him to."

Whoa, this was getting down and dirty. Part of me wanted to get out of there, but the other part felt rooted to the spot. Suddenly my phone rang. I stuck it in my pocket and dashed down the hall away from the fighting family, hoping the ringing hadn't drawn their attention to me. There was no way I wanted to have to explain why I was standing there eavesdropping on their argument. I didn't look back to see whether they had noticed me, just headed for the front door and ran out through the rain to my car.

Chapter 35

The call was Lacey again but I didn't pick up soon enough to get it. When I called her back, she sounded ticked off. "I've been trying to reach you all morning," she complained. "Where are you?"

"I was at your grandfather's funeral, so I had my phone turned off. Shane said you and Angelica got stuck in the mountains and couldn't make it. What happened?"

"We had the worst luck," she wailed. "October in the mountains. I should have checked the forecast, but I had so much on my mind, I forgot. I can't believe we missed Grandad's funeral." Lacey was crying and I heard Angelica in the background trying to soothe her.

"Lacey, I'm sure you did your best to get here. Your grandfather would understand. Do you want to tell me what happened?"

"We started back from Aspen late yesterday afternoon, but we ran into a monster snowstorm. The driving was getting pretty hairy, so I decided to stop at a motel in Dillon. I figured we'd get up early and easily make it to the funeral, but when we got up we heard that a truck had jackknifed on the highway and the road was closed."

"Have they gotten the road open yet?"

"Yes, they opened it about half an hour ago, but it was too late to make the funeral by then. We're on our way down now and we should be in Boulder in about an hour. We have to talk to you as soon as we get there. It's really urgent. Can we come right to your office?"

"For sure I'd rather talk to you in person, instead of talking on the phone while you're driving down a snowy mountain highway," I said, "but you know I can't have Angelica in my office."

"It's sunny up here this morning and the snow is mostly melted now. Also, Angelica is holding the phone for me, so no worries about the driving." She had started speaking calmly but her voice began to rise as she went on. "But we have to meet with you. We need help and you're the only one who will understand. This is beyond urgent! No one will ever know Angelica has been at your office."

"Can you tell me what's so urgent?"

"You're not going to believe this, but Glenna called me early Saturday morning to tell me she had Mom's new will. She said I shouldn't say anything to anyone else except Angelica, and I needed to come get it right away. I told her I'd rather tell Dad and let him get it from her, but she started yelling at me that if I told Dad or Shane, she'd destroy the will and deny ever finding it. She sounded so out of control, I didn't want to argue with her," Lacey groaned, sounding a bit out of control herself. She took a deep breath and continued, "Whatever might happen, I couldn't risk losing a new will that contains Mom's last wishes about her estate. So we picked it up on our way to Aspen, and Angelica read it out loud to me on our way up. Mom made some big changes and we're not sure what to do about it. That's what's so urgent."

After what I'd just heard in the angry exchange among Glenna, Derrick and Shane, I wondered whether Glenna was manipulating everyone in the Townes family for her own purposes. On the other hand it was hard to see what Glenna would have to gain from Mirabel's will, whether it was the original version or a new revised one. "Why didn't she want you to tell your father or Shane?" I asked. "And now that you have it and she can't destroy it, what's to stop you from giving the new will to your father or taking it to a lawyer? I think you should let them decide what should be done. I don't know anything about wills."

"We're not ready to do that yet," Lacey said, her voice rising again to almost a shriek. "Angelica and I can't agree on what to do with this will." She gave an exasperated sigh. "I'll let her tell you. I think she can explain her point of view better than I can."

Angelica came on the phone, speaking patiently in the deliberate manner of someone who has been repeatedly misunderstood. "Cleo, it's Angelica. Let me explain. The energy surrounding this will is muddy and its provisions are not harmonious. The universe has arranged for Lacey and me to have Mom's new will when other people don't know about it. I have a strong feeling that this will doesn't represent Mom's true intentions. Lacey thinks we have to take the will to a lawyer, but my intuition tells me that bringing out this will may cause great harm."

What the heck did that mean? I felt like I was in over my head again, drowning in complications with two messed-up kids. My immediate response would be to take the new will to a lawyer. But Vernon was a lawyer, so he certainly knew what he should have done. He had done great work for my grandparents and he had been eulogized as a man of high ethical standards. Why would he keep the will a secret? Why had he continued to insist that there was no new will? And if he wasn't going to report the new will, why did he keep it? Did he somehow feel that keeping the will secret was acceptable but that because it was a legal document destroying it would be going too far? Given that he made the choices that he did, was Angelica right that the new will was harmful?

My curiosity and my desire to help were strong. I did want to meet with them, but I was very worried about violating Derrick and Judith's strict instructions not to see Angelica again—especially at my office. I made what seemed at the time like a smart compromise, but was actually a rash decision. I said I would meet them at my house.

They showed up at 1:30, both looking worried and tired. I welcomed them into my kitchen, where I had laid out some muffins and fruit that I had picked up on my way home. Once Lacey and I were settled with coffee and Angelica with some lemonade, I asked Lacey to tell me as much as she could remember of what Glenna had said about the new will.

She closed her eyes briefly in thought, then began. "Apparently Grandad left his house and all its contents to Glenna. When she was cleaning out his office on Friday, she found several boxes stuffed with legal papers. For some reason, she decided to look through them before she took them to the lawyer handling Grandad's estate. And she found Mom's new will in one of the boxes."

"Amazing! Did she say whether she already knew your Mom had made a new will or whether finding it was a big shock?"

Lacey grimaced. "She said she didn't know anything about it. But I have no idea whether or not that's true. She can be cagey."

"Did she have any idea why your grandfather had kept the new will secret and told everyone your mom didn't make a new will?"

"She said she didn't know. But she said Grandad was much more forgetful than any of us knew—had big problems finding things around the house, forgot people's names and how he knew them, and sometimes got lost driving right here in Boulder. He was good at covering up so other people didn't notice. She said she urged him to get an evaluation of his memory, but he refused. She also said she tried to get him to cut down on his drinking because he was much more forgetful when he was drinking. But he said drinking as much as he wanted was one of the pleasures he'd earned after working hard all his life."

"So Glenna thinks Vernon forgot your mom made a new will?"

"Right. The new will is dated in June of this year—only a couple of months before Mom died. So you'd think he would have remembered. But Glenna said his forgetfulness had been getting much worse this spring and summer, and he forgot recent things more than longer-ago ones."

I could actually believe that Vernon Evers could have forgotten having drawn up his own daughter's new will. Having lived with Gramma's Alzheimer's for years, I knew quite a bit about short-term memory loss and how people who have it can be much worse than they seem. And when they start to notice their forgetfulness, they learn ways to cover up. It sounded very believable to me that a powerful man like Vernon Evers wouldn't want anyone to know how forgetful he was. Glenna knew what he was like day-to-day a lot better than we did. If she thought he'd forgotten making Mirabel's new will, it was likely she was right.

"We'll probably never know why he didn't bring out the new will," I said. "But whatever his reason was, Glenna doesn't seem to have any reason to lie about it. What I don't understand is why after she found the will she decided to give it to you instead of your Dad and told you not to say anything about it to anyone except Angelica."

"She said Dad and Shane had been accusing Grandad of not remembering and he was furious about that. Grandad was mad at Dad anyway for moving Judith into our house, and he was disgusted with Shane's lifestyle—thought he was a slacker. They knew Grandad was angry with them and they weren't getting along with him. Glenna figured that if she told them about the will, they'd be saying they were right all along about his memory. She accepts they'll have to know about the will soon, but she said they've never liked her and they treat her like a whore. She detests them both and she didn't want to deal with them or have to discuss Grandad's memory problems at his funeral. So she gave it to me and asked me not to tell anyone until after the funeral."

Angelica had been quietly eating a pear and a raspberry muffin while Lacey was talking. I wanted to get her into the conversation, so I asked, "Angelica, what do you think is harmful in the new will?"

"One thing is that in this will, Dad gets most of the money. He talked her into that. I know because I heard their arguments. Mom told him she had written him out of her will except for what she had to give him under Colorado law And she told him she was thinking of getting a divorce. Dad kept begging her to reconsider, told her he had given up Judith. After a while she believed him and told him she would stay with him and that she had made a new will. But he was lying. He never gave up Judith and he never planned to."

"I guess that's what your grandfather thought, too," I said. "But this will is a legal document. Even if your mother made a mistake, we can't keep it a secret now that we have it."

"That's what I think, too," Lacey said. "Plus in the new will Mom disinherited the Scientologists. If we don't turn it in, they'll get money Mom didn't want them to have."

Angelica put her hand on Lacey's arm and spoke slowly and clearly.

"But if we do turn it in, Judith will get money Mom didn't want her to have. We may not like the Scientologists, but they did help Mom when she needed help, which is more than Dad did. And all Judith ever did was hurt her." Angelica paused, staring into space. Then she said, "There's also Faye Whitton to think about."

"What about Faye?" I asked

"She said some very bad things in the will about Faye and the way she manages the West End Gallery. Mom said Faye had been warned but she hadn't changed so Mom was no longer leaving her the gallery. I think they weren't getting along lately, but I don't think Faye deserved that.

I turned to Lacey. "What's that about?"

"Mom said in the will that …"

"All of you sit right where you are and put that will at the end of the table," a loud male voice demanded. Brian stood in the kitchen doorway pointing a gun at us.

Chapter 36

I jumped up and confronted him, trying to sound confident, despite my pounding heart. "Brian, what are you doing? How did you get in?"

"You left the front door open," he sneered, "so I just walked in. Get back in your chair, Cleo. I'm here for the will." Keeping the gun carefully trained on us with his right hand, he walked up to the table, used his left hand to push me down into my chair and then to grab the will.

Lacey had begun to cry, but Angelica sat stoically, observing him. Sweat trickled down my chest. What had I done? Not only had I allowed Angelica to come to my house against Derrick and Judith's orders, I had gotten her into a life-threatening situation. I had to take charge.

"How did you know about the will?" I demanded.

"Don't be naïve, Cleo. Do you think we leave this sort of thing to chance? I've had your cell phone tapped for weeks."

Huh? "How did you get hold of my cell phone?"

"I didn't have to do anything to your cell phone. I have software installed on my phone that lets me see who you call and who calls you. I can listen in to all your conversations. Most of them are pretty boring, but I hit the jackpot today."

Brian never took his eyes off us as he put the will in his pocket, reached down into a bag he had dropped on the floor next to his feet, and pulled out several long pieces of rope and tossed them on the table. "Stand up, Cleo," he barked. I stood. He motioned at Lacey and said, "Put your arms together and hold them out in front of you." She complied. "Okay, Cleo, take one of those pieces of rope and wrap them tightly around her arms several times and then tie it so she can't get loose."

My gut was churning and I felt dizzy with fear, but I stayed put. Did not pick up the rope. He couldn't be serious about shooting us. If I refused to cooperate, maybe he'd take the will and leave. "Brian, you don't have to do this. You have the will. Isn't that enough?"

He took a half step in my direction. "Shut up, Cleo and do what I say or I'll shoot you in the foot." He pointed his gun at my right foot. Looks like his new level of spiritual awareness doesn't stop him from inflicting pain and suffering.

"Okay, you don't have to get violent. I'll do what you say." I reached for a piece of rope, walked over to Lacey's chair and bound her arms together. She sobbed and twitched, but didn't say anything. Brian watched closely to make sure I was tying her arms tight.

"Now the kid," he said pointing at Angelica. I picked up another piece of rope and turned to Angelica. I touched her shoulder softly to reassure her before I tied her arms. She sat quietly gazing intently at Brian the whole time.

Brian matched her stare. "What are you looking at?" he demanded.

"Your aura," she said. "It's a muddy forest green. That's a sign of jealousy, resentment, insecurity, low self-esteem, and feeling like you're a victim."

This guy is pointing a gun at us and she's making derogatory comments about his aura? "Angelica, I don't think he really wants to hear this right now," I said, hoping she'd take the suggestion and let it go.

Brian clenched his jaw, but didn't answer her or respond in any way. Instead he turned to me. "Back to your chair, Cleo," he said, pointing to where I had been sitting across the table. I walked over there and sat. Brian put his gun in his pocket, picked up a piece of rope and headed toward me. I knew the drill and could see no point in resisting. I held out my arms. I did try to leave a gap between my arms, but he wrapped the rope so tightly that it not only pulled them together, it burned my skin. I didn't flinch. No way was I going to give him the satisfaction.

He checked and tightened the rope on both Lacey's and Angelica's arms. Then he returned to the head of the table, took the will and the gun out of his pocket, put it on the table in front of him, and sat down. "I'm going to read this will," he said. "You can all watch my aura or whatever. Just sit quietly and don't bother me."

As he read his face flushed, his nostrils flared, and his arms and shoulders tensed. As I watched his anger build, I desperately tried to figure out how we could possibly escape. Maybe if we all tipped over our chairs at once, he'd be so distracted one of us could kick him while one of us scooted her chair to where a knife would be within reach. But that would take planning and coordinating our actions, which there was no way to do. And realistically our arms were tied too tightly to grab a knife and use it. Maybe if we all screamed at once, someone would hear us, but my house is thick stone and not really close to any other houses, so that wasn't likely to work. Plus, he'd probably shoot us if we screamed.

He looked up at me as if he could hear my thoughts. "You can stop worrying," he said. "I'm not planning to shoot you. My interest is in preserving the Church of Scientology's inheritance by destroying this will." He snatched up the will and ripped it in half. Then he stomped over to my gas stove, lit a burner and touched the will to the flame. With a flourish, he tossed the burning document into the sink and smirked as it turned to ashes.

"No! Stop! You can't do that!" Lacey screamed. "That's a legal document. Destroying it is a crime."

What was she thinking screaming at him like that? Just because he said he wasn't going to shoot us didn't mean he wouldn't. And he clearly wasn't concerned about committing a crime.

But now that he had destroyed the will, his anger had turned to gloating. "How are you going to prove I destroyed anything—or even that there was a new will?" he sneered. "No one has seen it but you three—a strange kid and a couple of women who talk to spirits—and Glenna Corn, a seductress who preys on old men. I doubt any of you would convince the police. Even Cleo's annoying boyfriend thinks you three are deluded."

I hated to admit it, but he might be right. It would be hard to prove what he had done. Brian always was an accomplished liar who knew how to cover his tracks.

Angelica glowered at him. "You are caught in a tide of evil," she said. "You act in darkness, which prevents your spiritual growth. Evil opposes the life force, kills human life or the human spirit. I believe you killed my mother so the Scientologists could get her money."

Brain gave her a surprised look. Then he launched into a lecture. "You know nothing about human life or the human spirit or spiritual growth," he said, patronizingly. "Humans are immortal spiritual entities who have fallen into a degraded state as a result of past-life experiences. Through Scientology we become free of our past-life traumas and recover past-life memory, leading to a higher state of spiritual awareness. Your mother understood that. But then she filled her body with toxic substances, left Scientology, and went back on her promises to us. She had to be stopped. As far as the church goes, I could have killed your mother with no spiritual consequences. A Scientologist can ethically trick, lie to, or destroy a critic or former member who is considered a suppressive person."

This sounded like a load of bullshit to me. I knew I should keep my mouth shut, but somehow I heard myself speaking out. "The police and the courts don't care about Scientology rules," I said. "You can't just kill someone and have no consequences."

"But I didn't kill her," Brian said. "She is responsible for her own death. She died because the toxic substances in her body dulled her awareness and blocked her mental alertness so that she slipped under the water and drowned."

He walked over to the counter, grabbed a long sharp knife, and brought it over to my chair. I panicked. My entire body trembled and my teeth chattered uncontrollably. Was he going to stab us? But didn't he say he wasn't going to kill us? And why would he stab us when he had a gun?

"I didn't kill Mirabel and I'm not going to kill you, but your spirits are trapped—tied up as tightly as your arms are right now. I can free your arms but only you can free your spirits," he said, slicing through a piece of the rope on my arms and unwinding the rest of it. He threw the knife on the table then ran for the front door and was gone.

I quickly freed Lacey and Angelica, gave them each a quick hug, then grabbed my cell phone. But I remembered the Scientologists had it tapped. They probably had Lacey's tapped as well. "I guess we'll have to find an uncompromised phone to call the police," I said.

"No, wait," Lacey said, as we all rubbed our wrists to restore circulation. "If we call the police, Dad and Judith will find out all about this and they'll bring charges against you for having Angelica here and especially for exposing her to this dangerous maniac."

"But he pulled a gun on us and destroyed your mother's new will," I said. "We have to report him."

"Wait," she said. She ran to the front window and looked out. "He's gone. Let's take a walk outside, get some air and think about this."

A strange suggestion perhaps under the circumstances, but the outdoors always helps me clear my mind. The day had cleared and the sun was shining, so I couldn't see any reason not to take a short walk before we called the police and all hell broke loose.

We stumbled out and onto the short path from my house to Settler's Park. The trees and bushes were a mosaic of yellows, browns, and golds. I looked up at the red rocks at the top of the trail and felt my inner-self click into alignment.

"Let's walk up the path to that big tree," Lacey said, pointing to a tree about fifty yards away. When we got there, she looked around carefully. "I wanted to be somewhere where we could be sure we could talk freely," she said with a smile.

"You look happy," I said. "What's up?"

"Brian only thinks he destroyed the will," she said.

"I know," Angelica agreed with a grin. "Can you believe it?"

"That wasn't it?" I asked.

"Being the topnotch lawyer that he was, Grandad had Mom sign two copies of her will. He may have been forgetful, but he was still a pro. Both copies were exactly the same, both signed and witnessed. The other one is in my car. We may not be able to prove the Scientologists murdered Mom, but at least we can keep them from inheriting. I'm going to take that will directly to our lawyer.

Angelica frowned and held her hand up in front of Lacey's face. "No, wait. Don't take it to the lawyer yet. Let's at least take another day to be sure we want this new will to take the place of the other one."

"We need to have the new will where it is safe," Lacey said. "And surely you don't want the Scientologists to inherit after what just happened." She sounded exasperated. "If we don't turn in the new will, the Scientologists win."

I was watching Angelica. She looked hopeless, like she had slammed into a wall. "But if we do turn it in, Judith wins," she said, "Dad will get all the money and she'll marry him. Judith is a nasty rotten woman. I don't want her and Dad to have any more of Mom's money than they're already getting." Angelica dropped to the ground, sobbing.

Lacey and I immediately sat down and put our arms around her as she cried out the pent up grief, anxiety and stress that must have been building inside her. This little girl had been so centered and so strong for so long that I had been expecting a breakdown at some point. Even Indigo children have their limits.

Lacey rubbed Angelica's back with a soothing motion. "It's all right, Angelica," she said. "I won't take the will to a lawyer yet. What's one more day? You and I can talk it through tomorrow when you're feeling better. Come on, let's go home."

We stayed on the ground for one more group hug, then got up and walked slowly back down the path to my house.

Chapter 37

As soon as Lacey and Angelica left, I headed over to the Verizon store to see what I could do about getting my phone untapped. Oops—they said the tap couldn't be stopped by doing anything to my phone. Apparently, the way someone taps a cell phone is by intercepting the signals the phone is sending out. As long as the person tapping it has my phone number they can keep listening to my conversations. It's illegal, of course, but that's a different issue.

My best solution was to buy a prepaid personal cell phone with a new number. I figured it would be only temporary until the Townes family mess was cleared up. Most of my usual business calls were unlikely to be of any interest to Brian, so I would only give the new number to a few people like Lacey, Angelica, and Pablo.

I took the new phone out to my car, where I called both Pablo and Lacey from the new number and left voicemail messages telling them to use that number to reach me. In Lacey's message, I reminded her that my old number was tapped. But Pablo didn't know any of that, so I just said I was having some problems with my phone and he should use this new one for now.

It was dark by then and the air had a chilly rawness from all the rain that had fallen earlier in the day. I couldn't wait to get home to my warm cozy house. Once I got there and closed and locked the door behind me, I realized I was too exhausted to think or talk to anyone. I turned off both cell phones, gulped down some soup, and collapsed into bed. Nothing kept me awake that night—not spooky dreams, not worries about Gramma, not Brian's evil actions, not anxiety over Angelica and Lacey's safety. I slept that deep healing sleep that sometimes follows a traumatic day.

Tuesday morning dawned sunny and breezy, which matched my energy level when I woke up. The cold front that had brought Monday's rain to the Front Range and snow to the high country had moved on with the help of some gusty winds. I had clients scheduled back to back until midafternoon so I hustled off to my office.

For most of the day I forced myself to put Gramma's plight and the Townes' family issues out of my mind so I could give my clients the attention they deserved. At 3:00 when the last one left, I grabbed my usual apple and yogurt for a late lunch, fixed a cup of tea, sat at my desk and turned on my new phone to check messages. The first one was from Lacey sent at 9:00 a.m. She sounded uncharacteristically cool and collected.

"Hey, Cleo, smart thinking about the new phone number. Hope you've recovered from yesterday. Angelica and I still haven't told anyone about what happened or about the new will. She wanted to stay home from school so we could work out what to do about the will, but I convinced her that she needed to go to school because there was no good way to explain her staying home. So I dropped her off there and I'm on my way to my yoga class. Talk to you later."

I was encouraged that Lacey was taking such a deliberate approach. And this on top of her finessing Brian by having a secret second copy of Mirabel's will. Maybe I had misjudged her ability to remain in control in a crisis.

But it turned out to be the proverbial calm before the storm.

Before I got to Lacey's next message, there was one from Pablo confirming what we'd found on the internet about the difficulty of prosecuting eBay art fraud. "Sorry babe, but what I'm hearing is that it's tough to regulate commerce when the seller can be anywhere in the world and so can the buyer," he said. "That means it's not clear what regulatory body has jurisdiction. It looks like it would take years to get any resolution. I'll keep looking for the seller and we can try to go after them but it's not going to help Martha's need for cash right away."

Disappointing, but pretty much what I expected to hear. I clicked on to the next message, sent at 1:30 pm. Lacey had reverted to her hysterical self. "Omigod, Cleo," she shrieked. "Angelica's school just called here to the house to ask if we'd picked her up early from school. They said she's not in class and no one has seen her since lunch." Her voice took on an angry tone as she continued. "Shane isn't answering his phone and I haven't been able to reach Dad or Judith either. What if they took her out to send her away to school like they threatened to do?" She paused, and then said exasperatedly, "But if they'd done that, wouldn't they be here packing her things? She's not with you, is she? Have you heard from her? Do you have any idea where she is? Call me!"

I called her, but it went right to voice mail. I left a message saying I hadn't heard from Angelica or anyone else in her family.

I didn't have any more messages on that voicemail, so I checked my old phone and listened to a few messages from clients—nothing urgent. Then I sat back to think about what to do next.

Would Derrick and/or Judith take Angelica out of school without telling the school staff? Probably not. With a sigh, I reflected on Angelica's propensity for unconventional independent action. She had probably left on her own for some reason. But where would she go? I didn't know her well enough to even make a list of possibilities. The school and Lacey and probably Derrick and Judith, and maybe even Shane were already looking for her. I was worried about her but what could I add to the search? I couldn't think of anything at the moment. And I really needed to use my time and energy to find a way to help Gramma.

What I really wanted to do was call my good friend Elisa and have her help me brainstorm ideas for getting the money Gramma needed. But I knew if I called her, I'd have to tell her about what happened with Brian and she'd be all over me about how she'd warned me about the dangers of helping Lacey and Angelica, and how I should back off before something worse happened. I didn't want to hear that lecture, because Lacey and Angelica still needed my help and support.

I also knew Elisa would push me to tell Pablo or the Boulder police about Brian pulling a gun on us and burning Mirabel's new will.

But Lacey was right that I would get myself in trouble by admitting that I had been at least partly responsible for getting Angelica into a life-threatening situation. And Brian didn't hurt us or manage to destroy the only copy of the will, so in the end there was no serious harm done. Of course Elisa would point out that Brian had tapped my phone, threatened us with a gun, tied us up and destroyed what he thought was the only copy of the will. And she'd be right that all of that was illegal and wrong.

The more I thought about it, the less sure I was about what to do about Brian. If he was capable of doing what he did, who knew what else he might do? I shuddered. Could he be responsible for Angelica's disappearance? Should the authorities be alerted?

I sat there holding my phone and feeling more and more stuck. I needed to talk to someone who could help me figure all this out. Pablo was the obvious choice to talk this over with, but I couldn't call and tell him about Brian. I'd get even more of a lecture than I'd gotten from Elisa, plus Brian would probably be arrested and the whole thing would become a public matter. Lacey and Angelica would be questioned by the police, Derrick would be informed, and I'd be in big trouble.

I told myself that if I thought it would help Angelica, I'd be willing to talk to the police about Brian, but I couldn't see any reason why he'd be involved in her disappearance. He'd let us all go yesterday, so why would he turn around and grab Angelica today?

"Yo, Cleo. You're stuck in the channel. Can't walk home from here. Might as well hit the surf." I looked up to see Tyler riding some invisible wave back and forth across the room.

"Tyler! What are you talking about? Do you mean I should tell the police about Brian?"

"No, that current is pushing you out into waves out of your range. You need to take the next one in."

"What's the next one? What should I do?"

"When the wave pulls you forward, stand up and keep your balance. Don't get blinded by the spray," he said as he surfed up to the ceiling and disappeared.

"No, wait," I yelled. "I don't understand. You need to explain."
But of course he didn't reply.

I sank back in my chair, closed my eyes and tried to make some sense of Tyler's cryptic advice. He had talked about balance and not getting blinded by the spray. Maybe he was telling me not to let the Townes family problems get in the way of thinking about how to get the money Gramma needed. Maybe Gramma's situation was the wave pulling me forward—it was already Tuesday afternoon and I needed to confirm with the Shady Terrace staff by the end of the week that Gramma would be buying in.

But what to do? I didn't see any wave to ride. As my thoughts went round and round, I kept ending up at the same place. For some reason, Faye wasn't taking Gramma's situation seriously and wasn't doing as much as she could to help.

Was this because she was ripping off Gramma by not telling me the truth about how many paintings she'd sold and for what prices? Should I try to follow up on Shane's allegations? And what about Pablo's thought that Faye might be somehow involved in the eBay fraud? I'd always liked Faye and trusted her, but people in desperate financial situations sometimes act rashly. If Shane was right and Faye had been taking more money than she should have been from the gallery, she very well might also have been defrauding Gramma.

I was startled out of my deliberations by my phone ringing. The ID said Faye calling. Wow—like somehow she tapped into my thoughts. Or maybe Tyler somehow got her to call. "Hey, Cleo," she said when I picked up, "I had some new ideas about how to raise money for your grandmother. Can you take a break and come over to the gallery for a few minutes?"

Perfect. It was 4:30. I closed up my office and walked over to the gallery. I would listen to her ideas, which would hopefully be good ones. But I'd also be watching for any signs that she wasn't being honest. If I needed to I could always confront her with Shane's email evidence and see what she had to say.

Chapter 38

When I got to the gallery, Faye was with a customer, so I wandered over to Pablo's exhibit to see whether he'd sold any more pieces. In addition to the four I already knew about, I was excited to find another three red "sold" stickers. I was thinking to myself that there was no way Faye could lie about the prices these works had sold for, which meant Pablo would definitely get his fair share of the money from these sales.

Whoa! Why was I even thinking Faye would rip Pablo off? I realized that I was accepting Shane's view of Faye without giving her a chance to defend herself. Since I'd known Faye forever, and I'd only recently met Shane, why would I take his word as the truth?

I noticed Faye and her customer heading for the front door. As soon as the woman left, Faye locked the door behind her and put up the "closed" sign. I felt a wave of apprehension. Did I really want to have this discussion with Faye about Gramma's money right here with just the two of us locked in to her gallery? But I took a deep breath and told myself I was way over-generalizing from yesterday's encounter with Brian. Why would I be nervous about talking to Faye?

As if to further quell my doubts, Faye approached me with a big smile. She looked stunning as usual. Today she wore a chic short grey cashmere dress over lacy black tights and high-heeled suede boots. Her jewelry—silver and turquoise necklace and earrings—looked to be handcrafted and expensive. I mused that for someone who was having financial problems, she was certainly keeping up appearances.

"Here's something to be happy about," she said. "Pablo's work is selling well. Look at all those red stickers." Then she lost the smile and sighed as she looked around the gallery. "It's been a hard day. Let's go to the back room and have a glass of wine while we talk." She beckoned me to follow her.

As I walked behind her, my new phone rang. Only Lacey and Pablo had that number, which meant the call was important. "I'll be right there," I said, stopping and pulling out my phone. "Just let me quickly get this call."

It was Pablo. I walked back over to his exhibit as I answered. "Hey, I'm standing here in Faye's gallery looking at all your red stickers," I said. "Very exciting."

There was a long silence. Then he began to speak slowly and carefully. "Cleo, I'm hoping you haven't talked to Faye about the eBay fraud. Just answer yes or no whether you have or not. Don't say anything else."

"No," I said.

"Good," he said quietly. "Now I need to give you some information and you need to listen carefully. It's very important that you stay calm and don't react to anything I say. Got that?"

"Okay," I said in my very calmest therapist voice, as I walked away from his exhibit to get where Faye couldn't hear me so easily.

"I found out more about the eBay fraud after I left you that message earlier," he said. "Now remember not to react when I tell you this. It looks very likely that the eBay seller TheBestArt4U is Faye Whitton."

Omigod! I stifled a huge gasp by turning it into a deep breath. My head was spinning. "How do you know?" I asked in a whispery voice.

"I can't go into that now," he said. "You need to leave the gallery right away."

I had worked my way into a corner at the front of the gallery by then, where I was looking at a large oil painting of a brown and white cow. I didn't notice Faye come up behind me until she put her hand on my shoulder. I jumped about a foot and pulled away from her touch.

"Hey," she said, laughingly. "I didn't mean to scare you. Who's the important call that's keeping you away from that wine?"

"It's Pablo," I said. "I'll be done in a minute."

She grabbed the phone out of my hand. "Pablo, Cleo has to go now," she said. "We have some wine to drink. She'll call you later." Then she disconnected my call and danced off to the back of the gallery with my phone in her hand. I heard it start to ring again as she went.

"Wait a minute, Faye. I need to go now and I need my phone." I dashed after her as she disappeared into the back room. My phone was still ringing. "I need to meet Pablo. That's probably him now, so I'll have to pass on the wine and the talk," I said as I pushed aside the curtain that covered the doorway into the back room.

"No problem. There isn't any wine anyway," Faye said. I looked in and gasped in horror. Faye stood facing me with a gun in her hand and next to her was Angelica tied to a chair with a gag in her mouth. Impossible! Tied up and threatened with a gun two days in a row! This was way too much for a ten-year-old, even if she is an Indigo child. Angelica had been at her breaking point yesterday. What must she be feeling now? I wanted to rush over and wrap my arms around her, but Faye's gun kept me rooted where I stood.

Panic shot through me like a lightening bolt. Sure we'd gotten away lucky yesterday, but what are the odds of escaping armed capture two days in a row?

"What's going on Faye? You can't keep us prisoner. Pablo knows I'm with you and he'll probably head right over to find me since you hung up on his call and I haven't answered since. You know he can be here in about thirty minutes."

"He won't find us here," she said sharply, "because we're leaving right now. Go untie and ungag Angelica. We're going somewhere private where we can talk without interference from Pablo or anyone else."

I was shaking so hard that I could barely walk over to where Angelica sat, and when I did get there my trembly fingers could not untie the knots.

"Quit stalling, Cleo," Faye barked. "If you waste any more time, I'll have to shoot you both right now."

She must be crazy. Would she really risk shooting one or both of us right here where someone would be sure to hear? If I had been her only prisoner, I probably would have called her bluff and tried to make a break for it. But I couldn't take that chance with Angelica. I pulled myself together enough to get the knots undone and give her arms little soothing pats. Angelica sat quietly even after her gag was out. I wondered whether she was in shock.

"Walk to the back door, Angelica," Faye said. "I'll be right behind you with the gun, so don't even think about trying anything. Faye picked up a black jacket and threw it over her right arm to cover the gun as she walked over to stand behind Angelica. "Here's what we're going to do," she said. "My car is in the underground parking behind the building. Angelica will open the door and we'll all walk out. "Cleo, you will close the door behind us and lock it." She tossed me a set of keys. "It's the key with the red thing at the top."

"Faye, think about what you're doing," I said. "What do you want from us?"

"You don't need to know the details now," she snapped. "Open the door, Angelica. And if we see anyone, both of you better act normal. I have my gun pointed right at Angelica's back."

Angelica opened the door and walked through. Faye followed close behind her. I walked through, closing and locking the door behind me as instructed.

"Now hand me the keys," Faye said, reaching back with her left hand. I put the keys in her hand, then remembered my phone.

"Wait. My phone. We left it in there. Give me back the keys so I can get it."

Faye laughed. "Don't be ridiculous, Cleo. Do you really think I want you to have your phone?"

Duh. What was I thinking? I shut up and followed along behind her. Out of the corner of my eye, I saw a couple on the sidewalk at the end of the alley. I turned my head in their direction and made silent faces. Please let them notice and come over. But no such luck. They disappeared from view and we continued across the alley into the underground parking. When Faye clicked the remote door opener on her keys, a black SUV in the front row blinked its lights and beeped in response.

"Get in the back, Cleo," Faye said. Once I was in, she opened the driver's side front door and pushed Angelia in and over to the passenger seat. Then Faye got in, slammed the door, and pulled out into the alley, driving with her left hand and keeping the gun in her right.

Angelica and I sat in silence. I had no idea what was going on in her mind, but I was frantically racking my brain for some way to get us both free. Hitting Faye while she was driving could get us all killed. Way too risky. I couldn't abandon Angelica by opening the door and jumping out. Suddenly I realized that my other cell phone—the one that Brian had tapped into—was in my purse. Faye probably hadn't thought I had two cell phones. I carefully and quietly reached into my purse and grabbed that phone. Of course I couldn't make a call, but I might be able to get away with sending a text message to Pablo.

I had no idea how much time I had before Faye stopped, but I figured it wasn't long. She had been driving north on Broadway for several miles. I started typing: *911 hostage w/faye gun her SUV.* The thumb typing was slow and awkward for me, because I'm not a frequent texter. I silently cursed the cell-phone keyboard. If Faye turned around, I was cooked. I could barely think over the pounding of my heart as I typed on: *n on bdwy help asap.*

I sent off the message, turned off my phone, and jammed it back into my purse just as Faye pulled in to a small strip mall, where she drove around back and parked. Now I could only hope Pablo would be checking messages and that Angelica and I could somehow hang on until the police found us.

Chapter 39

Faye stepped out of the car, keeping her gun trained on Angelica. "Get out," she snapped, motioning Angelica out through the driver's side door. "You too, Cleo. Come over here. Right now! Move!" She stepped up to a door in the middle of a squat building and handed me a key. "Unlock the door."

She shoved us into a long dimly lit room lined with modular cabinets fitted with mesh panels and racks that stored artwork. The cabinets were open on both sides to allow the art to slide out easily and I could see scads of paintings in them. It looked like the holdings of a much larger gallery than Faye's. Maybe this was where she stored the illegal copies she sold on eBay.

Faye noticed me scoping out the space. "I rent this building to keep paintings that I don't have room for in the gallery," she said as if she were having a normal everyday conversation with a visitor. "Rents are a lot lower out here, and the building is climate controlled." Suddenly Faye had swung from kidnapper to tour guide. She sounded so much like her usual self that for a minute I almost thought this whole thing was a joke.

But she waved her gun at me again and reverted to her sharp authoritarian tone. "Don't just stand there staring, Cleo. Lock the door and give me back my keys." My goal at that point was to stall as much as possible, hoping a delay would give Pablo time to find us while we were both still alive. But I didn't want to drag my feet so obviously that Faye would notice. So I locked up as slowly as I thought I could get away with and handed her the keys. Once that was done,

Faye pointed to a corner of the room. "See those chairs there. Bring three of them over. I'll stand here with Angelica."

Again, I cooperated like a kindergarten kid hoping for a sticker. I didn't see what else I could do. I couldn't risk Angelica's life by refusing to obey Faye's orders. Plus I had a naïve hope that if I followed her instructions without making a fuss, she'd eventually let us go the way Brian had the day before.

Before we sat down, Faye had me arrange the chairs so that we sat side-by-side and she faced the two of us, gun in hand. Once we were seated, Angelica looked Faye in the eyes and spoke. "You are surrounded by muddy blue energy, Faye," she said quietly. "It tells me that you're scared and worried, and not facing the truth about your future. I've seen that negative energy around you before, but not always. When I saw it I thought you were having a bad day or not feeling well, but now I know that you are seriously troubled. I've tried to give you positive energy, but all you can see is your fear."

Seriously troubled? That's the way Angelica describes a woman who is holding us at gunpoint and threatening to shoot us? This brave sweet child had guts enough to try to help a madwoman regardless of danger to herself, but I was terrified that her candor might get her shot.

I wanted to distract Faye and I wanted to keep her talking to buy more time for Pablo to show up. "We've followed your instructions. You've gotten us out here. Now I need to know what this is all about," I said firmly.

Faye's eyes narrowed. "I don't have to tell you anything," she barked.

I didn't answer or react, letting my silence exert a subtle pressure on Faye to fill the space. Sure enough, in about a minute Faye spoke up, her face contorted in anger. "Angelica came to the gallery this afternoon to let me know that Mirabel—my former friend and partner—made a new will that leaves me hanging out to dry. I'm furious that she would do that. Her expectations were ridiculous." Faye leaned forward menacingly, gun front and center, voice shaking. "Mirabel never understood gallery finances. Every time we hit a low point, she accused me of mismanagement. Apparently she took her revenge by not leaving me the gallery I've devoted all these years to building. But I'm not going to let her get away with that."

What had Angelica been thinking, telling Faye about the new will? Did she think her mother had made a mistake disinheriting Faye? Did she think that Faye could convince Lacey to destroy the new will? Did she think this was the best way to hurt Judith?

I still wanted to keep Faye talking. "Even if there is a new will," I said as calmly as I could manage, "we can't change it and neither can you. What do you hope to accomplish by threatening us?"

Faye smirked. "It's too bad I have to threaten you, but I need your help." Her eyes still blazed, but her tone was more civil. "From what Angelica says, Derrick and Judith don't know about the new will yet—only you, Angelica and Lacey know. So, you're going to help me get that will so I can destroy it. Then we'll all go back to the old will, and I'll let you and Angelica go. If you tell people, it won't matter because you'll have no proof."

Wow. Déjà vu all over again. Only this time if the new will was destroyed that would be the end of it because it was the only remaining valid original. I couldn't see any way she could get the new will without involving other people. Then to get away, she'd probably end up taking Angelica as a hostage. I couldn't let that happen. Maybe if I raised the stakes she'd back off.

I confronted her firmly. "Faye, think about what you're doing. You're in way too much trouble to save yourself by getting rid of Mirabel's new will. Pablo and I found out a lot of stuff about you that I'm thinking you don't want people to know—especially the artists you represent. Like that scam you're running on eBay. What do you think would happen to you if that got out?"

She didn't even look shocked that I knew about the eBay fraud, just annoyed. "Stop right there, Cleo," she demanded, pointing her gun directly at my face. "You have no idea what you're talking about. Artists just create and leave all the messy business details to the gallery owners. We have to do whatever we can to stay in business.. You know I'd never want to hurt any of my artists. But my hands were tied. The gallery was losing money, Mirabel was pressuring me, and

I was drowning in unpaid bills. When the opportunity opened up to be part of the eBay thing, I had to do it so I could make the money I needed to keep the gallery open."

Amazing. She thought her scam was justified. "Whatever your reasons, you're conducting a fraud and now you'll have to face the consequences. But that's nothing compared to the trouble you'll be in for kidnapping a child at gunpoint. If you take us back and let us go now, no one has to know about this."

"No. I'm not going to let Mirabel cheat me out of the gallery I've worked for all these years. Everything I've done has been for that gallery." Faye stood up, grabbed her purse, dug inside, and pulled out a cell phone. She walked over and stuck it in Angelica's face. "Call Lacey's cell number," she said. "No tricks. I'm watching."

Angelica typed in the digits, hit send, and held the phone to her ear. "Voicemail," she said.

"Leave a message," Faye said. "Tell her you're in trouble and she needs to call this number immediately. And she can't tell anyone else."

What? Faye was leaving that message with her own cell number? She was flying blind here!

Angelica left the message and handed the phone back to Faye, who took it and went back to her chair.

"Are you going to ask Lacey to bring the will out here?" Angelica asked. "What if she won't do it?"

"Of course I'm not going to have her come here," Faye said crankily. "She could bring the police or who knows who else. I'll arrange to meet her somewhere to get it from her."

She was sounding crazier and crazier. I interrupted with a dose of reality. "Look, Faye, even if you destroy the new will so you still inherit, you're not going to be able to run a gallery in Boulder—or anywhere—after all you've done."

Faye jumped up again, scowling and waving her gun in our faces. "Shut up, Cleo," she said angrily. "I know more about the art business than you ever will. I ran that gallery successfully for years. Then we hit one rough patch and Mirabel was all over me, threatening to dissolve our partnership. Now a new will turns up where she went back on her promise to leave me full interest in the gallery with no rent. Who did she think she was? She put up a great front, being all socially conscious, saving the environment and endangered species. But she couldn't be bothered with her own friends and family. We're better off without her. She was toxic to all of us. Think about it. Her husband's been having an affair for years. One of her kids died of anorexia, and the others live off her money and create problems wherever they go. Lacey stars in her own pointless hysterical life drama, Shane rips off people's identities and scams their credit cards, and Angelica here thinks she's some kind of specially chosen child who can do whatever she wants."

Her cruel poisonous tongue stunned me. What kind of monster says this stuff to a ten-year old about her mother? If that's the person Faye really is, it's no wonder Mirabel was on her case.

During Faye's tirade, Angelica had been staring at her, eyes wide, face frozen. Now she jerked to her feet and confronted Faye. "No! You're wrong! She was a beautiful person. But when she saw you for the evil person you are, you murdered her. I can see it now. You pushed her under the water and killed her."

Faye lashed back. "No! I'm not evil. I didn't want to kill Mirabel, but she left me no choice. She was going to shut down the gallery. I cared about the artists, she didn't. You're both artists. You should understand. I have to keep the gallery open. Now you can help me or I can kill you both and make it look like an accident."

Angelica leapt at Faye, scratching and kicking her. I sprang up to stop her, but before I could, Faye swung around her right hand that was holding the gun and smacked Angelica in the side of the head. Angelica slumped to the floor, hitting her head on the cement.

Fury exploded in me. I put aside concerns for my own safety. Angelica was my only focus. I had to defend her—do whatever it took to keep her safe. If Faye put a bullet in me, that would be the price. I kicked up at the gun in Faye's hand. It flew off in a high arc toward the back of the room. Faye and I both dashed after it, but her high-heeled boots weren't a good choice for running on slick concrete. I not only got to the gun first, I managed to stick out my leg and trip her, sending her sprawling to the floor. She landed with an "oof," and lay still.

I grabbed the gun, ran back and knelt next to Angelica, feeling for her pulse. She was breathing regularly and her pulse was strong, but her head was bleeding and she had lost consciousness. I stroked her face gently. A surge of love welled up in me. Before that moment I'd seen her as an interesting and often delightful child. I didn't really understand her but I cared about her and I wanted to help her. Suddenly as she lay there, this sweet, vulnerable, motherless child transformed in front of my eyes. She was me as a child, my inner child, the children I don't have. I wanted justice for her. I wanted her to be safe and happy. I wanted her to get the resolution and love and good life that she deserved. I vowed to make that happen.

I turned away from Angelica, grabbed my purse and pulled out my cell phone to call 911. But before I could make a call, the phone rang. Pablo calling. I answered.

"SWAT Team outside," he said. "Put Faye on so we can negotiate with her."

"Tell them to back off," I said. "I have her gun. I'll open the door for you. Angelica is hurt. We need an ambulance right away."

Faye hadn't moved or spoken. I seized her purse from where she'd left it by her chair, got her keys out, darted to the front door and unlocked it. What a welcome sight. There stood Pablo along with two Boulder PD SWAT Team members. Now that we were safe, they looked slightly overdressed in their bullet-proof helmets, vests and groin protectors. But I knew it was standard for hostage situations.

I ran back to Angelica, who was beginning to stir. Her eyes were still closed and her face was white. Suddenly she vomited. I rolled her carefully onto her side to keep her from choking, and grabbed Faye's black jacket from her chair to wipe Angelica's face. Then I sat with her on the floor, holding her hand and speaking quiet soothing words to keep her still until the ambulance arrived.

The police were checking on Faye, who abruptly awakened with a shout. "Damn you, Cleo! You and that bratty kid will regret sticking your noses into my business. Who do you think will believe your lies about me after they find out you two talk to ghosts?"

The rest of her outburst was drowned out by the scream of the ambulance siren as it pulled into the parking lot. Pablo directed the crew to Angelica and I stayed right with her as the medic checked her vital signs. "Are you her mother?" he asked.

"No," I admitted. "Just a friend. Her mother is dead, but I can call her sister and try to reach her father. Is she going to be all right?"

"We need to get her to the hospital," he said, as the other crew-member ran in, pushing a stretcher. They lifted her on, strapped her in, and wheeled her toward the door.

I ran frantically along beside. "Please tell me how she is," I implored. I knew they couldn't tell me anything about her condition—they weren't doctors and she was a minor and not my child. But I could and did insist on riding with her to the hospital.

"I'm staying with Angelica until her family gets to the hospital," I yelled over to the police who were questioning Faye on the other side of the room. "I'll give you a statement at the hospital or later at the police station, but not now," I said in my strongest don't-mess-with-me voice.

More Boulder police had arrived by then, but Pablo waved them away from me as I headed out to the ambulance. "I'm right behind you, babe," he said giving me a quick hug. "Call her family from the ambulance, but don't give anyone details until you've made your statement. I know none of this is your fault, but her family might not see it that way."

As I sat in the back of the ambulance, holding Angelica's hand, the wail of the siren washed over me like a tragic Greek chorus bemoaning my mistakes. I sagged in anguish. I deserved whatever consequences I might suffer from all this. I had ignored both Pablo's and Elisa's warnings. But Angelica—who had already suffered so much at such a young age—did not deserve to be hurt. And my failure to keep her safe stung like a sharp thorn in my heart.

Chapter 40

Staff at the hospital emergency entrance whisked Angelica off to a treatment room and sent me to the intake desk to provide basic information. The waiting room was a madhouse. Two college women had fallen from the roof of a three-story sorority house during an early-evening drinking party. Their not-so-sober sorority sisters jammed the tiny waiting area—crying, talking, laughing—all at an ear-splitting level.

As I fought through the crowd to the desk, one voice from the front door was loud and frantic enough to stand out above the cacophony of young female voices. "Cleo, where is she? Where's Angelica? I was on the phone with Dad when you called from the ambulance. Your voicemail made me crazy! I ran at least three red lights getting over here. Please say she's okay!"

Lacey and I shoved through the crush to get to each other, and I pulled her back with me to the desk where the receptionist sat behind a glass panel. Lacey looked sweaty and frazzled and very, very scared. I put my arms around her and spoke quietly into her ear. "Angelica's in a treatment room. I'm sure they'll let you go there as soon as you tell them who she is and what insurance she has."

Once the woman behind the desk understood who Lacey was, she took her behind the glass separator to fill out the forms in a quieter space. I was left alone with the boisterous after-party crowd. The adrenaline that had sustained me during our capture and escape was wearing off. I was shaky and dizzy, but I managed to slowly make my way through the mob to the front door. I wanted to get out and call

Pablo. He'd said he'd be right behind me and I desperately needed a huge Pablo hug.

Just as I got to the door, it swung open in my face. I looked up hoping to see Pablo's caring face, but instead I got a surly glare from Derrick Townes. "I told you to stay away from Angelica," he snarled, pausing briefly to glower at me. "But you didn't listen. And now she's hurt, maybe dying." Before I could even think about what to reply, he put his hand out to silence any response from me. "I don't have time to deal with you now," he said menacingly, "but you'd better believe there will be consequences." Then he pushed off through the throng toward the reception desk.

I opened the door again, walked out into the quiet parking lot, sagged against the wall, and vomited into a trashcan. My phone rang. Pablo. By the time I got a tissue from my pocket, wiped off my face and picked up the call, it had gone to voicemail. I sobbed in frustration and total misery.

A familiar voice broke into my melancholy. "Yo, Cleo."

I looked up. Suddenly Tyler materialized in the dark sky. Crouched low on his board, he surfed gracefully over a parking-lot lamppost and hovered in front of me.

"Awesome. You didn't bail in the impact zone."

"Tyler! I wish I had bailed. Angelica is hurt. What if she has a serious head injury? What if she dies? I should have stayed out of this whole mess."

"Hey, you're no poser. You're the badass. Cruncher didn't wipe you out. Now you can paddle back out and shoot the curl."

"Tyler, I have no idea what you're talking about," I cried. "You're not helping me one bit. It's bad enough that Angelica is hurt. Now Derrick blames me. I could lose my license or worse."

I got no response. Tyler had surfed off over the hospital roof, leaving me as usual stuck trying to decipher his message.

But I was too worried about Angelica to think any more about Tyler or to stand outside wallowing in self-pity. I pulled myself together, tried calling Pablo again and got his voicemail. I checked my voicemail and got his message saying he had to make a report to the

Boulder police before he could come to the hospital and he'd be there as soon as he could.

As I turned to go back inside, the sorority girls came streaming out en masse. I stood back to let them pass, then headed in to the empty waiting room and looked around for a ladies room to clean myself up. I washed my face, rinsed out my mouth, then went back into the waiting area and over to the desk to find out about Angelica. The woman behind the desk apologetically told me that Angelica's father had insisted that the hospital was not to give out any information about her condition.

"Can you at least tell me if she's alive," I begged.

"I'm sorry," she said, kindly. "We can't."

I found a chair and sat, staring bleakly at a rack of dog-eared magazines. How had it come to this? I only wanted to help Angelica and now she and I were both in jeopardy. I heard the front door open again. *Please let it be Pablo*, I said silently. But it wasn't Pablo. It was Shane.

He was wearing torn jeans and a rumpled gray tee shirt that said *I'm dressed and out of bed—what more do you want?* Pretty appropriate given how he looked. Unshaven, hair sticking up, eyes red. He scanned the room frantically, saw me and dashed over.

"What's going on with Angelica?" he demanded. "I just listened to Lacey's messages saying Angelica was missing and then that she's in this hospital. What happened?"

"It's a long story," I said. "Angelica's in back with the doctors. Lacey and your dad are there too. I don't know how she is. They won't tell me because I'm not family. But I'm sure you can find out if you go over to the desk. And if you do, would you please let me know? I'm so worried about her."

Shane dashed over and quickly disappeared into the treatment area behind the desk. Didn't even look in my direction. I thought about trying to call Pablo again, but didn't. He'd said he'd be here as soon as he could. No use interrupting him with a call that would delay him more. I sat, staring across the room trying to use deep breathing and a soft focus to calm my anxiety.

Finally the front door opened again. Pablo rushing toward me. Strong. Solid. Arms outstretched.

I ran to meet his hug. Wept in his arms. Told him what Derrick had said.

"It's okay, babe," he said, squeezing me tighter. "We can get this straightened out. Derrick doesn't know what happened to you and Angelica. Actually, I don't even know. And the Boulder police don't know, which is why we have to go to the Boulder Police station right now, so you can make a statement. They need the details to be able to hold Faye."

I pulled away, dug a tissue out of my pocket, dried my eyes and blew my nose. "I can't go now. I have to wait to find out about Angelica," I said.

"They're not going to tell you anything. And you don't want Derrick Townes out here yelling at you again. Let's go. While we're there, the Boulder police can call the hospital to find out how Angelica is and let you know."

Reluctantly I went with him. Told the whole story to the Boulder cops. With my statement added to what Pablo had already told them about the eBay fraud, they had more than enough to keep Faye in custody.

When I was done, Pablo came back to the interview room to take me home. "They called about Angelica," he said. "She's been moved to the intensive care unit. Still unconscious. They have her condition listed as serious."

I groaned. "What does that mean? Will she get better?"

"It means she's unstable, but not critical. And she hasn't been airlifted to Denver, so that's a good sign. For more than that, we'll just have to wait."

Chapter 41

We drove in silence to my house. Pablo suggested we stop for something to eat, but I was still feeling shaky and sick to my stomach. He grabbed a burger and fries for himself from the McDonalds drive-through on 28th. I didn't want anything.

Actually the smell of his food was making me more nauseous as we drove. When we got home, I sent him and his meal to the kitchen, while I headed for a hot shower.

After that, all I wanted was the oblivion of sleep to shut down my mind. I crawled into bed and was asleep before he got there. I woke up later, snuggled close to him and drifted back to sleep after willing myself not to think about Angelica until morning.

When I woke up at 6:30 a.m. listening to Pablo getting ready to leave for work, I had that icky feeling in my gut that you get when you wake up knowing something terrible has happened, but it takes you a minute to remember what. Then it all came crashing down on me.

I jumped out of bed and ran to grab Pablo before he left. "Can you call and find out how Angelica is doing before you go?" I asked.

He hugged me close. "I already tried, babe," he said. "The hospital wouldn't tell me anything and I couldn't get anyone at the Boulder PD who had a recent update. I'll try again after I get to work. I'll let you know as soon as I hear anything."

I was too worried to sleep any more, so after he left I grabbed my phone and went out for a run on the Boulder Creek Path. A bright sunny morning, cloudless blue sky, creek gurgling and splashing—all wasted on me. I was a prisoner of my own anxiety. Not only was I fearful about Angelica, I was apprehensive about Derrick's threats. And then, to top it all off, I realized it was Wednesday and I had only a few days left to find the money for Gramma to get a space in the new assisted living house.

I slogged along, willing my body to take over and get me out of my miserable mind. But instead I started feeling dizzy and sick again like last night. I realized I hadn't eaten anything for a long time, so I decided to go home and fix myself some breakfast.

I was finishing my eggs and toast when Pablo called. "I got an update from the Boulder cops," he said. "It kind of sounds worse than it is, so don't panic. Angelica has a severe concussion and the doctors are concerned she may have swelling or bleeding in her brain. They're doing a CT scan this morning to see if there's blood under her skull. Like I said, it sounds horrible, but they're expecting her to make a full recovery."

"You're right. It does sound horrible. Poor Angelica."

"I wish I could come stay with you, but there's no way I can get off today. Try not to worry, okay? I'll let you know as soon as I find out anything more."

"Thanks for wanting to be with me even if you can't," I said. "But I have to work, too. I have clients scheduled and I can't afford to cancel them. I've been doing that way too much with all that's been going on lately. Oh well, at least work will be a good distraction."

I met with a client at 9:00, then frantically checked my phone messages at the end of the session. Yes! A voicemail from Pablo saying Angelica's CT scan had gone well. She was still in the hospital for observation and more tests, but her condition had been upgraded to good. He also said he would be in a training course for the rest of the day, so he wouldn't be able to call again.

I had several other missed calls, but none was from Lacey or anyone in the Townes family. Apparently Derrick had cut me off from all of them. One call was from Tim Grosso. Maybe he had some new information about Shady Terrace. But I didn't have time to listen to any more messages before my next client, so his news would have to wait. Actually if I'd had any hint of what he was going to say, I would have erased his message without hearing it.

But I had no clue, so at 11:00 I grabbed my phone and hit voice-mail. "Cleo, what's going on?" Tim sounded seriously angry. "Faye's in jail and she says it's your fault."

That's right. Tim and Faye had a thing going on. He must be devastated at what she'd done. But all my fault?

The message went on. "She said she took you and Angelica out to her storage room to show you some art and you demanded that she give you the money you need for your grandmother and threatened to create big trouble for her if she didn't. When she refused, you at-tacked her and then set it up to look like she kidnapped Angelica and hurt her. Why would you do that to Faye when she's been so good to your grandmother all these years?"

Whoa, could Faye get away with this spin? I needed to talk to Pablo right away. But his phone went right to voicemail. Oh, right—I'd forgotten he was in training and unavailable for the rest of the day. His voicemail said to either leave a message he could return tomorrow or call another detective for immediate help.

I couldn't think what else to do, and my next client was waiting, so I went back to work. I kept on like that—seeing clients and check-ing phone messages in between—until my last client left at 4:00. I was proud of myself for keeping my anxiety at bay long enough to make it through the day, but once I was done, despair hit me hard. How could I have gotten myself into such a mess?

My phone rang. I decided that if it was Tim, I wouldn't answer. But it was Lacey. I picked up apprehensively. What if she also believed Faye's story?

But this call was good news. Lacey sounded relieved and cheer-ful. "Cleo, Angelica's doing much better. They're just keeping her here one more night to be on the safe side. She told us everything that happened. My dad is so sorry he blamed you and yelled at you. Angelica really wants to see you. Can you get away and come over to the hospital?"

Whew! Could I! I was on my way in less than five minutes.

Lacey, Shane and Derrick were all sitting around Angelica's bedside when I arrived. They looked tired, but very, very happy. Angelica looked pale and exhausted, but much better than she had last night. I went straight to her bedside, gave her a gentle hug, and said, "I'm so sorry Angelica that you got hurt. I wish I could have done more to save you from that."

She squeezed my arm. "You shouldn't feel bad, Cleo. It was my fault, not yours. I never should have gone to tell Faye about the will. If you hadn't showed up, who knows what she would have done to me."

I teared up a little as I moved back from the bed a little to face the others. "I'm so glad she's alright," I said. "I was so scared for her."

Derrick shifted in his chair, looking ill at ease. "Cleo, can you accept my apology?" he asked, awkwardly. "I know none of this was your fault and you probably saved Angelica's life. She doesn't know what happened after Faye hit her with the gun, but the police said you texted your boyfriend and he got them out there. Can you fill in the details for us?"

Shane went out and came back with a chair for me. I sat down and went through the whole story, ending with Tim's phone message about the story Faye was putting out.

"She'll never get away with that," Angelica said. "I can tell the police that what you said is what really happened."

"I just hope they believe us," I said. "I want Faye to pay big time for what she did.

"She killed my mom and tried to kill my sister," Lacey said, her voice rising. "She will pay. I'll make sure of that."

"Me too," Shane agreed. "And I can collect up the evidence of her financial mismanagement of the gallery and her Internet art scam."

"We'll all be there to back up your story against Faye. You have my word on that," Derrick said firmly. "We owe you so much. I hope you understand how grateful I am." He smiled. "And now that we have Mirabel's new will leaving our family all her money, with nothing to Faye or the Scientologists, I'm in a position to offer you a more tangible expression of our thanks. I know you want your grandmother to move into the new assisted living house now that Shady Terrace is closing. My dad is going to move there too, so I know about the $50,000 investment each family has to put up. Lacey says you're having a hard time coming up with the money for your grandmother's down payment. I'm going to call Mary Ellen at Shady Terrace today and tell her I'll invest the $50,000 for your grandmother as well as the $50,000 for my dad. I think it's a win-win. Your grandmother and my dad will be able to live in a new homelike group home, you won't be stressing about the down payment, and I'll be a partner in the venture and a co-owner of the house."

It was like a hundred-pound weight had fallen from my shoulders! I burst into tears of gratitude and relief, fueled by my utter exhaustion. Lacey came over and hugged me close as I sobbed out the stress I'd accumulated. Then I dried my eyes, thanked them all profusely and told them I needed to leave so I could visit my grandmother who I hadn't seen since Saturday.

"I'll walk you out," Shane said, getting up and following me to the door. "I have a couple more questions about the art fraud."

As we walked down the hospital corridor to the elevators, Shane pulled me over to a small sitting area. "I don't actually have questions," he said. "I wanted to talk to you about Grandad, but I didn't want to do it in front of Angelica. I don't want her thinking about any more upsetting stuff today." He sat and motioned me to a chair next to him.

I sat and waited silently for him to continue. "Dad and I met with the Coroner about Grandad's autopsy results and death report," he said quietly. "The official cause of death is listed as severe cranio-cerebral trauma with intracranial bleedings and cerebral contusions. The coroner ruled it accidental death resulting from a fall down the stairs. We pressed him about whether he could tell if Grandad had been pushed, and he admitted he couldn't. But he said that Grandad had been drinking—no surprise there—and that the police assessed the scene and found no evidence of foul play. So everything points to accidental death." Shane sounded exasperated.

"You sound annoyed with the findings," I said. Then I sat back to give him an opportunity to continue.

"I'm sure Glenna pushed him," Shane said, "but there's no way I can prove it. I was thinking that if you could help me contact Grandad, maybe I could get some evidence that would help us pin this on her."

What? He wanted me to help his family track down another murderer? Inside I was screaming *No! No way!* but I choked the words down and stayed silent. I forced myself to sit quietly in my seat. I knew he was coming from grief and anger. I understood and totally sympathized. I've been very close to my grandparents all my life, and I know how vulnerable old people can become. The idea of anyone taking advantage of them in any way disgusts me. But I knew I couldn't take on another cause.

I tried to let him down easy. "Did you know that Lacey already contacted your grandfather?" I asked.

He nodded. "Yes, but she didn't find out anything about who pushed him."

"Vernon told her it was his time to go," I reminded Shane, "and that's all he would say about the fall. Even if you do contact him, I don't think you're likely to get anything more."

"I just want to try," Shane begged. "Can't we just give it one more try?"

I couldn't face any more arguing with him, so I finally said; "I'll think about it and get back to you in a few days." But I knew I was done helping the Townes family. I needed to get back to my own life and spend some time reviewing and rethinking the choices I'd made.

Chapter 42

When you get a life-changing surprise, you want to share the news with someone close to you, ideally someone who has time to listen and talk. My bombshell came on Tuesday afternoon, a week after that horrible Tuesday when Angelica and I were kidnapped.

I had spent the morning moving Gramma into a comfy, sunny room at Glenwood Gardens–Mary Ellen, Joanna and Betsy's new assisted living house. As promised, it was small and homelike with a fireplace in the living room, plants everywhere, a resident cat, and a deck and a yard where residents could walk and sit. I especially loved the open kitchen where everyone could eat together family style at a large dining table. Gramma seemed at home there right away thanks to staff and other residents she knew from Shady Terrace.

I was home alone in the afternoon when I got my shocking news. I wanted to share it right away, but only in an in-person conversation. I called Pablo, but he said he was busy all afternoon and evening. Then I called Elisa. She said she had news to share too and could meet me later.

It was Halloween, so we agreed to meet on the Pearl Street Mall at 5:00 to see the little kids parading in costumes and trick-or-treating for candy at the stores along the mall. Then we'd go to the Rio for dinner and a long talk. Sounded great. I was looking forward to meeting up with Elisa. I hadn't seen her for nearly two weeks, mostly because she'd been out of town at a conference most of last week when everything was blowing up in my face.

After the crises were over, I'd filled her in by phone on Faye and everything that had happened. And accepted the tongue-lashing I knew I'd get for getting myself into a life-threatening mess yet again. Or in her words, "Honey, if you want to live to be old, you need to learn to back away from serious shit like that *before* it sticks to you."

What could I say? She had warned me to stay out of the Townes family drama, and maybe she was right. Still, now that it was over, I wasn't actually sorry that I'd followed Tyler's directives to stay involved and help Angelica. Despite the trauma Angelica and I went through, the overall results were positive. In the past week Faye had been charged with kidnapping and art fraud, and the police had reopened their investigation of Mirabel's death.

Best of all, Derrick had come to realize how precious Angelica is to him and started giving her priority over Judith, who had huffily moved back to her own place. There was no more talk of sending Angelica away to school. And she had an exciting new activity.

With Shane's help, Derrick had purchased a comprehensive art-gallery-software-management system to get the gallery's finances in shape. He had turned the day-to-day operation of the gallery over to Lacey to run with the assistance of a consultant. And, as long as she kept up with her schoolwork, Angelica was going to spend weekends helping at the gallery.

But I wasn't going to try to justify my actions to Elisa by listing off all these good outcomes. I hadn't seen her for two weeks and I just wanted to enjoy hanging out together on the mall, then go to the Rio, hear her news and tell her mine.

We strolled among princesses, Spidermen, Elmos, vampires, Batmen and other less-identifiable characters, some squealing in excitement, others crying in exhaustion. The kids were adorable, but also demanding. I was impressed with how handily parents steered them through the crowd while tiny voices clamored, "I don't like that kind of candy," "I need to go potty," and "I'm thirsty."

"Thinking of thirsty," Elisa said with a grin. "Let's head over to the Rio. I hear a margarita calling me."

It was early, so we got a table right away. A server wearing a unicorn Halloween costume brought us chips, salsa and water. Then a sexy-looking Wonder Woman in thigh-high red boots and a short blue skirt appeared to take our drink orders. "Rocks, salt," Elisa said, using Rio shorthand for a margarita on the rocks in a salt-rimmed glass. "Same?" she asked giving me a quick glance.

"No," I said slowly. "I'll have a ginger ale."

"No way," Elisa said, laughing. "She'll have the rocks, salt. She's just trying to get me going."

"No," I said firmly, waving Wonder Woman away, "I'll have the ginger ale."

After the server left, Elisa gave me her this-better-be-good look. "What gives? Have you converted to Scientology or what?"

"I'll tell you later," I said. "But first tell me your news."

"Only if you agree to explain your conversion from the world's best margaritas to ginger ale."

"I will, but it might take some time. So tell me your news first."

"Fine," she said with a sigh. "Here it is. Tim Grosso was hit so hard by finding out that Faye wasn't who he thought she was that he's taking a leave of absence to go off to a Buddhist retreat center for six months. And I'm going to be the interim chair of the Psych Department."

"Wow!" I said. "That's great. And kind of amazing since you just got tenure."

"I know. But department politics are strange, as you know. I guess he thought I'd be a good choice since I'm not part of one of the established factions. Anyway, that's my news. Now what's up with you?"

The server brought my ginger ale and Elisa's margarita, which sure looked tasty. After she left, I took a deep breath. "I'm pregnant," I said, "so no alcohol."

For maybe the first time in her life, Elisa was speechless. She stared at me, took a big swig of her drink, then finally spoke. "Is this good news? Are you happy?"

"Yes," I said thoughtfully. "I think I am."

"What about Pablo? What does he think?"

"I haven't told him yet. I just found out this afternoon when I peed on the stick. I didn't want to tell him on the phone, so I called him and invited him to dinner so we could talk. He said he couldn't come tonight because he'd promised to help a friend move after work. I'll see him tomorrow. But I wanted to talk about it today. So I called you."

Elisa looked thoughtful. Didn't make her usual quick comeback. Finally she said, "What do you want him to say?"

That was a good question that opened up a long conversation about life and love, choices and commitment, uncertainty, and planning for the future. Elisa pushed me in the good way that only she can to focus on what really matters to me. It was a satisfying talk, but I couldn't resolve what I wanted from Pablo.

Finally I tried to sum it up for Elisa this way, "On the one hand, Pablo's a very sweet guy who would make a terrific dad. He cares deeply about family and is a loving uncle to his nieces and nephews. We love each other and we have great sex. But on the other hand, we also have our issues with trust and commitment. Mia is a good example, and I still don't know what his relationship with her is."

Elisa listened thoughtfully, then asked, "What do you think is behind your and Pablo's hesitance to commit to each other?"

As soon as she asked, the problem was clear to me. "I think he's too bossy. He takes over and I feel swallowed up by him. He thinks I'm too flaky. I can't imagine him ever believing in my Contact Project or accepting that Tyler is more than a figment of my imagination." I stopped, took a deep breath, and said the scariest part. "I really don't know whether a permanent relationship—should I say marriage? —is in the cards for us."

Elisa nodded. No judgement that I could see. "But the baby?" she asked.

Again my answer was crystal clear. "Whatever happens between Pablo and me, I want this child," I said earnestly. "I'm thirty-seven years old and I want to be a mother. I didn't plan this baby, but I see her or him as a gift." I smiled. "Who knows? Maybe my child will be an Indigo."

Acknowledgements

Again I acknowledge Raymond Moody, M.D.'s *Reunions* (Villard Books, 1993), which was the inspiration for Cleo's Contact Project. Also, *Afterlife Encounters* by Dianne Arcangel (Hampton Roads Publishing, 2005), and *the Indigo Children*, by Lee Carroll and Jan Tober (Hay House 1999) were helpful references as I wrote this book.

Many thanks to those who read and edited drafts of this book, especially Marian, Janet and Andrea from my Boulder Media Women's critique group.

As always my husband, Allan, and my daughter, Laurel, were my go-to readers who went through draft after draft, giving me useful notes and unwavering support. I couldn't have done it without them.

For information about Lynn Osterkamp's other books,
visit her website at:

www.lynnosterkamp.com

PMI Books
Boulder, CO
www.pmibooks.com